I, KETURAH

I, KETURAH

A NOVEL BY

Ruth Wolff

THE JOHN DAY COMPANY
NEW YORK

© 1963 by Ruth Wolff

Library of Congress Catalogue
Card Number: 63-15904

Contents

Prologue

IT WAS a summer night I first knew the sudden enchantment of the stars. I was sixteen and away from the Orphanage for the first time, and if I had been alone and unwanted that morning, the stars seemed to prove to me that night it was no longer true.

The stars are stretched across the sky again tonight, like a map to set a course by. I never cease to wonder at the fact that they've been shining since the world began, that down through the ages men have found their way by them. They once led shepherds to a stable; they have lighted me up many a path.

I know the stars by the familiar names they keep in the country: the Evening Star, the Big and Little Dipper, the North Star, the Big Bear, the Little Bear, and that mesh of tangled light most visible in the fall of the year: the Milky Way. There was never a fair evening at dusk when we were coming up from the barn or sitting out on the lawn, that Mr. Denny didn't exclaim at a particular moment: "There she is. There's the Evening Star." He announced it each time that silver toe pricked the darkening sky, whirling in a private ballet of its own before it settled down to simply shine, as if it were an event of great importance. Mr. Denny was like that. Common, everyday things made up his life, and he made them uncommon and particular; he was as taken by the evening star as some people are by the curtain going up at the theater.

But that was all a long time ago. Mr. Denny is dead now. So is Martha, his wife. They were nothing but kind to me, and gave me a home when I hadn't any. I often come out in the evening and stand under the stars, and remember the Dennys and wonder what they would think about all that has happened to me since.

The big, white house is like a ship drifting on the dark sea of the lawn. "Mr. Denny," I sometimes feel moved to say to him, "here am I, Keturah. Would you believe it? But it's honest-to-God true. . . ." I can still hear Mrs. Denny's disapproval whenever I used that expression. I've learned not to say it aloud but it still holds in my mind. When Georgia Lee wanted to impress something upon you, it had to be honest-to-God so. And I wanted to be like Georgia Lee more than anything in the world once. Even talk like her. I wanted to be everything she was except her almost having a baby when she was thirteen, because she was the prettiest girl in the Orphanage, and I wished I looked like her.

She had the bed next to mine in the long row of beds, and after the lights were out and Mrs. Atwood had gone back downstairs, Georgia Lee would lean over the side of her bed and whisper to me in the dark. "He was honest-to-God good-looking, Keturah, he was," she would declare. Or, sighing wistfully, and I would hear her tiny voice lost and unhappy: "They were honest-to-God silk stockings. The only ones I ever owned."

One never escapes completely from what one has been, I

suppose. All the fine houses and clothes may cover up where I've come from but they won't erase it. The Orphanage will always be a part of me, and the Dennys, but I wouldn't be where I am if it weren't for them. Nor would I be able to give this new life stirring within me, this mysterious little life when it is born and growing up, the knowledge and the understanding to carry on the heritage of this house, if I hadn't been buffeted about a little. For this has not always been a peaceful place. Trouble has been here, and sorrow and unhappiness. That is all gone now. Yet who knows when it might not come again? We who are here now have been refined by the past like molten metal purified in the hot fires of passion and tragedy. But there were those not hardy enough to survive.

I still look in the mirror and ask myself: Who am I? Where did I come from? Who had the brown eyes? It leaves forever a question to know nothing about one's parents. And now that a part of me is to be part of a new life, I am keenly aware that I have nothing to hand on to it but what I am. My strong body must have come from my father. My mother must have been the frail one because she died when I was born, in a room she moved into only two weeks before. But perhaps it was just that her heart was too tired. It might not have been her body at all. The woman from whom she let the room brought me to the Orphanage, and handed me over in a soiled little blanket to the Atwoods. They buried my mother in a pauper's grave, and years later when I went back to find it, there was no marker for a young girl who had been known briefly to the landlady as Mrs. Brown.

Mr. Atwood told me these few details the day I was sixteen.

He called me into his office, which was as bare as a cell,

with a desk, two straight chairs, and a bookcase with moldy green books on the shelves. He sat behind the desk like a slab of ice. I used to wonder if he never smiled because if he did he might begin to melt. When he was through I asked only one question. I wanted to know where I got my name.

His long, cold finger—I knew it was cold, his hands were cold whenever he caught hold of me to shake me or to send me on my way—his long, cold finger moved slowly back and forth across his lips before he answered.

"Don't you like it?" he asked, his lips guarded by his finger.

"I hate it," I told him.

I could see him deciding to place the blame on someone else. He was never wrong. No matter what happened, Mr. Atwood was never wrong.

"Mrs. Atwood chose it," he admitted slyly. "From the telephone directory. She opened the book at the Browns, and put her finger down on Keturah Brown. Keturah is a good Biblical name." He tried to soften the fact. "Keturah was one of the wives of Abraham."

"I wish her finger had slipped," I said, "to something pretty."

"Pretty is as pretty does," Mr. Atwood quoted for the thousandth time I could remember but I didn't believe him for a minute. Georgia Lee was a little beauty, she was always in trouble, but it never made her one bit ugly.

This is the miracle of it all. A nobody can become somebody. Mr. Denny used to say: "Cream won't stay at the bottom, Keturah. It always comes to the top."

For a long time this puzzled me. Could there be any cream in me? I'd wonder, up in my little room with the sloping ceiling, trying to get warm under the feather comforter. And I'd go back and compare myself with Georgia Lee again. Georgia Lee looked like cream with her white skin and her soft features and her eyes that swam in their blueness. But she kept getting into all those scrapes that brought her nothing but hardship. And one day I realized that although Georgia Lee looked like cream, she was really only milk spilling over.

There are paths running in all directions. Paths uphill, paths downhill, and paths going around hills too. They are in everyone's life. Those you are pushed onto you have to get over the best you can, but those you get to choose are the important ones and take you where you should be going. Georgia Lee had beauty and she threw it away. Mr. Denny had contentment and he enjoyed every minute he was alive. I had only myself. I had been denied beauty, and then I found it on a summer night when I was past sixteen and saw the star-pricked sky for the first time. I had never known love until the Dennys warmed me with theirs. I prayed to a heavy-handed Being in unison with forty other girls, on bare knees, on cold, wooden floors I had helped scrub, pleading that our souls would go to Heaven if we died in the night. And then I learned of a God who fashioned a bud, unfurled a flower, and hung the little golden pears on the trees at the end of summer. Slowly, painfully, I began to emerge. Along the way I found that, no matter how small the gift you have to offer, if you give of it generously, it makes a place for you and opens a way.

~§ PART I §~

Summer Children

"GOING-OUT-FOR-SUMMER DAY" came in the middle of June. The rising bell rang half an hour earlier, at five fifteen instead of quarter to six. There was only fifteen minutes to dress, make our beds, wash, the usual order. At one minute after five thirty we had to be in the kitchen to start preparations for breakfast. There was no time for dawdling or an idle primp.

Martha Palter, the oldest girl, was out of bed before the bell stopped ringing, letting up the dark green blinds to the halfway mark. The blinds were pulled all the way down each evening although the windows were high and narrow, the sills even with the top of my head. No one ever could have seen in, nor could a Peeping Tom have scaled the high, red brick walls. But as if the world outside was an enemy, the Atwoods took every precaution against it. Perhaps within the iceberg of himself Mr. Atwood was forever tempted to melt, and Mrs. Atwood was forever fearful that he might, that she shut us up as she would have liked to enclose her husband, never realizing she was creating an atmosphere as dank and pallid as a cellar bed of mushrooms.

As Martha let up the shades the thin light of early morning greeted our sleepy eyes, revealing the stark, gray walls of the dormitory. At once everyone was out of bed. I had slept in my underwear so that I had only to slip into my dress and black oxfords, that had been carefully polished to hide the scuffs and placed at the foot of the bed the night before for Mrs. Atwood's inspection.

In the single, blistered mirror in the bathroom I combed my hair over the heads of the girls crowding for a glimpse of themselves. My long hair was unmanageable after it had been washed, there never being enough water to rinse the soap out. The water was carried up hot from the kitchen for our weekly baths and hair washings, and it was measured carefully. Exasperated with the straggling ends that would not lie flat, I combed water through it, and clasped it together on the back of my neck in the heavy, tortoiseshell barrette that had come in a missionary package one Christmas. Georgia Lee was usually beside me at the mirror but that morning she was not there. I never failed to cast an envious glance at her yellow curls that fell immediately into place. Her eyes were wide open and shiny blue. She was thin and small and delicately made. I had to stoop to see in the mirror but Georgia Lee could stand perfectly straight.

I was going out that summer for the first time. Always before I had had to stay behind when Mr. Atwood took the children to the picnic at Camp Springs to be put with families for the summer. I had to stay and work in the garden, help with the canning as the boys hauled in the ripe fruit and vegetables, and do my share of the cleaning. Summers offered no vacation. After the long, hot months in the fields and the roasting kitchen, I welcomed the fall and a return to classes. "We need you here," was the only explanation

Mrs. Atwood gave when the names were called of those who were to go, and mine was not among them.

Perhaps she let me go that summer because she felt I needed training in a home if I was to find a job as hired girl when I left the Orphanage in another year or so. Perhaps it was because there were others coming up who worked faster than I did. Mrs. Atwood timed everything we did: so many minutes to get the water boiling for the cereal, so many minutes to fry the eggs, so many minutes to scrub a floor, so many hours to hoe and weed. I was not a fast worker. To finish in time I always had to hurry at the end. Although Mrs. Atwood could find nothing to complain about in the results, this slowness of mine irritated her. She would stand beside me holding up her bony wrist on which a round, gold watch blazed. She would lift her black eyebrows before the question came.

"Miss Pokey not through yet? Just two more minutes."

And when I would finish in the nick of time she was cross because I had foiled her again. She had lost the opportunity to punish me. Maybe Mrs. Atwood let me go at last because she was tired of contending with me.

I slept scarcely at all that last night, questions running wildly through my head. What would it be like outside? What sort of world lay beyond the red brick walls of the Orphanage? What was a home like? Home was only a word to me. And would one be offered me? What if no one took me and I had to come back with Mr. Atwood on the evening train?

The boys were more fortunate than the girls. They were allowed to go to the county high school but the Atwoods would not trust the girls out of their sight. Mr. and Mrs. At-

19

wood and Miss Flory, Mrs. Atwood's sister, held classes for us in the first-floor wing under the girls' dormitory. All three of them were long, thin, evil-looking people, regarding us with distrust. Miss Flory had the least resistance against us but she was dominated by the Atwoods. She was afraid of both of them, and we had no respect for her. She giggled nervously in the classroom, and it was difficult for her to demand obedience.

Our classes consisted of cooking, sewing, arithmetic and spelling. About once a week there was reading. Mrs. Atwood claimed we wouldn't have time for it after we went out working anyway. Miss Flory had a passion for spelling matches. There was a constant rivalry in spelling and I had at least a dozen blue ribbons, which I had won in matches, tucked away under my bed in the flat box that held all my belongings. I learned to spell hundreds of words I never knew the meaning of.

For pastime we looked through the worn magazines that had been donated to the parlor. They were kept on a special table, and we were allowed to look at them only on Sunday afternoons. I hovered over the bright pictures in the dim room, the dark shades half drawn behind the coarse lace curtains, squinting my eyes to see. There were few books. Once in a while a package of them would drift in but they were always old books someone no longer had any use for, books with dingy covers, mildewed pages, straggling in from the shelves of old houses that had been put up for auction after the last owner died. No one ever opened them.

"I'm going away. . . . Far away. . . . On a train . . ." In the darkness of the dormitory, in the long row of beds, in the rise and fall of breathing of those who slept openmouthed, the words wound through my head.

2

Georgia Lee was grim with disappointment. She was not allowed to go. She had been in trouble when she was thirteen, before she came to the Orphanage, and no matter how good her behavior was at times, she was constantly regarded with suspicion. Georgia Lee had been forbidden to talk about her past. But she was not one to confine herself to silence forever. The drabness of her days left her no alternative than to remember with longing the few shoddy but gay months she had known when she had skipped from her aunt's house to the false security of her boy friend. By hanging our heads over the sides of our narrow beds we could whisper after lights were out, and Mrs. Atwood was safely downstairs again. In the little space of time before our tired bodies demanded sleep, Georgia Lee, on occasion, regaled me with her past.

"I hate . . . hate . . . hate . . ." she whispered hoarsely, after a day of punishment, a day of peeling potatoes in the steamy kitchen. The day before, on Sunday afternoon, with nothing to occupy her time in those few free hours allotted to us, immeasurably bored, she had taken a bit of red crepe paper left over from Christmas, held it under the faucet in the bathroom, and pressed it to her lips until the color was transferred. In the little square of blistered mirror she became fascinated with herself, and some stubborn streak in her made her leave it on. She had dared to appear at supper with reddened lips. I gasped when I

21

saw her. Mrs. Atwood was just about to offer grace when she spied her. Georgia Lee had to leave the table and wash it off.

In the dark, after the day of potato peeling, she had let loose a flow of savage revenge. The word hate covered not only the Atwoods but the whole world. I leaned over as far as I could without falling out of bed, and tried to offer her some consolation.

"Honest-to-God you looked like a picture in a magazine." This bit of honest flattery had an immediate effect.

"Did I really?" She snickered. "Wasn't Mrs. Atwood the jealous one? Mr. Atwood's eyes fairly bulged out of his head."

She was not in the least bit sorry, and I was glad of it. I hated the Atwoods as much as she did.

"You'll get married soon as you're out of here," I assured her.

Between her teeth she muttered, "No."

"But you wouldn't have to go out for hire then."

"I hate being married."

"How do you know?"

"I was same as married once."

I caught my breath. "I don't believe you."

"I almost had a baby once. Do you believe that?"

"No."

"I jumped off the steps two solid hours to shake it loose."

Mrs. Atwood chose that moment to come back upstairs for something she had forgotten. She carried a lamp, its light flashing up ahead of her as a warning as she came up the steps. Her long, thin figure appeared in the hall clad in a long, black robe, her black hair uncoiled down her back like a snake. Her hair reached clear to her knees. Georgia Lee had the giggles once wondering if Mr. Atwood got tangled up in it in bed. We slid hurriedly under the covers pretending to be asleep while Mrs. Atwood came into the room, found what she wanted on a table near the door, and went back downstairs again. Immediately the last flicker of light was gone we were over the edges of our beds, and Georgia Lee, no longer able to restrain herself, having found a sympathetic ear just when she needed it most, told me what had happened to her.

"It was the silk stockings I hated giving up the most," she reflected after the bitterness had died down in her. We would be half asleep next day in classes but nothing could stop her once she'd started. And I had listened with both ears cocked in shocked silence. "I wore them till they looked like chicken ladders. When I had them up good and tight my legs looked like honest-to-God dancing legs."

When I finally crawled down into bed again, half frozen from the cold room, I was chilled in my very bones. The coldness would not leave. My teeth chattered. Hard as my life had been I was now aware of dangers that lay beyond. I began to say my prayers again for something to turn to. I had never received any comfort from them before nor did I then. In the middle of them I stopped, and leaned over the edge of the bed again.

"Did it hurt very much almost having a baby?" I asked.

Georgia Lee lay rigid in her bed. She was probably too cold to inch out from under the covers again. Or maybe she was crying. But Georgia Lee never cried. Her spirit was tough and defiant, and tears were neither her weakness nor her trickery. She said without moving: "It like to cut me up in pieces."

3

The Drury twins were waiting for me to help them, sitting on the floor with their shoes on the wrong feet. Ethel's socks were on inside out. They were undisturbed about the trip before them. Only four years old, they had been at the Orphanage less than a year. They were to be in my charge for the day but I knew they would be no trouble. Mrs. Atwood hoped someone would adopt them as she had little use for the smaller children.

Their shoes and socks on straight, I brushed their fine, fair hair down in bangs over their foreheads. They were the same size, shape and coloring. Even their expressions were the same. The only visible difference besides their haircuts was a small triangular scar on Billie's forehead. I asked him about it again as I brushed his hair, never having received a satisfactory answer.

"I fell," Bill replied.

"He fell off a train," Ethel piped up, always ready to aid him. But neither would she elaborate.

"You're not going to fall off the train today, Billie," I assured him.

He nodded his blond head and stuck his thumb in his mouth. Ethel stuck her thumb in her mouth. There the two of them sat with their thumbs tucked away, placidly waiting for whatever might happen to them. I had never seen them laugh or cry. They merely stuck their thumbs in their mouths and solemnly regarded their shifted-about lives

24

from round, light blue eyes faintly fringed with golden lashes.

I had just one moment in which to say good-bye to Georgia Lee. She had avoided me from the time the bell rang—in the bathroom, through preparations for breakfast, at the table. As we lined up for the long walk to the station, I saw her slip out of the kitchen door. I went after her. I could not leave without telling her good-bye.

I found her huddled together on the back stairs, holding her head in her hands. Her yellow curls fell over her face. She would not look up.

"Don't feel so badly," I begged. I ached for the right thing to say to her. All excitement left me at having to leave her like that. "I might come back this evening," I told her, almost wishing suddenly that I would. "I doubt if anyone will have me."

"I hate Mrs. Atwood to the day I die," Georgia Lee muttered behind the screen of golden hair. "Don't come back on my account."

I put my arms around her tense little body.

"I'll get even with her," she declared. "I'll get even with her sometime. See if I don't."

I heard Mrs. Atwood calling my name in her high, shrill voice.

"I have to run," I said quickly. I had to let go of her. I had to leave her sitting there like a little stick, stiff with hate.

❧ 4 ❧

We marched out of the building two by two except for myself and the Drury twins bringing up the end of the line. As I had a twin by each hand, three of the boys had to carry our suitcases as well as their own, suitcases Mrs. Atwood had had brought down from the dusty attic, and parceled out to us. Mine had to be tied with a clothesline to keep it from falling open. The boys were in blue shirts and overalls. Their faces shone from diligent scrubbing, no dirt lingered behind their ears, there were no high-water marks. The girls marched behind them in dark calico dresses and wide-brimmed black straw hats with a tail of ribbon hanging down each back, hats handed down from year to year, stored away in boxes in the attic from one year's outing to the next. As the line trailed down the road, the black shoes and stockings picked up a film of dust. Wasted were the hours of shoe polishing the night before.

At the head of the line Mr. Atwood strode, lifting his long legs, his black hat down over his eyes to shade them from the sun, like a demon marching us off to some unhappy encounter of his own devising. Behind us the red brick building stood revealed in the bright morning light, ugly, discolored, a misshapen thing against the blue sky. I gave it a last look. The dark green blinds were all halfway up, even as a ruler. The bed of cannas in front of the porch were still only stiff, uncurled spikes. If there is anything to remember about the place, I decided, it's how ugly it is.

Mrs. Atwood inspected us again at the station, full of high hopes we wouldn't be back for three months. Her searching glance came back and rested on me as if she had forgotten something. I flushed under her cold gaze. Mrs. Atwood had scolded me back in the kitchen for coming late to line. She wanted to know where I had been, and I had lied and said to the bathroom. She had had no time to do anything but believe me but now the accusing glance returned. She picked up one of my hands attached to a twin's. "You forgot to clean your nails, Keturah."

I had. I had weeded the garden the afternoon before, and I had relied on the bath and hairwashing to get the dirt out as I had no time to clean them. Both had failed to do the job.

"I'll clean them on the train," I told her.

"See that you do." She dropped my hand, and our eyes met. Hers were as sharp as the railroad tracks beside us. "You'll have to get a move on if you expect anyone to keep you. No dawdling and rushing it up at the last minute. If you break a dish they'll make you pay for it."

I had broken only one dish in all those years of dishwashing, an old saucer that had had a crack in it and had come apart in the water and cut my hand. I saw again how much Mrs. Atwood disliked me. I knew it the first time she had said: "I washed your diapers, Keturah. I cared for you when no one else would. You have an obligation to pay."

Did I? I often wondered about this when she treated me unfairly. I had not been asked to be born. I had been taken to the Orphanage because there was no place else for me. The Atwoods were paid for taking care of us. Oh, I thought longingly, standing there before her on the station platform, if only someone would take me in that day, I would scrub, clean, milk, hoe. . . . There wasn't anything I

27

wouldn't do for someone who would take me away from the Orphanage for three months.

Way off in the distance the train whistled. We watched it puffing up the tracks, scarcely visible at first, looming larger as it drew near, its shiny steel nose fairly pushing back the morning as it rumbled by and hissed to a stop. The big brass bell on top the engine clanged noisily as we boarded the day coach. I lifted the Drury twins up the steps and climbed up after them. We took the first empty, red plush seat we found. The boys came around and pushed up the flyspecked windows. Out the open window I saw Mrs. Atwood again. She was frantically waving at all of us. She kept waving her hand up and down and I wondered if it wasn't getting tired. There was a queer smile on her colorless lips. The conductor was standing on the cinders beside her, and she was showing a self foreign to the one I knew. She went on waving until I thought her hand would break off but I did not wave back. The twins had taken their thumbs out of their mouths and automatically lifted their hands to her. I looked at their smoothly brushed blond heads and hoped fervently some kind people would want to take them. They were still young enough to have the tarnish of their past removed.

The conductor called "All Aboard, All Aboard . . ." and the train began to move. The wheels clicked, the whistle blew, the conductor slammed the door shut. We were on our way. Mrs. Atwood hurried along beside the train for a few seconds. The last I saw of her was the heavy coil of dark hair sticking out from beneath her flat, white straw hat, the front of the brim dipped with a red rose as out of place as a fly in January. Her hand was still waving. But almost at once we had passed her, she was gone from sight. If I had known then about people what I know

now, I would have waved. In that last moment at least, I would have waved. Mrs. Atwood had no love for children and she was confined with almost a hundred of them.

5

Farms stretched to life under the morning sun: cows flank-deep in daisies, sunbonneted women hanging snowy wash on crisscrossed lines, farmers behind plows turning up the rich, dark earth; dogs wagged their tails and barked at the train; children looked up from their play to stand and stare. Along the banks of the railroad tracks honeysuckle bloomed, and touched by the warming sun, loosed a sweetness that drifted in through the open windows. Once a pair of white horses, manes and tails flying, galloped along beside us. I nudged Billie and Ethel to see. "Where?" they asked, having to take their thumbs from their mouths first, the horses out of sight before they got their eyes around to them.

The children sat quietly in their seats. There was a water cooler up at the front end of the car, the water sloshing in the big, inverted glass with the movement of the train. But no one went up to get a drink. There was scarcely any talking. In all those little minds, inside those well-brushed heads, behind those wide-eyed gazes, the questions must have been desperately going around: What will become of me today? Under whose roof will I sleep this night? Will it be hard, will I be lucky and get a good place?

I remembered my dirty fingernails. I had nothing to clean

29

them with. I spied a pink train ticket on the floor beneath our feet. Picking it up I ran the edges under my nails. My rough, red hands with the broken nails were a horrid badge of the Orphanage. I hid them in the folds of my dress, wondering if they would ever match the pale, smooth skin of my arms above them.

The train stopped at half a dozen little disappointing towns. A few stores, a straggle of men in overalls, women under sunbonnets, market baskets on their arms, a dirty yellow station. I was always glad to get out into the country again. For the country fascinated me, the little streams curling between mossy banks, the dark wooded hills where shadows had not yet been routed by the sun, the sweep of daisy-starred meadows, the fields of yellow mustard in bloom, the wide, deep blue sky. I loved the big red and white barns, their tin roofs glistening like water, topped with weather vanes and lightning rods.

Mr. Atwood came through the car, warned us we were reaching our station, gave us a few last-minute instructions, and went back up to the front and waited for the train to stop. The ride was over too quickly. I had taken off my stiff hat and leaned my head against the back of the red plush seat. Going round a bend I had seen the engine far up ahead of us puffing black smoke into the blue sky, the big wheels churning round and round. And I had had the fanciful thought that by some stroke of magic the train might carry us on and on, past our station, past the towns, the country, until it had carried us too far ever to bring us back. We would be forever children riding on a train. With a jolt the train stopped. And I had the Drury twins by the hands again, and we were standing on another cinder platform under a blazing sun.

Lined up as before, we started off, Mr. Atwood's black

hat at the head of the line leading the way down another dusty road. I began to perspire in the tight, long-sleeved calico dress; damp spots spread under my arms. Our shoes were gray with dust. Ethel began to whimper before we were halfway there. She said her shoes were too tight and her feet hurt. It was the first time she had ever complained and I knew it must be true. I picked her up and carried her. With each step my dress became more wrinkled and damp. But I no longer cared.

We marched in under the grove of beech trees where the picnic had already begun. Women in bright dresses flitted under the trees, men stood in groups talking, children ran in and out among them. We marched right up to the benches in front of a platform draped in red, white and blue bunting that had been reserved for us. As if they had been waiting for our arrival, the band on the platform began to play. People hurried to find seats. I had to hold Ethel on my lap and Billie rested his round bottom on the corner of the bench. No sooner were we settled than the band struck up the first notes of "My Country 'Tis of Thee," and we all had to stand up again. But we were in the shade at last, the hot sun no longer beamed down on us and, tired as I was from having carried Ethel, I sang. The music lifted my weariness. It was so gay and loud after Miss Flory's struggling attempts at the piano to accompany our hymn singing on Sunday morning, I could not help but sing. Immediately after the singing the speaking began.

Mr. Perkins, who had welcomed us as we entered the grove, welcomed us again from the platform, then introduced the speaker of the day, a man running for a local office. The speaker pounded and thumped the wooden stand in front of him and shouted to sway the people to vote for him. He talked for a whole hour. Nothing he said made any sense to us, but under Mr. Atwood's watchful eye we sat patiently. Babies cried, children sneaked in and out of the red, white and blue bunting, fans flipped back and forth, sticky flies settled on us and provided the diversion of chasing them away. When the man finally finished, everyone clapped. We all clapped too, although I'm sure none of us enjoyed a word he said.

Mr. Perkins stood up again and announced dinner. "I know everyone's hungry." He beamed down at us. "Especially these boys and girls who had a long trip before they ever arrived here this morning." He spread his smile over us. "Now boys and girls, I want you to march up to those tables and eat all you want. You won't find any better food anywhere."

Every dish you could think of was set out on those long tables over which the sunlight sprinkled like golden raindrops falling through the beech trees. I had never seen so much nor such a variety of food. Heaped-up platters of fried chicken, pineapple-laced hams, great bowls of potato salad topped with sliced eggs and bacon crisps, sliced tomatoes, baked beans, macaroni and cheese, cole slaw, cottage cheese, deviled eggs sprigged with parsley, and a rainbow of jelled salads. The desserts were the most wonderful of all. Three- and four-layered cakes iced finger thick with pink, chocolate, white and yellow icings, decorated with jelly beans, red cinnamon drops, fresh flowers and candy rosebuds. There were mince, apple, gooseberry, raisin, and coconut cream pies. At the very end of the tables fresh fruits were piled high, the finest each farm had to offer.

It was too much food. It was so beyond our meager fare, our thwarted imaginings, that we could only walk dazedly down the line unable to make up our minds what to put on our paper plates. We reached the desserts and suddenly realized that we had come to the end of the dazzling display. In a desperate effort to be sure of having something to eat, we helped ourselves to cake and pie, so that we all stuffed ourselves on sweets and afterwards longed for the fried chicken we had passed by.

The Drury twins fared better than the rest of us. Seeing they were so small and barely able to reach the table, some of the ladies came to their rescue. The twins came away with a little bit of everything on their plates and much more than they could eat. I looked longingly at their fried chicken as we settled ourselves on the grass under the trees. Two of the older boys, Harry and Ival, sat down beside us. They worked in the fields and never had enough food to fill their big, rawboned, growing bodies that were almost man-sized. They ate their three slices of pie and two pieces of cake and a peach apiece, and then hung over the twins like buzzards, waiting to see what would be left. There was a whole piece of fried chicken on each twin's plate when they plopped them down in front of us.

"I'm full," Billie declared, holding his round stomach.

"I have to go to the toilet," Ethel announced.

I looked over at the boys. They were grinning sheepishly, their eyes on the two pieces of chicken.

"Will you do me a special favor sometime?" I asked.

"I'll fill the water buckets for you for a whole week," Harry eagerly offered.

"I'll carry your stove wood for a month," Ival promised.

I pushed the plates over to them. I took Ethel's hand and pulled her up. I reached down for Billie. If I didn't take him along he'd want to go as soon as I came back. I led them off, glad not to have to watch the boys devour the chicken. I was still hungry.

It was not until the middle of the afternoon, after a round

of choir singing (in the evening the best competing choir would be chosen), that we were put up on the platform, the smaller children in front, the taller in the back rows.

Mr. Perkins had shed his coat as the day warmed; his long, white sleeves were held up by striped bands above the elbows, his pants by matching striped suspenders. He helped arrange us, more at ease than Mr. Atwood who kept unnecessarily cautioning us to sit quietly. The people who had been milling around during the singing gathered onto the benches again, stretching their necks to see us, whispering to each other behind their hands. Mr. Perkins raised his arms for quiet, then began urging the farmers to take a child for the summer. "All you have to provide," he told them, "is a place to sleep and three meals a day." He turned to Mr. Atwood who was sitting on the edge of his chair. "And now, Brother Atwood, will you pleasure us with showing the children."

Mr. Atwood paraded us around that afternoon as if we were livestock at a fair. I never hear the good points of a show animal declared but what I think of that afternoon. I didn't think Mr. Atwood had it in him. He never gave a word of praise no matter how hard we worked. There was something almost evil in the display he made of us, as if we were nothing more than puppets and had no more souls or feelings than a placid cow. I have treated the few Negroes I have known with extra kindness because of that day. I have only to look into their patient, humble faces to remember that their ancestors were auctioned off in the same cold-blooded way we were.

The smaller children received no response from the audience. Mr. Atwood had begun in high spirits and talked fast but to no avail. It rankled him a bit when the third child had to go back and sit down again. The back of his head with the thinning, black hair through which his unhealthy white scalp peeped, and the back of his pale neck, began turning red. But Mr. Atwood was not one to be vanquished easily. He took out his handkerchief, wiped his balding head as the sun, squeezing in between the trees, was beaming down on him too, adding to his discomfort. He wiped the back of his neck. Sticking the rumpled handkerchief back in his pocket he went over and took one of the Drury twins by each hand and led them forward. They had their thumbs in their mouths. Clasped to Mr. Atwood they stood stolidly waiting as they had waited so many times for something to happen to them.

"This year," Mr. Atwood's voice rang out with renewed incentive, "we have something to offer we haven't had in a long time. Twins! A boy and a girl. Look at them, ladies and gentlemen. Did you ever see two finer specimens? Well behaved, sturdy . . . Look at their legs. Solid as bedposts. Never been sick a day in their lives." (He had had them less than a year. I wondered how he could be so sure.) "Never heard them cry either." He let go of the twins and spread his arms wide. "Now won't some warmhearted young couple whom the Lord hasn't seen fit to bless with children of their own, open up their hearts and take these two young ones? Take them for the summer. See how you like them. Might be you'll want to have them for keeps." He placed a hand on each head. "Two finer children the good Lord never made. Left orphans when they were born. Came to us direct from their grandparents who were getting too old to care for them."

Again there was no response. I saw a pretty, young woman in the second row wiping her eyes. She sat close to a big, blond man, his sunburned arms folded across his blue shirtfront, his gaze intent on the twins. The other faces gazed dully up at the platform. My heart sank. I prayed that someone would offer to take them. I didn't really expect God to hear me. He never had before. But I had to appeal to someone.

Mr. Perkins tried to come to Mr. Atwood's rescue. Mr. Perkins had never seen the twins before that day, and I wondered how he knew so much about them but I didn't care if he was making it all up. He was on their side. He got no further than Mr. Atwood had. He finally led Ethel and Billie back to their seats.

Mr. Atwood wiped his head and the back of his neck again. He began on the second row. He was working on the third boy when Mr. Perkins called him aside. I hoped fervently since the affair was going so poorly, they had decided to call the whole thing off. Mr. Perkins whispered to Mr. Atwood, and then Mr. Atwood stood up straight and squared his shoulders. He turned and beamed at the twins. He went over and jerked their thumbs from their mouths and handed them over to Mr. Perkins who lifted them down from the platform.

"Thank you, ladies and gentlemen," Mr. Atwood exclaimed, his enthusiasm returned. "Thank you kindly. Thanks to the young couple whose hearts were touched by the spirit of charity." Then he went on exploiting the boy beside him who stood head down, hands shoved into overall pockets, twisted with embarrassment.

I saw the blond man who had sat beside the pretty woman in the second row, leading the twins away. Ethel stumbled over a tree root and he picked her up in his arms. Slung over his shoulder she stuck her thumb back in her mouth. I tried to see where they were going but they were swallowed up in the crowd. When I looked back at the audience I saw the woman's seat was empty too. God had heard my prayer! If I was the only one not chosen because I'd doubted Him, I would not complain. Ethel and Billie had a place.

Once a move had been made, others began coming up and asking for children. A few who had been out the summer before were quickly spoken for. All at once everyone seemed to have a place to go, even the younger ones that had been passed over at first. As his success mounted, Mr. Atwood became more garrulous. He even joked a bit, warning the people not to feed their boarders too well or they might become lazy. Finally only three of us were left, two twelve-year-old girls who were out for the first time, undernourished and small for their age, and myself.

I wanted to shout to Mr. Atwood: "We'll go back. We'll gladly go back. Only don't make us stand up there in front of everyone and beg them to take us." Mr. Atwood, however, was charged with triumph. He dragged those two scrawny girls out there on the platform and said things about them that no one could believe seeing their thin, sallow faces, their poor teeth, their skinny arms and legs. The girls twisted and hung their heads, and looked as if they would burst into tears. Mr. Atwood had to give up at last and let them go back and sit down. I closed my eyes. If only the platform would open up and swallow me.

"Keturah!"

My eyes flew open. Mr. Atwood was crooking his finger at me. Dully I stood up in my wrinkled calico dress with the damp stains under the arms.

"Here is the last one." Mr. Atwood's voice had a note of relief in it. "A big, strong girl able to do the work of any woman. Healthy as a horse. Just take a look at her hands. She's worked in the fields, cut wood, carried water. Here is a real prize, ladies and gentlemen."

For a moment, hauled up in front of those staring faces,

I thought I was going to faint. Mr. Atwood, seeing something wrong, put his hands on my shoulders and gave me a shake that brought me roughly to. "See here," he whispered hoarsely. "Don't act a fool."

"Please let me go back," I begged under my breath.

Anger rose in his eyes, then he gave me a little shove as if he were tired of trying to get rid of us. "You'll pay for this later," he snapped, his back to the audience.

I sat weakly down, lowering my head to hide my flushed face, burying my wretched hands in my lap. The two girls beside me got up and left. I heard Mr. Perkins clapping for quiet, announcing there was to be one more choir before supper. The feet of the choir marched up on the platform, and all that I saw was their shoes. Someone began to play the piano. The choir sang: "Oh what gladness we'll know over there . . ." The voices rose shrilly on the air. I wished I were dead. They sang three numbers, then the feet marched off again, and I was alone on the platform.

I sat gazing at my hands tangled in my lap. If Mr. Atwood had not called attention to my hands, if he had not said, "Look at her hands," I might not have panicked. But all eyes had fastened on them, what I hated most, my rough, red hands. I realized someone had tapped me on the back. Mr. Atwood probably wanted me to get off the platform. I wondered if he was still angry with me, what penalty I would have to pay. Sighing, I rose from my seat. Whatever it was it would probably last all summer long.

6

"Aren't you going to have a bite to eat?" a kindly voice asked.

I swung around. A strange man stood below the platform. Behind his steel-rimmed glasses a pair of friendly blue eyes peered up at me. "Come along," he invited. "There's still plenty left. I know you must be hungry." He held up a hand to help me down.

I wasn't hungry. But I could not resist reaching out and taking the offered hand. I jumped down beside him. I was taller than he was. He held my arm and steered me over to the tables. Taking up a paper plate he began filling it without asking me what I wanted. I walked stiffly along behind him. At the end of the line he had to hold the plate with both hands to keep it from caving in. "Now you come over here and join us," he bade me, and meekly I obeyed him.

He led me over to two ladies sitting on the ground under one of the big trees. They were dressed almost alike in starched gingham dresses and white straw hats with summer flowers on the brims. In each hat an enormous black hatpin was stuck through from one side to the other.

"I'm Cyrus Denny," my rescuer introduced himself. "Been carrying the mail around here for most forty years." He grinned, his weathered face breaking up into a map of pleasant lines. "This is Mrs. Denny." The heavyset woman with thick, shell-rimmed glasses nodded. "And her sister, Mrs. Wayburn." The thin woman with sharp, black eyes stretched a smile across her face. "Sit down here with us and make yourself comfortable."

I sank down beside the ladies, smoothing my dress over my knees, wishing the wrinkles would disappear. Mr. Denny handed me the plate. I stared bleakly at the piled-up food, wondering what I would do with it.

"Don't know why they left you up there by yourself," he said, easing himself down beside me. "But we didn't want you going back hungry." He picked up his own plate that he had left lying on the grass.

"You're not eating." Mrs. Denny noticed I had not touched my food.

Mr. Denny peered over at my plate. "That looks like a piece of Mrs. Denny's chicken. If you don't eat it she's going to be mighty disappointed."

"Maybe the girl prefers the ham," Mrs. Wayburn offered.

"Bet you don't often get fried chicken like this." Mr. Denny ignored her remark. His eyes twinkled behind the steel-rimmed glasses. "Do you now?"

I shook my head. "No," I admitted. After I spoke one word I felt better. Mr. Denny had the kindest face I'd ever seen. There was something contagious about its friendliness. Slowly I began to catch it.

"You haven't told us your name."

"Keturah." I never had occasion to use my last name. I scarcely knew I had one.

"Keturah." He pronounced it carefully.

"I don't like it," I informed him.

"Oh come now," Mr. Denny said. "It's a good fundamental name right out of the Bible."

"Aren't you going to try my chicken?" Mrs. Denny persisted.

If only to please her I picked the golden breast up in my fingers and took a small bite. The crisp crust was scarcely in my mouth when my hunger returned. I picked the bone clean.

"Mrs. Wayburn here made the potato salad." Mrs. Denny continued in her conspiracy to have me eat.

Mrs. Wayburn peered over her sharp nose. The summer flowers on her wide-brimmed hat trembled as she nodded her head.

"I can always tell mine by the cream dressing. It stays so nice and moist."

I ate the potato salad.

"We've taken a boy from Mr. Atwood every summer," Mr. Denny said, making conversation while I ate. "But there's not much work on our place anymore. Sold off all but twenty acres. Enough for Martha and me. Keep two cows and my old horse Nelly who used to pull the mail wagon. Garden just big enough for us to take care of. 'Spect we really don't need extra help." He scratched his thick, iron-gray hair. "Seems kind of strange not to be taking anyone home with us."

"Going to be kind of lonesome this summer," Mrs. Denny mused. "I always enjoy someone extra to cook for."

Both Mrs. Denny and Mrs. Wayburn were pulled into and pushed up by tight corsets that would not permit them to bend easily. Their hands and arms were sunburned and freckled, their plain faces creased with fine lines. But they bestowed on me such welcome I thought they were beautiful.

Mrs. Wayburn flicked her eyes over me. "What's going to become of you, Keturah?" she wanted to know.

I looked away from her quick, black eyes. "I'll be going back with Mr. Atwood," I managed to say lightly.

Someone came along just then and stopped and chatted with Mr. Denny. I ate quickly, remembering that Mr. Atwood would be hunting me up soon, and he might come before I finished.

"You're hungry after all," Mrs. Denny noted happily. "Do you mind going back, Keturah?"

The question was too nicely put. I could feel her sympathy without her saying so. I couldn't answer. I pretended to have too much cake in my mouth.

"Run along and get yourself another piece," she urged, immediately I'd swallowed it, seeming to know I couldn't answer. "Take the one with the light pink icing. It's Mrs. Wayburn's. Light as a feather."

I hurried over to the table, glad to escape for a moment. I helped myself to a huge piece of cake with light pink icing, and a paper cup of lemonade. When I came back, I saw that Mr. Denny had moved over beside his wife and was quietly talking with her. Across the grove I saw Mr. Atwood with the two other girls who had not been taken. He was stretching his neck, and I knew he was looking for me. I took the last bite of feathery cake and washed it down with the lemonade. "I have to go," I blurted out. "Mr. Atwood's hunting for me."

I rushed off forgetting to say good-bye. I had not even thanked them. But it was too late to turn back.

Mr. Denny came catching up with me. "I'll go along with you," he panted, short of breath. "I want to see Atwood before he leaves."

We threaded our way through the crowd, the men smoking, exchanging talk, the women packing baskets, the never tired children still running helter-skelter. The sun was halfway down behind the beech trees, casting horizontal rays across the grove. I saw some of the children I had come with that morning attached to families. I wished I could see the twins again but they were nowhere in sight.

"Keturah," Mr. Denny was saying. "I don't think you ought to go back. Why don't you stay and spend the summer with us?"

I walked on as if I had not heard him. I stopped short as the full meaning of his words swept over me.

"You mean you'd have me?"

He scratched his gray head. "It just don't seem right for us to go home alone, Martha and me. We never did before."

I stood staring at him. I had to be perfectly honest.

"I eat a lot. I'm slow. I have to hurry up at the last to get done in time."

He gave me a long look. "You do appear as if you had a pretty good appetite. Don't like a puny eater. Never been one myself."

"But you don't need anyone." I could not accept the good fortune being offered me.

The flat rays of the sun struck his glasses and I could not see his eyes. "Oh," he drawled, "we could use a girl, I guess. Martha needs help around the house although she won't admit it even to herself. Getting older, we are, but don't like to tell ourselves so. She oughtn't to be out in the sun so much anymore." He folded his arms across his chest, his workworn hands nestling on his sleeves. "The fact is, we like someone young around. The Lord didn't send us children of our own. Guess he meant for us to look out for other people's."

Mr. Atwood came swooping up beside us like a dark shadow.

"Well, here you are, Keturah," he cried cheerfully. He was displaying his best manners again. The day had gone well for him, and filled with fried chicken, homemade cake and pie, he could well afford another expansive gesture. Yet I thought I saw his anger hidden away inside of him, smoldering, ready to pounce upon me once he had me alone. "Been looking everywhere for you. About time to start for the train." He pulled out his heavy gold watch which was fastened with a gold chain to his belt so no one could ever steal it. "Mrs. Atwood will be mighty glad to see you coming back."

Would she? Had he reconsidered, remembering how much help I would be in canning time? I stood silent before him, the joy of a few moments ago swept away.

"Look here, Mr. Atwood," Mr. Denny said quietly. "We've decided to keep this girl with us for the summer. Don't know how she happened to be passed up this afternoon but the luck's all ours."

Mr. Atwood strangely enough did want me back. It was almost funny. If Mr. Denny hadn't wanted me I'm sure he wouldn't have been half so anxious to have me either. Once he had the reins, Mr. Atwood wanted to hold them. He changed from his genial, false front in the twinkling of an eye. I saw he thought I had pulled a trick on him.

"Oh, but I'm taking her back with me, Mr. Denny," he said archly, keeping control of his voice. "We just brought Keturah along to help with the little ones. We need her this summer."

Mr. Denny remained unruffled. "I think it might be good for her to stay here for a change."

Mr. Atwood gave me another sharp glance. "She'll have one soon enough she's eighteen."

"Now look here." Mr. Denny planted his feet more firmly on the ground, and I saw he was a man of strength as well as kindness. "You stood her up there like a show horse this afternoon and tried to auction off her good points, and

44

now when I've made up my mind to take her you've changed yours."

Mr. Atwood also planted himself more firmly. "I have."

"Suppose," Mr. Denny offered, not raising his voice, "I call in George Perkins about this. He collects for the Orphanage around here. Gets a pretty good contribution each year too. Maybe he has enough authority to have a voice in this matter."

The color came darkly into Mr. Atwood's already sullen face. He pursed his lips tightly together, stretched them back toward his ears and let them snap back into their down-turned corners. "I'll tell you what we'll do, Mr. Denny," he said, backing down cautiously at Mr. Denny's proposal. "We'll let Keturah choose. If she wants to stay, she stays, If she wants to go back, I take her." He did not wait for Mr. Denny to agree. He turned to me with as much friendliness as he had ever shown me. "Keturah, it's up to you."

I don't know what made him think I would ever choose to go with him. Pure egotism must have fooled him into thinking he was not really hated. Or maybe he thought I was that afraid of him. I looked at Mr. Denny. "I want to stay with you, sir."

Mr. Atwood brushed his hands with an exasperated air of good riddance. Then quickly he changed again.

"Settled," he cried. "You can have her, Denny. But don't say I didn't warn you. She'll eat you out of house and home. You'll be wanting to send her back before I'm after calling for her."

"Anytime she wants to go," Mr. Denny said, smooth as silk, "she is free to leave."

Mr. Atwood turned on his heel and left, disappearing into the crowd.

"I never did like that man," Mr. Denny said. "And the more I see of him the less I do." He pressed my arm. "Glad it turned out this way, Keturah?"

<h2 style="text-align:center">7</h2>

I fell upon the stars that night going home with the Dennys. We had stayed until the program was over. I sat between Mrs. Denny and her sister while the choirs competed for first prize, scarcely hearing what they sang. Someone had asked me! For three long months I would be free of the Orphanage. I had to keep closing my eyes and opening them to realize I was still there. As we were leaving the grounds I saw the Drury twins fast asleep in the arms of the young couple who had taken them that afternoon.

"The Campbells will never send them back," Mrs. Denny prophesied. "They've been wanting young ones ever since they married seven years ago."

I went over and gave Ethel and Billie each a little pat. Even in sleep they sucked their thumbs.

"They won't be any trouble," I told Mrs. Campbell. "They never cry."

She smiled sweetly back at me from under the dark wings of her hair. "They've been like angels ever since we took them."

"If they had some decent clothes they'd be real pretty," I assured her.

Mrs. Campbell smiled again. "You just wait until I get to sewing for them."

Bouncing over the dark country road in Mr. Denny's Model T, which he proudly told me had replaced a horse-drawn wagon to carry the mail, I put my head out the window and took a long, deep breath of the fragrant summer night. Looking up, I saw the stars. They were scattered brightly across the sky. One of them winked at me.

"Look at the stars," I cried, never having seem them before. The car bounced over a hole in the road, and I bumped my head on the window frame, knocking my jaws together. I sat back in the seat rubbing my head, seeing if my teeth were still in tight.

"You've got to hold on over the bumps," Mr. Denny warned, never slowing down. "Wait until you get up on our hill, then you'll really see the stars."

We took Mrs. Wayburn home first. Once she was out of the car she continued talking to Mrs. Denny through the rear window. I became sleepy listening to them. All the tiredness of the day caught up with me. Dimly I heard Mr. Denny tell the two women they'd already discussed everything there was to be discussed, and he wanted to get home that night. When Mrs. Wayburn was safely in her house and the lamp lit, Mr. Denny backed out onto the road again. After a few miles we turned off onto a narrow, unpaved road, and almost at once the headlights flashed over a long, white fence.

"Here's where our place begins," Mr. Denny said, and I was wide-awake again, wanting to see all of where I was going. We turned up a steep driveway and stopped. Mr. Denny leaned out the window, pulled on a pole dangling from a pulley, and before my startled eyes the fence broke and a white gate swung open. We drove inside, and Mr. Denny reached out and pulled on another pole and the gate swung shut behind us. The Model T chugged up the hill. At the top the car lights revealed a white cottage under a gabled roof in the center of a fenced-in yard. Mr. Denny flung open his door.

"Well, here we are, Keturah. Welcome home!"

A dog came running up to meet us. He jumped up on the Dennys, sniffed curiously at me. "Down, Romany," Mrs. Denny ordered. "Down. Now behave yourself."

Mrs. Denny went up ahead and in the side door and lit a lamp in the window, while Mr. Denny took the baskets and my suitcase out of the back of the car and rolled up the windows. He reached in and switched off the headlights. "Now look at the stars, girl."

I leaned back my head. Above the trees they sparkled dazzlingly close.

"See the Big Dipper up there to your right." Mr. Denny pointed it out. "Holding water tonight. No rain tomorrow."

I couldn't find it at once and he helped me locate it by the large North Star.

"Beautiful sight," Mr. Denny murmured. "Never get tired looking at the stars."

At that precise moment a star fell from the sky. It slid across the heavens like a bright arrow and was gone. I clapped my hands over my ears and screamed.

"Make a wish," Mr. Denny shouted. "Make a wish on a falling star."

"It hasn't exploded yet," I gasped.

Mr. Denny didn't laugh. He teased me about it later but he didn't laugh at me then. He said: "Pshaw, it's not going to explode. It fell way over on the other side of the world, the China side probably. It's already shining in some other sky."

I was still trembling. "Don't they ever blow up?"

48

"Never heard of one that did. Haven't you ever seen a falling star?"

I told him I had never seen the stars before. I told him about the blinds being pulled down at dark, that I had never been outside at night. "Well imagine," he said. And I felt suddenly as if he were someone I could always confide in, that he understood. His not laughing at me in my fright cemented a bond between us.

Mrs. Denny took me up to my room underneath a gable. She went up the little winding stairs ahead of me, carrying the lamp. She set it on the dresser that had a foggy mirror above it and carved oak leaves for the handles of the drawers. Shadows thrown by the lamp flickered on the sloping white ceiling. There was a small spool bed to match the dresser and a marble-topped washstand with a painted china pitcher and washbasin on it. The white curtains moved with the breeze that came in when Mrs. Denny propped the window open on a stick. I closed my eyes. When I opened them the room was still there.

"We'll have to clean it good tomorrow," Mrs. Denny said. "I wasn't expecting anyone to sleep in it tonight. You won't mind being up here alone?"

The thought hadn't crossed my mind. True, I had always slept in a room full of other girls but the idea of having a room of my own left no place for fear. I assured her I wouldn't be.

When she had gone back downstairs, I undressed and blew out the lamp. I sank down on my knees at the low window. Above the trees I caught a glimpse of stars. In their misty light I could see the white barn and two pale cows nosing down the hill beyond it. I started to say my prayers from habit but my heart was too full for the usual words.

"God," I broke off abruptly. "You don't seem to be around very often but you sure were today."

Nothing was timed except getting up, going to bed, and meals. While Mr. Denny milked and tended his cows and horse, I fed the chickens, hurrying back to the house to carry in the breakfast Mrs. Denny had prepared. During the morning Mrs. Denny and I worked in the garden and flower beds. Mrs. Denny would have to sit down in the shade at intervals and fan herself with a palm leaf fan she always kept handy, wiping the perspiration from her face with her apron. At noon Mr. Denny was back for a hot dinner. He carried a few lumps of sugar from the table for Nellie, his old horse, always somewhere near the yard fence waiting for her treat. "She pulled the mail wagon long as she could," Mr. Denny explained, evidently feeling I might question the wisdom of his keeping such an old horse. "She's got a right to a pension same as any other retired government employee."

From the front of the house there was a fine view of the river flowing through the valley below. The river changed color with the weather and the time of day. Early in the morning a silver mist rose from it, like a veil being slowly lifted; at noon it was brightly blue; in the evenings it was as flat and colorless as a mirror. Barges of coal and oil pushed up and down the river by spanking white stern-wheelers passed frequently, and occasionally a pleasure boat, tiered with gingerbread railings, bearing a prow as snowy as a swan's breast. Down in the valley the green cornfields were split through the middle by shining railroad tracks over which the trains rumbled day and night. Sometimes in the afternoons I rested under a shade tree in the yard, the birds drowsily twittering in the leaves above, and I wondered what Mrs. Atwood would say if she saw me doing absolutely nothing in the middle of the day.

I loved the evenings best of all. We carried the rockers down from the porch and set them on the lawn where it was cooler, rocking to and fro while Mr. Denny regaled us with the news he had gathered during the day, or commented on what he had read in the newspapers. He read every postcard he delivered but with him it wasn't a matter of snooping. He considered himself a bearer of good news and bad, and he liked to know what sort of news he was taking. He also read two newspapers thoroughly, the daily from the city which he brought home with him, and a local weekly that came every Thursday.

Mr. Denny had a vital interest in everything that was going on in the world. As a young man he had gone to the city to study law, but had had to give it up because of ill health. He became a rural mail carrier instead of a lawyer, but he never relinquished his love of law and politics. We were given a Mr. Denny's-eye view of the news, buttered up with his cheerful optimism.

At nine thirty the Flyer to Washington, D.C., sped by in a string of lights that marked bedtime.

ᴁ 8 ᴂ

J. P. Sims, Esq., Owner and Proprietor of the General Store, as it was painted on the front window in which also hung a sign: ASK FOR IT, WE HAVE IT, was a big, bustling, hulk of a man who had only been fooled once in his life, and Mr.

Denny had played a part in the joke. Mr. Sims told me about it the first time I went down to the store.

The store was stocked from floor to ceiling and wall to wall with everything imaginable. That some of the things had been on the shelves for years, outmoded, gathering dust, never bothered Mr. Sims. He never took inventory, able to remember everything he had, and the new products were simply stacked up with the old. It was a maze of fresh food, canned goods, knickknacks, farm tools, clothing, household goods and patent medicines, and I wandered through it all as dazed as Alice in Wonderland.

Mrs. Denny had asked me to go down to the store for a piece of bacon back for cooking beans. She had not discovered she was out of it until after Mr. Denny had left at noon. Almost reluctantly she had asked me to go to the store, never wanting to put me to any extra trouble. With a feeling of adventure I went down the hill, pulled down on the pole and watched the gate swing wide for me to pass through. I had never been anywhere alone before. Romany came racing down the hill and out the gate before it swung closed. He trotted along beside me, his plumed tail waving like a flag of protection.

A strap of sleigh bells tinkled as I opened the screen door and stepped inside the store. Strips of gummed paper, black with dead flies, hung from the ceiling. Mr. Sims was leaning against the drygoods shelves apparently waiting for a customer. His big hairy arms were folded across his chest, the sleeves of his dark blue shirt were damp with sweat, a pair of striped suspenders held his loose pants up over his huge stomach.

"Howdy," he greeted me, the small black eyes in his fleshy face wondering who I was.

"Mrs. Denny sent me for a piece of bacon back," I announced myself, "to cook with beans."

"So you're the summer girl at the Dennys'."

I nodded.

"Good people." He shook his big head up and down to verify it. "I've got just the piece of bacon back for the Mrs."

While he went off to get it I looked over a rack of fly-specked picture postcards in front of me, wishing I could look at everything in the store. When Mr. Sims came back with the meat wrapped in thick brown paper, he asked if there was anything else. Mrs. Denny had given me a dime to bring back a bag of candy. She had a sweet tooth, and always kept a dish of candy handy on the sideboard.

"A dime's worth of candy," I told him.

The candy was under a domed glass case cloudy with fingerprints. I stared fascinated at the array of little glass dishes piled high with lemon balls, jawbreakers, licorice whips, mothballs, gumdrops, peppermint, horehound, chocolate drops. . . .

"Everything's two for a penny," Mr. Sims said. "Except the jelly beans. They're five for a penny."

Carefully I made my choice while Mr. Sims' fat, hairy hand reached in and took two of each from the dishes I pointed to. He counted out loud: "Two, four, six, eight, ten. One dime." He handed me the bag. Then he invited me to stay and look around. "Might see something you'd like to buy sometime. Got everything from pots and pans to long underwear. Anything a body needs except that friend of Cyrus Denny's." He stuck his thumbs under his striped suspenders. "Did he ever tell you about it?"

I shook my head.

"It's the only time anyone ever tricked me." He leaned

53

against the counter, unaware of how anxious I was to roam through the store. "Cyrus had this man out visiting from the city, lawyer friend of his. The two of them came in here one afternoon and this gentleman with Cyrus said he'd like some Caveat emptor. 'Never heard of it,' I said.

"He looks at me and says, 'You've got a sign on your windows: Ask for it, we have it.' We were standing in front of the canned goods and I got to thinking maybe it was some fancy kind of fish he wanted. They got those foreign names on fish cans sometimes. I turned around to look. 'Nope,' I told him. 'Guess I must be out of it.'

" 'Well then,' he says, spruced up like he was in his fine clothes, 'as a lawyer I had better warn you to take that sign out of your window. It's illegal to fraudulently advertise.' Those were his exact word, miss. 'I came in here for Caveat emptor because the sign says ask for it, we have it.'

"Doggone it, I got mad. Seldom lose my temper but that fellow standing there asking for some fancy stuff I never heard of stirred up my blood. 'By God, if there is such a thing I'll get some for you,' I told him." Mr. Sims let go of his suspenders and brought his big fist down on the counter, as he must have done when the lawyer was there.

I watched him fascinated, seeing the store forgotten. "It was too much for Cyrus," Mr. Sims went on. "Cyrus broke out laughing. 'Sims,' he says, 'he's joshing you. Caveat emptor's a legal term.'

"By God, I was mad then. Excuse me for swearing, miss, but that's exactly how I felt." He lifted his chin, of which there were two, and stood there defying his unseen adversary. After a moment he quickly scratched his head over which a few long strands of black hair leaped from one side to the other. "I still don't know what it is. Do you?"

I shook my head again. "No."

"Guess I was mad at Cyrus a while afterwards. They had a good laugh over it at the post office and around these parts for a time. But a body can't stay mad at Cyrus Denny. He's too good-natured. After I got good and calmed down, I decided it was all the other fellow's idea to begin with and Cyrus had just been along. Anyway, I ain't never took my sign down. No city fellow's going to tell me what kind of signs I can hang in my window." He lifted his big body from the counter. "Come on, I'll show you around."

I followed him down one long aisle and back up the other as he proudly showed me his wares: a white glass hen with a red comb, sitting on a glass dish; a double eggbeater which he claimed beat eggs twice as fast; an oil lamp with a shiny brass base; a set of china with green apples painted on it; cowbells with different tunes; and a windlass hanging on the wall that tinkled like pieces of glass falling softly through the air. At the perfume counter Mr. Sims picked up a bottle of red lilac perfume with a rubber atomizer, and squirted some on my arm.

"Smell you up like a lady," he said.

The sleigh bells jingled to announce another customer, and the time had come for me to leave. I thanked him for showing me his store.

"Not at all, not at all. Like to show my wares to a new customer." He followed me to the door where Romany was waiting patiently on the step outside. "Hurry back," Mr. Sims called as I went out.

Two women passed me on the road, staring at me from under the brims of their starched sunbonnets. They did not speak. But I did not mind. I lifted my arm and smelled the red lilac perfume. "Smell you up like a lady," Mr. Sims had said. I held my head as high as they did theirs. Unknown to me then, Mr. Sims had watered a seed.

9

Sunday was centered around church. The Sugar Creek Baptist Church, a square, red brick building with an open bell tower on the roof, was over a hundred years old. So were the square panes of the long windows through which the light cast rainbow colors onto the oak pews. The windows were wide open in summer and flies and bees wandered in and out undisturbed.

Beside the church was an old cemetery under a grove of pine trees, the tombstones leaning forward and back. A low stone wall enclosed the graves. Mrs. Denny told me that a snake had stuck its head out of the wall one morning when she was decorating the family graves and she had thrown an apron over its head and pulled until the snake came all the way out. With the last jerk she had fallen over backwards, but got to her feet in time to kill it with a rock.

Mrs. Wayburn, standing beside us, shivered. "If it had been me, I'd have run a mile a minute hollering for help. Martha always was the brave one."

She took me over and pointed out her husband's grave to me. One of the newer stones marked it. "I miss the man for all the contention he gave me," she said.

I didn't know what she meant but she seemed to be quite sufficient without him. I had the feeling she must be as well off rid of Mr. Wayburn as she had been living with him.

Mr. Denny was superintendent of the Sunday school and read the Scriptures. I wondered if he used the same Bible

Mrs. Atwood had. The verses she read were always dry and dull and full of thou-shalt-nots. Mr. Denny put a lot of feeling into the words as he read so that everyone listened attentively. He would read: "I will lift up mine eyes unto the hills . . ." the words dropping into my mind like a picture, and sometimes when I walked around the front of the house, I would look at the dark green hills rising behind the river, and the words would come into my mind again. I would repeat them to myself: "I will lift up mine eyes unto the hills. . . ."

The Baptists liked to sing. They sang four or five hymns in a row. The very first Sunday I attended, Mr. Palmer came over and held his open hymnal in front of me while I was hunting for the page in mine. He never paused in his singing, merely pointing to the place, swinging his free hand in accompaniment. Mr. Palmer was a bachelor, his hair faded to a pale red, a rim of pink around his light blue eyes. His hands and face were covered with pale freckles. Down the front of his immaculate white shirt flowed a white, hand-knitted tie with a blue P embroidered on it. He was extremely shy when he wasn't singing. But while he sang his courage rose, his voice boomed out, his false teeth clicked, and every so often a spray dampened the pages of the hymnal.

"You've got a nice voice, young lady," he said, the hymns sung, the courage still in him. He extended a freckled hand. "Fred Palmer's the name. Welcome to Sugar Creek Baptist Church."

I shook his hand gratefully. To the Atwoods I had been a drudge. I had stood up under it, refusing to become a worm for them to step on. Mr. Palmer had called me "young lady." Mr. Sims had smelled me up like one. Beneath my tight calico dress I felt a surge toward something better than I

57

had been. I smiled into Mr. Palmer's pink-rimmed eyes, and he blushed until the freckles melted on his weathered face.

The classes met in the basement. I was placed in a circle of chairs with half a dozen girls around my age. Miss Lavendar, the teacher, was a sweet old lady, very deaf. She smelled of lemons. The girls eyed me askance and chatted among themselves all during the lesson, adding to the hubbub of all the other classes around us. Miss Lavendar couldn't hear anything distinctly in all that buzz, but she bravely went on giving the lesson she had prepared, unconcerned if anyone paid attention or not. She passed around a picture illustrating the lesson. Underneath it read: SUFFER THE LITTLE CHILDREN TO COME UNTO ME. The words were familiar. They were carved on the walls just inside the front door of the Orphanage. I had thought they meant the Orphanage was a place for children who suffered. I held the picture a long while before I passed it on to the next girl. I had never associated the words with a hand outstretched in welcome, children gathered at a man's knee. When the picture returned to Miss Lavendar she held it out to me.

"Would you like to have it, Keturah?" she asked. "Since you're a new girl I think it would be nice."

"You mean to keep?" I asked in amazement.

She smiled sweetly. She hadn't heard me right. "You could sleep with it if you want to, but it might get mussed."

The girls laughed. But I could not laugh at Miss Lavendar. She was giving me the picture. She had understood that it meant something to me.

After Sunday school the men went outside and the women gathered together to chat until time for church. The children ran in and out. At five minutes to eleven the bell in the open steeple rang again. The pews were filled and the service began. The minister was very young and had a weak voice to be preaching. But he seemed to believe what he was talking about. His failure was his voice. What he said came out in such an even, steady flow that before the sermon was half over, heads began to nod, children squirmed and whimpered and had to be taken out, and my thoughts wandered away to Mr. Wayburn lying out in the yard where he could hear only the soft murmur of the wind in the pine trees, the birds singing back and forth, and the insects ticking away in the grass. I wondered what sort of contention he had caused his wife.

After church we either went to Mrs. Wayburn's house for a chicken dinner or she came to ours for one. While we waited for dinner to be ready in Mrs. Wayburn's parlor, I could scarcely remove my eyes from the mantle where there was a picture of Mr. Wayburn in his coffin. He looked very long and stiff in his black suit, his head resting on a white satin pillow, his hands crossed on his flat stomach. The picture gave the room a solemn air. I could almost smell the flowers in the wicker baskets standing at either end of the coffin. Voices were lowered as if no one wanted to disturb Mr. Wayburn. I was always glad when Mrs. Wayburn called us to the dining room.

The second Sunday the Campbells were at church with the twins. Mrs. Campbell had been busy sewing. Ethel fairly bloomed in a yellow dress with white flowers appliquéd on it, a yellow bow tied on her straight blond hair. Billie had on a yellow suit to match. I went over to speak to them.

"Now what do you think?" Mrs. Campbell asked proudly.

I patted their heads. For once they weren't sucking their thumbs. "We've got cows," Billie told me. "And kittens,"

59

Ethel beamed up at me. I could scarcely believe the change in them. Love had opened them up like flowers.

Mr. Palmer was back again with his hymnal no sooner than the singing began. But when we broke up for classes, he disappeared again, taken in tow by his two maiden sisters who kept him safely between them for the rest of the morning. Somehow he managed every Sunday to escape them long enough to sing beside me. The Dennys teased me about it.

"Seems to me Brother Palmer can't get over fast enough with his hymn book," Mr. Denny would remark casually enough.

"Wonder if that old fool will ever stop being silly," Mrs. Wayburn fussed. "He used to come sidling up to me when I was a girl, Keturah. Before he got his false teeth and started spraying."

"He was real stuck on you, Bertha," Mrs. Denny recalled. "If you hadn't met Armor Wayburn when you did, I think you might have took up with him."

"Why Martha!" Mrs. Wayburn exclaimed, horrified. "I'd have been an old maid first." Her round straw hat with summer flowers on the brim bobbed on her head despite the hatpin stuck clear through it. "I just hope Keturah has as much sense as I did."

It was my turn to be shocked. "Why, he's older than Mr. Denny."

"Almost," Mrs. Denny agreed. "We're just having fun, Keturah. No offense."

10

I had been at the Dennys' a month when Mr. Denny gave me a dollar one morning. Carefully he took it out of his little, worn leather purse at the breakfast table, as carefully unfolded it, smoothing out the creases, and laid it beside my plate.

"I thought you might like to buy something for yourself down at the store," he announced.

I did not dare to touch it. There had never been even a penny of my own, and here was a whole dollar beside my plate. Mrs. Denny came in from the kitchen and set the platter of bacon and eggs on the table. "I'm sure there's something you'd like to buy," she said, and I realized she knew what Mr. Denny had been up to. They must have talked it over together. "Maybe a can of talcum powder and some shampoo for your hair, or a new comb."

Slowly I reached out and touched the bill. "It's an honest-to-God dollar," I said.

Mr. Denny laughed. "It sure is, Keturah."

Mrs. Denny sat down quickly. "Why, Keturah," she said, suddenly brusque. She never corrected me, never made remarks about my upbringing at the Orphanage, but when something I did failed to please her, she simply said "Why, Keturah," and I knew I had made a mistake. I flushed under her remark and for a moment there was silence. Then Mr. Denny said: "It's yours to do with what you like."

"Thank you kindly, Mr. Denny," I said. "But I haven't done enough work to deserve it."

His blue eyes twinkled from behind the steel-rimmed glasses. "Seems to me you've been making yourself pretty useful around here. Martha hasn't had a headache since you came. The hot sun always gave her a headache. Hen house looks as good as it ever did; the yard's as neat and trim as if we had a hired man." He paused to take a sip of coffee from his cup. "But you didn't get the dollar because you earned it. It's a present. That's different, you know."

There were two things I had been wanting, a postcard and a one-cent stamp so that I could write to Georgia Lee. I had thought about her often, wondering who was sleeping beside her, if she was keeping out of trouble. I also wanted to let her know I was not having a hard time of it. I slipped the dollar bill in my pocket and thanked Mr. Denny again.

That very afternoon I went to the store. Mrs. Denny was almost out of white thread for her crocheting, enough so that she could use it as an excuse to send me off. She gave me the usual dime for a bag of candy so I wouldn't spend any of my dollar to buy her some. "You don't have to hurry," she said when I left. "Nothing needs to be done until supper-time."

It was a long, hot walk to the store in the middle of the afternoon under the blazing sun, but it was all downhill. Romany came rushing through the gate to trot along beside me, his plumed tail waving. At the store I looked over every single postcard on the rack, turning the spindle slowly around, going up and down the rows. Mr. Sims was busy with some other customers and didn't hurry me. I finally chose a colored picture of the Statue of Liberty. I liked the blue of the water under it. Besides, there were no flyspecks on it. I found Mrs. Denny's white thread, then wandered through the store looking at everything I might buy.

"Need any help, Keturah?" Mr. Sims came along behind the counter, mopping his dripping forehead with the damp sleeve of his blue shirt.

I shook my head. "I'm looking for something for myself. Mr. Denny gave me a whole dollar to spend."

"Look as long as you like," he offered, and moved down the counter. In a little while he was back. He leaned toward me over the trays of sparkling jewelry. I could smell the sweatiness that stained his clothes. "How do you like it here by now?" he asked.

I assured him I liked it very much.

"No orphan fares better anywhere than at the Dennys'," he said.

There was no malice in his voice, but he had called me an orphan, the word that set us apart from other people. It dimmed the pleasure of the afternoon. Perhaps it was because for the first time, with a dollar of my own, I didn't feel like an orphan.

Mr. Sims became aware he had said something amiss. He put both big, hairy hands flat down on the counter and poked his face so close that I could see way back into his small black eyes that had no whites around them.

"Don't let being an orphan put you at the bottom of the pile, Keturah," he said kindly. "I was one too. My own mother's people raised me but it wasn't much better than an institution. Put me out in the fields from morning to night and never a kind word from anyone. But look at me now." He straightened up and stuck his thumbs under his striped suspenders and snapped them against his broad chest. A glow of pride spread over his hot face, and I saw at the same time what he had been and what he had become. "I got a fine family of my own, three girls, two boys. Got this store stocked from floor to ceiling, from front door to back; never any lack of food on the table. I might have to work a little harder than some but got a good place to rest when I do get home." He paused. "You'll make it too, Keturah. There's that about you."

I stood staring back at him, becoming slowly aware of what he was trying to tell me. I felt something stirring around in me, like some deep well receiving another's struggling childhood. And slowly rising from the well, the knowledge that he saw a way out for me too. I could not smile, filled with a wistfulness.

"Do you really think so, Mr. Sims?"

He nodded slowly. "In fact, I'm sure of it."

I bought a blue silk hairnet crocheted in big, open squares with a blue silk bow on the front, to put my hair in at night. I thought the girls in the dormitory would be fascinated by it and think my summer had been truly prosperous. I had enough left to buy a can of lily-of-the-valley talcum powder, a bottle of green shampoo and a pink powder puff. I knew Mrs. Atwood would take the puff away but I could put a little powder on my nose on Sundays until she did. I still had a dime left, and with it I bought a nail file, remembering my dirty nails that day at the train. I would have them well cleaned when I went back.

Mr. Sims wrapped the packages carefully. "Enjoy them," he said, as he handed them over. Then he gave me a wink from one of his little chipmunk eyes and hurried over to wait on another customer.

I leaned against the wall desk at the post office and tried to think of what to write to Georgia Lee. Nothing I had planned sounded right now. After what Mr. Sims had said

I realized that Georgia Lee was a worse off orphan than I was, and I couldn't think of anything to cheer her up. The man behind the barred window was watching me, wondering, I suppose, what that orphan girl from the Dennys' was up to standing there so long. I also had to be sure it would be something that Mrs. Atwood would allow Georgia Lee to read, if she ever gave Georgia Lee the postcard. It would all depend on how she had been behaving. Mail came so seldom to the Orphanage, it would be a real event for Georgia Lee to get a colored picture postcard of the Statue of Liberty.

I could not tell her how much I liked it at the Dennys'. Mr. Atwood had probably been hoping all along that I was having a miserable time and would come crawling back to him when he came for me. He would tear the card up in his anger. Suddenly I knew what to write.

"Dear Georgia Lee," I wrote, the long, black pen with the rusty point scratching across the card. "Don't let it put you on the bottom of the pile. Your friend, Keturah." I thought Georgia Lee would know what I meant.

It was the end of August too soon. It was the end of August and almost time for Mr. Atwood to come back. We never spoke of it. The days passed in pleasant routine. The vegetable garden was still flourishing; there was still canning to be done; the flower beds were neat as a pin. Once a week I cleaned the hen house, but Mrs. Denny had to chop the heads off the chickens she fried. I couldn't even bear to watch her. Nor could I watch her drown the litters of kittens that were produced during the summer. She would tie them up in a brown paper bag with a weight inside and put the bag down in a tub of water. What she did with them afterwards I never knew, I was always off as far away as possible.

65

During the hot August days a thunderstorm came up almost every afternoon. Mrs. Denny and I huddled on the daybed in the dining room until the storms were over. Mrs. Denny was a firm believer in feathers as a protection against the lightning, and she kept a featherbed on the daybed all summer long.

One Saturday afternoon a storm came up just as Mr. Denny was ready to take us over to visit some of their relatives, and we had to wait until the storm was over. Mr. Denny scoffed at the featherbed.

"Nothing in it," he declared, and sat in his favorite rocker beside the window, watching the storm, enjoying it as he did all manifestations of nature. "Look at old Nelly standing right out there in the rain. Got sense enough not to stand under a tree, either. Likes a good washing off." A flash of lightning split the sky, and I clapped my hands to my ears but they did little to shut out the crash of thunder that followed.

"Struck near here," Mr. Denny noted calmly. He rocked a moment, his pipe between his teeth. "Ever hear about Rip Van Winkle, Keturah?" And while the storm raged Mr. Denny told the story of Rip Van Winkle, who had climbed up into the mountains and found the little men playing at ninepins, and how they frolicked over the thunder their crashing balls made for the people down in the valley far below.

"Always think of those little men at their game when it thunders," Mr. Denny said. "Laughing over people scared of the noise."

I knew it was not a true story but afterwards I was calmer during the storms. Whether it was Mr. Denny's lack of fear or the story he told me I don't know, but always afterwards during a storm I thought of the little men rolling ninepins and I dared sit in Mr. Denny's rocker, leaving Mrs. Denny on the featherbed.

The second Friday in September Mr. Denny came in for dinner without stopping to pat Romany when he ran up to meet him. He came in the house and washed his hands in the basin at the sink without saying a word. When I carried the food into the dining room he was standing at the window with his back to the room.

"Mr. Denny," I announced timidly. "Dinner is on the table."

He waited until Mrs. Denny and I were seated before he came over and sat down. He folded his hands and mumbled the grace he usually spoke so reverently.

"Something go wrong this morning, Cyrus?" Mrs. Denny asked cautiously as she handed him the bowl of mashed potatoes.

Mr. Denny helped himself, then covered his potatoes with gravy. He reached for the dish of watermelon pickle. "There was a card at the post office from Mr. Atwood. He's coming Monday."

I gripped my fork. So it was going to be over.

"My, how the summer's flown," Mrs. Denny murmured. "Seems like Keturah just came."

"The Campbells are going to keep the twins," Mr. Denny said.

"Oh, I hoped they would," I exclaimed, forgetting my own predicament for the moment.

"They'll have a good home," Mrs. Denny allowed. "And the Campbells couldn't have done better if they'd had children of their own."

The meal continued in silence, each mind busy with its own thoughts. I wondered what the Dennys were thinking. I suppose they wondered as much about me. We finished our dessert of sliced oranges and bananas mixed with marshmallows and coconut and brightened with maraschino cherries. Mrs. Denny made it more often than any other dessert but it was still their favorite. Mr. Denny wiped his mouth with a paper napkin, crumpled it into a tight ball, and dropped it on his plate. He pushed back his chair, crossed his legs, and poked his teeth with a wooden toothpick.

"Well, Keturah, are you ready to go back?"

I shook my head. "But I have to go," I tried to say lightly, afraid their silence had meant they were afraid they might have trouble getting me to go.

Mrs. Denny was still at her dessert. Her spoon clicked against the little glass dish. Mr. Denny reached over on the sideboard for his pipe and can of tobacco, carefully filled the pipe and held a match to the bowl. He puffed three or four times until he had it going. He hooked an arm over the back of his chair.

"You don't have to go back, Keturah," he announced in his easy way so that it did not seem anything momentous he was saying. "Mrs. Denny and I, in fact, would be sorry to have you leave."

"But we don't want you to stay if you don't want to," Mrs. Denny hastily added. "I know it's lonesome here for a girl your age."

I looked from one to the other. I could scarcely believe my ears. They were offering me a home if I wanted to stay. What had been worrying them was the fact that I might not want to, that I was lonely. . . . *"You mean you want me?"* I cried.

Mr. Denny smiled sheepishly. "Of course we want you. We've wanted you to stay ever since we saw how well you fit in with us. We'd be mighty lonesome if you decided to leave."

Mrs. Denny brushed the edge of her apron across the end of her nose. "You've been a mighty good help this summer, Keturah."

I jumped out of my chair. I threw my arms around Romany who rushed up to me, thinking I was going to feed him. "I'll never leave," I declared. "I'll never go away from here."

⊷ 11 ⊶

I did not see Mr. Atwood again. Mr. Denny made the final arrangements with him and I was released from the Orphanage.

"I don't think anything ever gave me more pleasure than telling Mr. Atwood you were going to stay," Mr. Denny told us after things were settled. "He didn't like it, Keturah. I guess you did more than your share of the work."

"They never thought anyone would have me," I said, secretly amused at Mr. Atwood's anger. "I didn't either."

I was no longer a summer child. *I belonged.* I had to go down to the store and tell Mr. Sims about it. He beamed at me from behind the counter. "That's your first step up," he advised me, and gave me one of his small-eyed winks.

The Dennys discussed sending me to school. But I would be behind in everything but spelling, and I didn't want to be the oldest and largest girl in my class. Since I was past sixteen, the matter was dropped.

"I'll tell you what," Mr. Denny said one evening as we sat out on the lawn under the stars. There had been company earlier—a Mr. and Mrs. Fornash and their children Dick and Claudine, the latter my age. She was in my Sunday school class but she had never bothered to speak to me. Neither Dick nor Claudine was blessed with good looks, but under their perfectly combed, straight hair, their active minds blazed with knowledge. Their parents impressed upon us the fact that Dick and Claudine were at the head of their classes.

They had taken them to Washington, D.C., on the Flyer during the summer as a reward for their high grades. Dick told about the session of Congress he had attended, and Claudine related every little detail of the interior of Mount Vernon. I don't believe she left out a vase. Mrs. Denny yawned behind the corner of her apron she had forgotten to take off, but Mr. Denny, always eager to learn anything new, listened attentively. Whenever Claudine might possibly skip something her mother interrupted. "You forgot the little cherry whatnot, Claudine, in the upstairs front corner bedroom, the one by the north window." "Oh, yes," Claudine would recall immediately, "I did almost forget it, Mother. But how could I? Martha Washington's picture was on it. A little miniature of her as a bride."

When they finally left, trailing the glory of their summer trip behind them, Mr. Denny knocked the ashes from his pipe. "I'll tell you what," he said. "Keturah has as good a mind as that Claudine has. If she had her opportunities she'd outshine her."

He never said in so many words that he would help me to accomplish this, but when it became too cool to sit out in the yard, the three of us gathered in the dining room in the evenings, Mr. Denny in his favorite rocker, Mrs. Denny at the table embroidering pillow slips or crocheting, myself on the horsehair settee struggling to cross-stitch a towel. Mr. Denny read aloud. He had a bookcase full of books in the hall—they were all old books, worn from much reading, books he had bought in his youth in the city or books that had been given to him as gifts long ago. He began with *David Copperfield* and followed it with *Silas Marner*. I lived these stories of people who had faced hardship and unhappiness and triumphed over them. I continued to live them up in my room at night, after I had turned out the lamp and snuggled down under the feather comforter, the wind blowing around the little gable.

Although Mr. Denny kept us informed of the news, he encouraged me to read articles in the newspapers. Struggling through them, I found many of the words were familiar from spelling matches, but I didn't know their meaning. I would underline those I didn't know, and Mr. Denny would go over them with me, using a dictionary if he wasn't sure of the meaning himself.

Mr. Denny also began reading aloud from the Bible every morning at breakfast. He read most often from the Psalms and the New Testament, as these were his favorite parts. During the day I would find myself repeating some of the words that had caught in my mind. "Under his wings he shall hide thee," or, "whiter than snow," or, "As far as the east is from the west." They were akin to the surrounding hills, the valley, the birds, the snow that came in December and lay on the ground for days at a time. They were words to treasure and store and think about.

As the days shortened and the cold settled in, I went down to the barn with Mr. Denny to help with the evening chores so he could get back to the warm house sooner, to supper and our reading. I milked one cow while he milked the other. We gathered armfuls of the sweet, dry hay from the loft for the cows and Nelly. In the privacy of the winter barn with the lantern light flickering on the whitewashed walls, the wind seeping in through the cracks, the muffled stomp of hoofs on the earth floor, shut away as we were, Mr. Denny told me more about his life. Maybe it was that as he worked with his hands he could better express his identity, or maybe it was that when Mrs. Denny was present, her chuckles and snorts at some of his musings disturbed him from revealing too much. But there in the early winter evening barn I learned of Mr. Denny's struggles as a young man, his hopes, his ambitions, how he had once felt that his illness had defeated him. He yearned sometimes toward the law he had relinquished, it was true, but his knowledge of it gave him a prestige in the community where few men had much education. At election time and in legal matters, people sought his advice and respected it.

"I would never have made a topnotch lawyer," Mr. Denny confided to me as Nelly crunched the lumps of sugar she had nuzzled from his coat pocket with her few teeth. "I'd never have caught on to all the tricks. I wasn't slick, not having been trained that way." He fondled Nelly's ears, which twitched under his caressing fingers. "In the country your competition's with nature and you soon find out you can't outwit her. If it hails just before you cut the wheat and the crop is flattened down, you just accept it. Count it so much loss that year and hope for better the next."

He gave Nelly a final pat on her bony flanks. "You grow to know your limitations struggling with something bigger than yourself. Nature keeps a man humble. You don't get to boasting, not knowing what day the lightning might strike your own barn."

We picked up our buckets of warm, foamy milk and went out into the cold night.

"Nope," Mr. Denny went on, without any interruption to his thoughts as we went up under the stars. "I'd have been just a pebble on the beach. I'd have struggled and strained, and the strides I might have made would have been dimmed by the effort. I did have the ambition once to try it. But I was a fish out of water."

We stood at the yard gate looking up at the stars. "It's best not to rebel against your destiny, Keturah. I came back home and found I was in the right place. With my kind of people. Never been sorry. I wasn't made for city life. Even the sidewalks hurt my feet." He lifted the gate latch. The cozy lamplight swam down from the house. "No place like home on a winter night, is there?"

Later, upstairs in my room, I stood in front of the little round mirror that hung above the walnut dresser, my flannel gown drawn at my throat and wrists, the blue silk crocheted net holding up my heavy hair, the perky blue bow perched on my forehead. In the yellow lamplight I stared at my reflection, not too clear in the peeling mirror. What would life hold for the girl gazing back at me? I wondered. Where would she step to from this room with its slanted ceiling, its virgin innocence? I had no ambition but to stay where I was. Yet Mr. Denny's talk had set me to thinking. If I ever had to be something else what would I be?

I remembered a picture I had once come across in a magazine on a Sunday afternoon at the Orphanage. It had left a deep impression on me for some reason. I had often gone back to look at it. A girl in a gold satin dress rested on a gold couch. She had golden hair and golden eyes. She was completely beautiful. *Portrait of a Lady*, I read under the pic-

73

ture. In some way she had become for me an unattainable ideal.

I swung about in front of the mirror, admiring myself in the cobwebby hairnet. I lifted my chin and the girl in the mirror lifted hers. I smiled and the girl smiled back at me. I remembered how Mr. Sims had smelled me up like a lady, how Mr. Palmer had said, ". . . young lady." I leaned close to the glass so the girl on the other side would hear. "Someday," I dared to tell that lamp-lighted image of myself, "someday I'm going to be an honest-to-God lady. See if I don't."

⊷§ 12 §⊷

I shall always remember my first Christmas at the Dennys'.

Late in November Mrs. Denny baked her fruitcakes. Candied fruit was snipped into tiny pieces, walnuts and hickory nuts we had gathered in the October woods were cracked and shelled; the heavy dough was stirred with a big, wooden spoon in an earthenware mixing bowl lined with tiny cracks of age. While the cakes were baking the house was charged with a wonderful spicy odor. Coming in from the cold outdoors and smelling the cakes rising in the oven was to sniff of an exciting time to come.

Mrs. Wayburn came over to help with the cookies. As we rolled out the floured dough and cut it in the shapes of stars, wreaths and animals, sprinkling the tops with pink sugar, cinnamon drops and raisins, Mrs. Denny and Mrs. Wayburn exchanged gossip. They speculated on the matrimonial prospects of the single, the difficulty of expected births, the life expectancy of the sick. In her quick, sharp way Mrs. Wayburn reminded me of a bird with sleek head cocked, beady eyes alert. A kindhearted woman, her tongue often beat her heart in relaying a piece of news. She had a way of saying "He'll be dead and six feet under by Christmas, mark my word" that startled me. She would predict with assurance: "If he lives the week I'll be surprised." Death was her favorite subject. She gave detailed reports of last moments spent on earth and what happened at funerals. I suppose living constantly with the picture of her dead husband in his coffin, she felt closely associated to death. To me, who had never seen anyone die or had ever been to a funeral, the subject was fascinating. But at night up in my room, the bare trees tapping against the frame house, I would crawl down under my feather comforter until I could scarcely breathe, trying to shut out the visions her recitals drew into my head in the dark.

Reading was put aside as we pored over mail-order catalogues. Mrs. Denny would slyly let Mr. Denny know what she wanted by lingering over a certain page. In the same way he made his desires known to her. Mrs. Denny told me to choose a dress to wear to the entertainment at the church on Christmas Eve. The Dennys had bought clothes for me in the fall—warm dresses, a coat, shoes, three pairs of lisle stockings, underwear, and a green felt hat. The morning the boxes arrived, I tried everything on for Mrs. Denny, who saw that it fit and approved. I tried everything but the underwear on again for Mr. Denny when he came home. "Now you do look fine in that green hat, Keturah," he exclaimed, calling forth a pride Mrs. Denny felt unnecessary to stir up in her approval. I tried the green hat on every night for a week before the mirror in my room, Mr. Denny's praise singing in my ears.

I could not choose between a black wool jumper with a red silk blouse and a navy-blue serge dress with a white collar, for the entertainment.

"Don't go worrying yourself any further," Mrs. Denny said finally, no doubt tired of my dilly-dallying. "We'll surprise you with one or the other."

Two days before Christmas, Mr. Denny and I went out to the woods to cut a tree for the bay window in the parlor. There was a light snow on the ground. Mr. Denny whistled as we walked through the snowy woods, his cheeks rosy, an ax over his shoulder. He knew the tree he wanted. He had not taken it the year before, wanting it to grow a bit more.

Surrounded by the snow, the fir tree stood strong and beautiful in the winter afternoon. Mr. Denny gently touched the feathery branches. I could see he hated to cut it down.

"But think of the pleasure it will give us," he said, having to have a reasonable excuse to take it from its native woods.

He swung the ax expertly at its base and in a few minutes the tree toppled over onto the snow. We carefully fastened it on the sled we had brought along, and I pulled it behind me.

"I'm sure this tree never dreamed it would grow up to be a Christmas tree," I said as we trudged up the hill toward home.

"Nope," Mr. Denny agreed. "And all it did to acquire the privilege was to grow tall and straight."

After a moment he asked: "Ever thought about what you

76

want to be, Keturah? You'll soon be seventeen, going on eighteen. Time you were thinking about it."

I glanced at him quickly. "Will I have to leave then?"

"Not if you don't want to."

"Then I'll stay here forever," I assured him.

"I'm glad you feel that way. But Mrs. Denny and I won't be here forever," he warned. "We're getting up in years. When we're gone you'll be on your own."

I looked up at the gray sky holding more snow. The wind blew across my face. His solemn words saddened me. I didn't want to think about them. I remembered that night in my room when I had made a vow to the girl in the mirror. Dared I tell Mr. Denny? His face was only kind. "I want to be a lady," I told him.

His eyebrows lifted as he sucked on the empty pipe he had stuck into his mouth. "Well now," he mused, again not laughing at me as he had not laughed the night I was terrified of the falling star. "A lady is a fine thing to be."

A sigh escaped. "But I'm not beautiful."

Mr. Denny remained serious. "I've seen many a homely lady who could sit herself beside a queen." He stopped to rest a moment at the top of the hill. "Do you know what a lady is, Keturah?"

"I saw a picture of one once. In a magazine."

"A real lady is a kindness to others," he went on, skipping over my remark, "a joy to her husband, a good mother to her children."

"All of that?"

He nodded. "But it's not out of your reach. Remember, cream always rises to the top."

I would lift the flimsy cheesecloth covers from the pails of milk set out in the summer kitchen, to see if the cream

77

were ready to be skimmed, and I would wonder how the cream coming to the top could have anything to do with my being a lady, the rich, thick cream that was the best part of the milk, adding to a dish of strawberries or a bowl of cereal, whipped up into a thick froth to set off a dessert. It never failed to come to the top. Was it like the best part of a person rising up from within until it finally showed? But how did one get the first drop of cream to begin with? I wondered. Or was there something good in everyone that could meld and increase and slowly rise until at last it appeared on the surface? For a long time it was a puzzle to me.

After the tree was set up in the bay window, we popped corn, strung it, and wound it around the branches. Mrs. Denny brought out a box of ornaments she kept from year to year, carefully unwrapping them from tissue paper, and Mr. Denny and I hung them on the tree. Last of all, the little candle holders were clamped on the tips of the branches and a red candle placed inside each one. Just at dark on Christmas Eve Mr. Denny touched a match to each candle. When they were all lit the little green tree was more beautiful than it had been in the snowy woods. Its candles burned twice, once on the branches and again in the windows. I thought how proud the little tree must feel standing there with its strings of popcorn, its glistening ornaments, its reflected candles. It had come out of the lonely woods where it had been showered by rain, warmed by sun, decked with winter's snow, where it had shivered in the sharp cold, holding up its branches under the darkest sky. And I felt a kinship toward the tree, its origin shrouded in mystery as my own.

Mrs. Denny handed me a big box.

"We'll open our gifts in the morning, Keturah. But you need this for tonight."

With trembling fingers I undid the green ribbon, unfolded the tissue paper and carefully lifted the lid. Neatly folded inside was the black wool jumper and red silk blouse. I shut my eyes and opened them again. They were still there. I touched the blouse with my fingertips.

"It's honest-to-God silk," I marveled.

"Hold them up against you," Mrs. Denny said brusquely. "See if they're going to fit."

But it was Mrs. Wayburn who came to my rescue and held the blouse and jumper to my shoulders, my hands clumsy all at once seeing I had provoked Mrs. Denny by my outburst. "It's just right for her," Mrs. Wayburn declared. "Run and put it on, Keturah."

I fled upstairs. I was longer coming back than I should have been but I couldn't tear myself away from the image in the glass, the dark-haired girl in the red silk blouse, skin fairly blooming above it, the black jumper fitting snuggly at the waist, revealing my full bust and curving over my hips. I could scarcely believe it was I, Keturah. I skimmed the powder puff over my nose and ran downstairs.

Mr. Denny beamed. "Well, well, Keturah," he exclaimed, and I knew he was pleased without saying more. Mrs. Denny approved cautiously. "Not too snug, is it?" I shook my head. "Oh not at all," I assured her. "Goodness!" Mrs. Wayburn clapped her hands together, her eyes darting over me. "You might catch yourself a real beau tonight, Keturah, if you don't watch out."

I did catch a beau that night if two pairs of eyes meeting across a crowded room, if two people coming into brief, exciting contact with each other, could be called catching a beau. But it was a beginning, a seed planted, a seed that had to be hidden in the dark earth of ignoring before it could take root and send up a shoot and produce a flower. There was a long period of waiting: for the right day, the right place, a warmth of springtime bestowed.

The basement of the church was hung with red and green crepe paper. In the center of the room stood a great tree lighted with white candles. Around it the folk of the countryside gathered and sang carols, while the candles brightly burned and reflected on their upturned faces. The voices rose until it seemed as if the ceiling would be lifted by their joyful praise. Around the tree stood men who wrestled with the earth from dawn to dusk, women who spent their lives in hot kitchens, in cleaning big, old-fashioned farmhouses, in rearing children; old folks with lined faces, hands relieved of the reins of work; young people who would follow in their parents' footsteps, others who would go out beyond the limits of their birthplace to seek their fortunes, who would never spend another Christmas Eve around the big tree at the church; wide-eyed children clinging to grown-up hands, trying to catch the words of the songs; babies soundly sleeping in strong arms.

"Hark the herald angels," we sang. Such a joy surged

through me that I was only dimly aware of a pair of eyes staring at me from across the room. Their persistent gaze finally held me, and I saw they belonged to a tall, blond boy who sat with his family each Sunday, one row in front of us on the other side of the church. I did not know their name. As I stared back the boy ducked his head, lifted it again for a quick glance. The song finished, heads bowed as the minister offered a closing prayer. When I looked up again the boy had disappeared.

Refreshments were passed around. I took a sugared doughnut and a mug of steaming coffee from the tray. As I lifted the doughnut to my mouth, someone passing through the crowd bumped my elbow and the doughnut flew to the floor. I stooped to pick it up. Down among the skirts and trousers, crouching on the floor beside me, was the boy who had stared from across the room. We spied the doughnut in the same instant, our hands touched reaching for it. Our eyes met close up. "Sorry," the boy murmured. Then quickly he rose and vanished in the throng of people.

"Floyd Beesom can't see where he's going," Mrs. Denny said as I stood beside her again. "Always got his mind off daydreaming."

His name is Floyd, I thought.

But I did not see him again. I suppose he was too embarrassed to show his face again. As we were leaving we passed the Fornashes at the door. Mr. Denny wished them a Merry Christmas. Claudine had on a new coat with a tan fur collar. She held her long neck proudly up out of it, not even bothering to smile. As we went down the walk, Mr. Denny remarked, "Now what did Claudine have her nose up in the air about?"

"Her new coat," Mrs. Wayburn said tartly. "That was a real fur collar."

Mrs. Denny tossed her head. "If you ask me, I think she was jealous of Keturah. Keturah outshone her in that red silk blouse."

I laughed. I laughed into the cold, clear, starry night. Pale shifts of snow lay in the meadows across the road. Who would ever be jealous of me? And yet if Claudine knew Floyd Beesom had stared at me, mightn't she be? I hadn't seen any boys hovering around her during the evening, for all her brains.

We waited for Mr. Denny to go over and get Mrs. Wayburn in the morning before the other gifts were opened. Mrs. Wayburn always had to go home at night to be sure her livestock were fed first thing in the morning. Mrs. Denny was more than pleased with the little pincushion I had cross-stitched for her, wondering how I had made it without her knowledge. Mrs. Wayburn was just as pleased with the one I gave her, and Mr. Denny lovingly fingered the red, white and blue flannel bookmark I had made for him, with his initial cross-stitched on it. He placed it in his Bible. Their gifts all opened, there were still three packages under the tree.

"Those are yours, Keturah," Mrs. Denny said. "We left yours till last."

I did not expect anything more. "But I had mine last night," I exclaimed.

"Just your dress." Mrs. Denny's eyes danced behind her horn-rimmed spectacles, enjoying my surprise.

I sat down on the floor beside the tree and opened the small, flat box first. In it was a green scarf from Mr. Denny, to match my hat. In the second box was a white cotton slip with eyelet embroidery at the bottom from Mrs. Wayburn. In the big box was the other dress I had admired in the catalogue, the dark blue serge with the white collar. I looked up at the three faces bent over me, three pairs of eyes happy with my happiness. I could not stop the tears. As they fell I became aware that something was happening to me, that inside of me somewhere a space was opening to receive what was being given to me. Not just the gifts, but everything. I had accepted the Dennys since I had come to stay with them; I had accepted what they had done for me. But now I was truly receiving it. There is a difference. You can give a stray dog food, affection, a warm kitchen to sleep in, and he will accept it readily and be gone at the end of a week, it never having mattered, really, where his needs were met. But in truly receiving, the heart is touched and forms an attachment for the giver. That was the way it was with me that day.

On Sunday morning I spied Floyd Beesom in the church-yard as we drove into the parking lot. He stood in a group of overcoated men, the morning sun pricking them out against the red brick building. As we went up the walk I waited until I was ready to pass him to raise my eyes and speak. When I glanced up I found Floyd gazing off into space, his eyes the color of the clear, morning sky. I went into church smarting under his coolness. When Mr. Palmer came over with his open hymnal, I gave him the warm smile I had reserved for Floyd. Only once did I dare to glance at the opposite end of the bench in front of us. There the Beesoms sat—all looking straight ahead.

Going home Mr. Denny took a turn at teasing again. "You and Brother Palmer sang mighty well this morning, Keturah. I think you have his sisters worried."

"I doubt it," Mrs. Wayburn snapped. "He's been tied to them since he was in diapers."

I was in no mood for teasing. "I can't bear the way his teeth click," I said unkindly.

"Pshaw now," Mrs. Denny chastened me. "All he needs is a better fitting. Mail-order teeth always do go to clicking."

I stared out the window. My red blouse had failed to attract Floyd Beesom in broad daylight. We ignored each other the rest of the winter.

⋖§ I4 §⋗

Spring came later that year than it was marked on the calendar, and by the time it arrived, Mr. Denny had finished still another book, *Tale of Two Cities*. It became my favorite story. I wept silently through much of it, while Mrs. Denny surreptitiously ran her finger up under the rim of her thick glasses. Mr. Denny read with added fervor at our distress, as if our tears were partly due to his reading. This was true in a sense. Mr. Denny read with a feeling for the story, although when he had opened the book to begin, he noted he would be reading it for the seventh time. He marked a number seven on the flyleaf. What Mr. Denny lacked in adventure in his own placid life, he found in the books he loved. In some way he transferred this to us, especially to me; I lived the stories as he read, and long after he finished the book, Sidney Carton remained my ideal.

When Floyd Beesom finally spoke to me, Sidney Carton

84

evaporated. There was no resemblance between the two, but it did not matter.

I had been to deliver a pat of Mrs. Denny's butter and one of her homemade coffee cakes to Miss Cordelia. Miss Cordelia was the last of her family living on an old farm on a hilltop, where there was an even better view of the river than we had. Her hill was higher. I never minded going over, because of the view. Miss Cordelia was an old lady, suffering with rheumatism. She was barely able to get around. The big, two-story frame house with its sharply gabled roof studded with lightning rods was the house she had been born in. She had not been out of it for years. Her garden and livestock were tended by a queer, silent man named Jack, who raised his head as I passed but never uttered a word. I was always glad when he was in the barn or off in the fields. There was something sinister about his sullen, dark face and black eyes that stared without recognition. He slept and ate at the house, and Miss Cordelia treated him kindly.

The house was crammed with old furniture and pictures but Miss Cordelia would never sell a thing, although everyone said she needed the money. She was always glad to see me, coming to the door at my knock, with a gray shawl around her thin shoulders, her gnarled hands barely able to turn the knob. She was so thin she was almost transparent, her thick, iron-gray hair, wound into a knot on the top of her head, having more life in it than her body. We sat in the musty parlor where the shades were pulled so far down scarcely any light came in. She had long ago done away with curtains, and the room had the naked air of being in the midst of housecleaning.

Miss Cordelia cherished every bit of news I brought her;

she knew all the old families, although she never saw anyone anymore except the few people who came bringing something to eat, feeling sorry for her alone and ill up on the hill with no one to talk to but the silent Jack. Miss Cordelia never failed to give me a dozen fresh, white eggs to take back to Mrs. Denny although we had plenty of our own. Miss Cordelia's pride would not allow her to accept without return.

Jack was still plowing when I left. I felt him watching me as I went down the road. When I turned to speak to him his sullen eyes gazed dully back at me. I waved and he gave the old horse a sharp slap with the reins and went on with his plowing. I shivered although the evening was warm, and walked faster to be out of his sight. His dark shadow slid away from me in the dazzling April evening. Earlier in the day a spring rain had lavishly washed the new greenness, and now it fairly shimmered as the slanting rays of the evening sun touched the fresh leaves on the dark boughs of the trees, the spring wheat quilt-patched in between freshly turned fields. Wild flowers blossomed along the road banks, and I stopped and picked a bunch of fragile bluets to take to Mrs. Denny. As I bent to pluck their tiny stems, as thin as wire, the warm, sweet smell of damp earth pierced with growing things swept up and over me, and I felt suddenly alive and tingling as I had on Christmas Eve at the singing. In that moment I escaped the long winter. A catbird singing wildly on a fence post put what I felt into song.

I stepped out onto the highway. Coming in my direction was Floyd Beesom. He was ambling along as if he carried all the time in the world in his pockets. If he recognized me he gave no notice. He picked up a stone from the roadside and tossed it up in the air and caught it again. The catbird's song was singing through me, the air was fairly ticking with life. As he neared I dared to speak. "Good evening," I said lightly.

He stopped, the stone caught tightly in his hand. His light blue eyes came flickering up to me. "Hi."

"What are you doing way over here?" I asked, wanting to keep him there.

He slipped the stone in his pocket and kept his hand on it. "Been over to see a man who had a horse for sale."

"Did you buy it?"

"Nope. It was an old nag." He looked at me curiously. "How come you don't go to school?"

So he had missed me at school. The little seed dropped on Christmas Eve had sprung a root. "I'm too old to go," I said, and felt myself flushing.

"I'm older than you, I bet." He pulled his hand out of his pocket and threw the stone in the air again. "I'm going in the Navy after school."

"You are?" I'm sure my voice dropped a note for he quickly added: "Won't be till fall though. Have to help my dad this summer."

Having said all there was to say at the moment, shyness flooded over us. All the things I had thought to tell him if we ever got to talking escaped me like birds flying away. I lifted the bunch of bluets to my face and studied the little yellow crosses in their tiny throats, so perfectly drawn in each small flower.

"You on your way home?" Floyd asked finally.

I nodded.

"Want me to walk up a piece with you?"

"If you want." I tried not to show my pleasure.

We went slowly up the road together. The meadows rose brightly green in the fading day, a lark poured out its eve-

ning tribute, along the Dennys' road the trees arched overhead, pricked with blue sky. At the gate Floyd leaned
against the post and dug his hands down in his overall pockets.

There was something I wanted to know before we
parted.

"Why did you stare at me Christmas Eve?"

He grinned sheepishly, took the stone out again and polished it on his sleeve. "Just wanted to, I guess."

"Why didn't you ever speak to me afterwards?"

He turned and made a long mark on the white post with
the edge of the stone. "I was scared to, I guess."

I squeezed through the gate without pulling the pole.
From the other side of it I said: "It was kind of you to walk
up the road with me."

He grinned again.

"You won't be afraid to speak to me now, will you?"

He stole a glance out of the corners of his eyes. "Guess
not."

I started up the hill. Halfway up I looked back. He was
leaning on the gate watching me. He waved, turned
around, and started off down the road. The evening star
popped out as I went on up the hill. I made a wish on it. I
wished Floyd Beesom would keep company with me.

That was the summer that revolved around Floyd Beesom. Like a farmer who concentrates on one crop expecting
it to be his best, I concentrated on Floyd. A strange, new
warmth rushed through me at mention of his name. My
body pricked with new sensations, so that along with summer, I seemed to ripen physically. I became as addled at
times as if I didn't have good sense. It often took
Mrs. Denny's brusqueness to recall me to my work.

"Daydreaming, Keturah?" she would exclaim. "Stewing because Floyd Beesom hasn't been up the hill since Sunday? It's a long walk from his house, you know. Did you get the seedlings watered?" I hadn't, and I would dash off to take care of them, not daring to admit to Mrs. Denny that she had guessed my thoughts.

Yet all summer long there remained a certain shyness between us. We lapsed into long silences we could not find our way through. Floyd was never talkative, and I often found it difficult to keep the conversation going. But his dullness was offset by the physical pull that drew us together. We needed only to touch hands, to brush shoulders, to sit close together on the porch steps, to know a racing pleasure. Sometimes Floyd's eyes fastened on me as if my body were a curiosity he would like to unravel. With my mature figure I must have been to him like a ripe plum that he was fascinated to pluck but frozen to climb the tree.

I wrote Georgia Lee a letter. I couldn't put on a postcard what I had to say. *I have an honest-to-God boy friend,* I wrote proudly. *His name is Floyd Beesom. He is 18 going on 19. He is going in the Navy soon but I will wait for him forever.*

◆§ 15 §◆

That was the summer I experienced birth.

Along toward dark one hot evening thunder clouds piled up in the west above the hills. Mrs. Denny fanned herself and predicted a bad storm. In the next half hour the sky darkened, lightning flashed behind the hills, and a low ominous roll of thunder rumbled across the sky. A stiff breeze sprang up, and while Mrs. Denny and I hurried to close the windows, Mr. Denny put the chairs up on the porch. As he came in the door Daisy mooed down in the barn.

"Daisy's nervous," Mr. Denny said. "Like as not the storm will bring on her calf. I'd better go down and see."

He went out to the kitchen and came back carrying a lighted lantern in his hand. "Want to come along, Keturah?" he asked. "I think Daisy will be having her calf tonight."

"In the storm?" All the frightening things Georgia Lee had told me about having a baby flashed through my mind.

"She doesn't want to go," Mrs. Denny came to my rescue.

Mr. Denny stood waiting for me, the lighted lantern swinging at his side. "I think it's something Keturah ought to know about," he said.

Without any more being said, we went to the barn leaving Mrs. Denny to wait alone in the storm. The wind blew in a sudden, wild gust, a streak of lightning forked through the sky directly overhead. The first drops of rain pelted us as we reached the barn, illumined before us in a flash of lightning. It looked rickety and ghostly in the eerie light, listing a bit to one side, scarcely seeming strong enough to protect us from such weather. A crack of thunder almost split the earth in two, and I leaped inside. The rain came down in torrents on the tin roof.

The lantern picked out the little green mail wagon, perched on high, spidery wheels, that Mr. Denny had used for so many years. He could not part with it either. A white rooster sat on the edge of a stall, his dark comb flopped over. He opened a beady eye and stared sleepily at us. Daisy mooed nervously in her stall as Mr. Denny held the lantern above her. She tossed her head, her sad eyes swimming in the light. Mr. Denny hung the lantern on a nail and pressed his hands against Daisy's bulging sides. She stomped her feet and mooed again.

"Daisy's due for sure." Mr. Denny patted her nose and fondled her ears. He spoke gently to her, and she switched her tail.

Every other moment a flash of lightning lit up the barn, the wind rattled the door and banged the shutters of the loft. Daisy stomped her feet at each crack of thunder. Mr. Denny continued to calm her, acting as if the storm wasn't going on at all. Finally I sat down on the milk stool and waited for what was going to happen.

"I hope Mrs. Denny's not minding it up there alone too much," Mr. Denny said. "Didn't like leaving her but this is Daisy's night." He struck a match, lit his pipe, and settled down to wait.

For a while the thunder took over but after a terrific crash that seemed to strike almost beside us, the storm began to pass away. The wind died down, the thunder rumbled in the distance, and there was only the steady, heavy downpour of the rain as if we were sitting under a waterfall. The fitful lightning flashed on and off at longer intervals. In the circle of lantern light the dimmery barn seemed suddenly cozy. The warm, dank smell of the stalls mingled with that of the fragrant hay in the loft. It was a smell I liked.

Daisy turned her head and rested her solemn eyes on me, her sides blowing in and out. Her eyes were like brown liquid in her tan face that had a white, star-shaped patch on the nose. Daisy *did* like us being there. Big, dumb cow that she was, she now seemed to have almost human qualities. Even as I watched, her eyes suddenly dilated, became stabbed with pain, her sides vibrated convulsively and she rocked back and forth on her legs. Mr. Denny spoke quietly to her again. He stroked the white star on her nose. "Now Daisy . . . Good girl . . . There . . . there Daisy . . . Now Daisy . . ." Daisy hunched in the shadows, heaving violently. The calf slithered from her onto the bed of straw. The wet bundle lay at my feet. I sat glued to my stool scarcely breathing. Almost at once Daisy was poking her nose into the glistening bundle. The little, thin legs miraculously unfolded, the furry ears pointed up. They twitched at the touch of Daisy's caressing tongue.

Mr. Denny took the lantern off the nail and held it down over the newborn calf. Its eyes shyly glistened up at us.

"What a darling!" I exclaimed, released from my terror. I sighed. "It came so quickly. I thought . . . I thought . . ."

Mr. Denny smiled, nodding his head. "The miracle of birth," he said, putting it all into the right words. "I never cease to wonder at it."

As we left the barn the lantern threw a circle of light up the hill ahead of us. The rain was over, the air cooler and heavy scented with wet honeysuckle. The water ran noisily in the gullies and dripped from the trees. As we climbed the hill with the circle of light dancing ahead of us, I realized that Georgia Lee didn't understand about having a baby. She had never known the good part like Daisy licking her calf, washing it clean, having it nuzzle against her to eat. Maybe it was because with Georgia Lee it had been all wrong from the beginning; she had been trapped into having a baby, she had willfully jumped on and off the steps; she didn't really know about birth at all.

When Mrs. Denny opened the door for us I caught her

by the shoulders. "The calf is here," I cried. "Daisy has her calf."

If she had minded being alone in the storm she did not fret about it to us. "Well that's just fine," she exclaimed, not quite knowing what to do with me in her arms but patting my shoulders nonetheless. "Daisy always has the prettiest calves. Now we'll have to get a name for it."

The next morning the calf was standing on its spindly legs sucking from Daisy's full udder. It was a beautiful calf, faun-colored with not a trace of white anywhere. Its shy, brown eyes rolled around in its pointed head as it nursed. Daisy contentedly chewed her cud, switching flies with her tail. I gave her a gentle pat and an extra ear of corn. "We're going to call the calf Delia," I told her. "And I won't let Mr. Denny sell it ever."

◄§ 16 §►

The corn grew tall, the fruit ripened on the trees, and as summer climbed toward harvest the fever mounted, and in the warm nights, the tight laces of shyness that had confined us snapped. Floyd and I were no longer satisfied to hold hands, to sit close. Awkwardly we kissed under the shadows of the trees and along the dark road. He was never gentle. There was a quality of roughness in him that held me at bay.

The hot night held on to summer as if it could not bear to let summer go. As Floyd held on to me. His mouth on mine, he pressed me against the side of the barn, tugging at my blouse, his hands roughening.

"Let's go in the barn," he whispered hoarsely.

When I hesitated he begged, "Aw come on."

Again, his very urgency struck a warning note. I struggled to free myself. "What's the matter?" he jeered. "You scared?"

I did not know what I was. But I could not go with him. "I can't."

He reacted as if I had slapped him. Letting go of me, he jammed his hands in his pockets and started walking rapidly down the hill. When he was halfway down I ran after him. "Don't be mad with me, Floyd," I panted.

I stumbled along beside him to the gate. As he reached for the pole I caught hold of his arm. For a wild moment we clung together with what passion remained. When it was spent he dropped his arms and started down the road, not turning to look back.

" 'Night, Floyd," I called after him.

" 'Night," he flung over his shoulder, his footsteps going on down the road, under the trees that finally swallowed him.

In the lamplight of my room I examined my bruised lips in the peeling mirror. There was a flush in my cheeks; my eyes were strangers to me. I blew out the lamp and knelt down at the window, resting my chin on the sill. Through the water maples I could see the outline of the white barn, the spot Floyd had pinned me against. I went over each detail, lingering over each touch, each revelation. I did love Floyd. I truly did. And yet at the very edge of my feeling for him the warmth dampened down, there was a little fringe like hoarfrost, a rime I could not

94

wipe away. Beneath the shyness in Floyd lay something that overrode me like a strong wind I had to protect myself against. The knowledge vanished, and I wanted only to be with him again.

We had planned to meet Friday night at the church social. When I arrived with the Dennys, Floyd was on the front steps waiting, in a white shirt and dark trousers, his light hair plastered down on his head. His eyes held a smothered excitement, so that he could only cast a furtive glance in my direction. As the evening wore on, Floyd broke out of his shell that still encased him when other people were around. He treated me to homemade ice cream and cake, and twice he bought iced bottles of soda pop. When Claudine spoke to us, hanging on the arm of a boy half a head shorter than herself, Floyd remarked, when they were out of hearing: "Gosh, she's skinny."

I looked at Claudine in her pale yellow silk dress that was much more fashionable than the light blue gingham I wore, hanging straight up and down on her, and I knew what Floyd meant. I blushed, not daring to look at him.

The Dennys left early but we stayed until the end. We giggled over the prizes we won at the fishpond, applauded the music, and strolled under the paper lanterns, holding hands, or sat close together on a wooden bench under the trees. Each time Floyd caught hold of my hand, a flame ran up my arm.

We walked home under the fading stars. The light from the late rising moon spread over the hills. "I don't want you to go in the Navy, Floyd," I said. In another month he would be leaving. "Do you have to?"

"I don't much want to myself anymore," he admitted. "But I'm signed up, so I guess I have to." He tightened his arm around me. "We got to make up for what we're going to miss." He trembled against me. "Go to the barn tonight."

All the way home I had sensed the barn lying in wait for us, the dark loft, the soft hay. . . . I pressed my hand in his side. We went on up the road kissing, and the moon came over the hill and glistened through the trees.

Someone was standing beside the gate. In the moonlight I could make out the figure of a girl in a light dress, her blond hair fluffed about her head. I gasped.

"Is that you, Keturah?" a soft voice called out.

"Georgia Lee!" Freeing myself from Floyd, I ran to her. We fell into each other's arms. "Where did you come from?"

"I ran away. I couldn't stand it any longer."

"But how did you get here?"

"I walked most of the way. Once or twice I caught a ride but not very far." She lifted a bare foot and rubbed it with her hands. "My feet surely do hurt."

Aware of Floyd standing behind me, I turned to him to explain. "She's my friend from the Orphanage."

"Is he your boy friend?" Georgia Lee asked. "The one you wrote me about?"

"Yes. Don't you have any shoes?"

"They're in my bag." I saw the big shopping bag on the ground beside her. "They got too tight and I had to take them off."

I was truly glad to see Georgia Lee but whatever I was going to do with her I didn't know. I was sure Mrs. Denny wouldn't like it that she had run away. She would probably have her sent right back.

"What are you going to do?" I asked.

She shook her head. "I don't know for sure. I thought

96

maybe you could help me get to the city so I could get a job."

I was thankful she didn't expect the Dennys to take her in. But it was midnight. And standing against the gatepost in her bare feet, Georgia Lee looked more like a child than a girl of sixteen. In the moonlight her shadowy appeal was apparent. Floyd seemed to sense it too.

"Maybe we could hide her in the barn tonight," he suggested.

"Are there any cows?" Georgia Lee asked timidly. "I'm scared to death of cows."

"They're out in the pasture," I told her. "You could stay in the barn until we figure out something."

Georgia Lee picked up her shopping bag, and the three of us climbed the hill to the barn. I led the way up into the loft. Georgia Lee handed Floyd the shopping bag and crawled up beside me. She threw her arms around me again. "I knew you would help me, Keturah. You're the only friend I have. Honest-to-God you are."

I held her close. It was good to be with Georgia Lee again. She was so sweet, so small, so affectionate. The fact that I was her best friend filled my heart to overflowing. I leaned over the edge of the loft and told Floyd to come up. He climbed up and made a place for himself on the hay beside me. The moonlight swept through the open shutters and made a halo of Georgia Lee's pale hair.

"What happened?" I asked.

"Mr. Atwood kissed me," Georgia Lee said simply. "He jumped out and grabbed me as I was coming from the washroom. Mrs. Atwood came sneaking around the corner without her shoes on, and caught us."

I drew in my breath. "What did she do?"

"She slapped me."

I could see her doing it. "Why didn't you tell her the truth?"

She sighed and rubbed her sore feet. "She wouldn't have believed me." She shivered, her whole body trembled in the moonlight, and her eyes were huge dark spots in her face. "Mrs. Atwood was going to send me to reform school. That's why I ran away."

"Gosh!" Floyd exclaimed.

"It's an honest-to-God fact," Georgia Lee assured him. She yawned sleepily. She swung around and put her head in my lap. "I'm so tired I could die." I stroked her forehead, and she closed her eyes. "Do you think I can get to town and get a job, Keturah?" she asked drowsily. In another moment she was asleep.

We spoke softly so as not to disturb her, trying to figure out a way to help her get to town. She would need some money until she got a job. When I mentioned it to Floyd he said he had twenty dollars saved up and offered to lend it to her. I was proud of him for being so generous. We decided he would bring it over first thing in the morning and hide it under a rock beside the gatepost. He'd get up early and be gone and back before his family missed him. Excitement mounted over our plans. I would milk for Mr. Denny, as he liked to get an early start on Saturday. I would bring food down to the barn when I went down to milk. If Georgia Lee had hitchhiked this far, we figured she could get the rest of the way.

It was growing late. The moonlight had slipped away from the loft door but it still crept in through the open cracks in the walls. It was mysteriously lovely there in the barn with Georgia Lee safely asleep in my lap, the sweet smell of the hay, the faint movement and stirring of small animals, the chorus of night insects humming away outside,

98

the little secret sounds of the summer night floating up to us. Floyd put his arm around me and edged closer. He slipped his hot hand inside my dress. I put my head back on his shoulder and his mouth found mine. We drew apart only to catch our breath, tangled in an excitement of coming together again. I glanced down at Georgia Lee on my lap. Her eyes were open. "Hi!" she said softly.

As we flew apart Georgia Lee giggled. "I won't squeal on you." She sat up and fluffed her hair. "When I get to the city I'm going to get myself a beau."

I got on my knees. "We have to go," I said quickly, trying to cover my embarrassment. "It's late."

"You sure there won't be any cows?" Georgia Lee asked again.

"I'll be down in the morning before they come in. I'll bring you something to eat."

"I am hungry," she admitted. "But I guess I can wait until morning."

Floyd told her about the twenty dollars he was going to hide at the gate for her.

"I'll pay you back every cent of it, Floyd," she promised. "Cross my heart and hope to die."

As I started down the ladder a scurrying noise drifted up from somewhere down in the shadowy barn. "Ooöo," Georgia Lee squealed.

"It's only a mouse looking for corn," I assured her.

"I don't know but what I'd rather sleep under a tree." She reached out and caught my shoulders. "Couldn't you sneak me up to your room, Keturah?"

I suppose I could have taken her up to my room, but I felt it was enough to do behind the Dennys' back to keep her in the barn. The more I thought of it the more I was sure that the Dennys wouldn't approve of Georgia Lee's running away. Mrs. Denny might not even believe her story. Nor did I think she would approve of Georgia Lee going alone to the city. They would send her back. There was nothing to hurt her down in the barn. I would have stayed with her myself but Mrs. Denny always dozed lightly until I came in. She would call to me when she heard me lock the door, to let me know she knew I was safely back in the house, before she fell into a sound sleep.

If I had risked taking Georgia Lee to my room that night maybe everything would have been different. My whole life might have been otherwise. I would probably have married Floyd and stayed on there. Life hinges on such small decisions: my deciding that Georgia Lee was to stay in the barn rather than in my room closed one door and eventually opened another. For a long time afterwards I thought I had made a terrible mistake. But it was simply a door slamming shut in my face. As the planets can move in only one direction for night and day to click, for the tides to ebb and flow, the moon to wax and wane—our lives are mysteriously pointed in one direction. The needle of our conscience is as good a compass as any. So small a decision, even, as deciding Georgia Lee should stay in the barn that night because I wanted to protect both her and the Dennys kept me on the path I was destined for.

Floyd and I said good night briefly at the yard gate. We were awkward and shy again, shaken by the knowledge that Georgia Lee had watched us in the loft. Floyd waited until I was inside the door. I looked back through the glass and saw him standing there, his hand on the top of the gate as if he hoped I might come back out and he could open it again. I turned the key in the lock. "In, Keturah?" Mrs. Denny called from her bedroom. "Yes," I called back softly. I went out through the kitchen to the outhouse. When I reached my room I knelt down at the window and pressed my face to the screen to catch a glimpse of Floyd going down the hill. Only the moonlight lay fading on the pasture. I thought of Georgia Lee down there in the big, white barn, safe at last from the Atwoods. I prayed that they would never find her. I crept into bed hoping that nothing would frighten her in the night.

◅§ 17 §▻

I might as well not have gone to bed for all the sleep I had. I was up as the first bird dropped a pearl-like note into the pearl-gray morning. Down in the kitchen I put some cold slices of ham between the leftover biscuits and stuck them in my pocket. I picked up the milk pails just as Mr. Denny came out to get them.

"I'll milk for you this morning, Mr. Denny," I greeted him hurriedly. "I couldn't sleep this morning. And you like to get an early start on Saturdays."

Mr. Denny was easily agreeable. "Well, that's mighty nice of you, Keturah."

Mrs. Denny appeared in the doorway, sticking a final hairpin into her knot. "That'll be just fine," she said, having overheard us. "I'm going to need more wood if I do any baking this morning. You can get me a little wood, Cyrus, instead of taking so long to shave."

"Looks like I'm trapped," Mr. Denny said in good humor.

I fled down to the barn. The two cows were standing near the door waiting to be milked. Delia, the fawn-colored calf, was just inside nuzzling along the floor for something to eat. I hoped Georgia Lee hadn't seen her. I hurried up into the loft. The hay was pressed into a little round nest where Georgia Lee had slept, but no one was in it. I called her name softly, but there was no answer. I ran over the whole loft but she was not there. Panicky, I went back down the ladder, out the back door of the barn, and looked around the trees. Still there was no sign of her. I could not believe that she had gone off without food, without waiting for me. Surely she was hiding somewhere. I felt something wet against my arm. Delia had followed me and was nudging me with her moist, warm nose. I threw my arms around her neck. "Delia, Delia," I cried. "Where is she?" Delia flicked her velvety, faunlike ear as if the words tickled her, and stomped her feet wanting something to eat.

I ran down to the gate. There was no stone beside the post, no sign of any money. There was nothing to do but go back up and milk and hope Georgia Lee would show up.

I went down to the barn a dozen times that morning hoping to find either Georgia Lee or Floyd. I was thankful that Mrs. Denny was busy in the kitchen baking, so she did not notice what I was up to. Each time I went back up to the house more disheartened than before.

At noon a car came up the road. As it was still too early for Mr. Denny, I waited in the doorway to see who it might be. When the car stopped at the gate I recognized, with a start, the Beesoms. Mr. Beesom got out wearing his overalls and a straw field hat. Mrs. Beesom slammed her door and came up behind him in a gingham dress and kitchen apron, a starched sunbonnet on her head. They would never ordinarily have come calling dressed like that. Fear clutched my heart. I didn't know Mrs. Denny was behind me until she spoke. "Why, it's the Beesoms. At this hour. Wonder if something's wrong? Howdy," she called down to them.

They stopped at the foot of the steps without returning her greeting. There was a stern, forbidding, troubled air about them. They fastened dull, accusing eyes on me.

"Our Floyd didn't come home last night," Mr. Beesom announced, the same accusation in his voice. "Do you know where he is?"

Mrs. Denny gave me a questioning look. All three pairs of eyes fastened on me so tightly I could not speak. Flashing through my mind was the thought: Floyd's gone. Georgia Lee's gone. They must have gone together. "No," I managed to say.

"He was here last night, wasn't he?" Mr. Beesom demanded.

I nodded.

"What time did he leave?"

"A while after midnight," Mrs. Denny spoke up. "Keturah came in just after the clock struck twelve thirty. I heard her."

Mr. Beesom kept his gaze on me. "Did he mention anywhere he might be going?"

"Where would he go but home?" I tried to hide the fear pressing down on me.

"Floyd's a good boy," Mr. Beesom said. "Never gave us any trouble. Can't figure him doing a thing like this."

"He was going in the Navy." Mrs. Denny tried to find an answer. "Maybe he ran off and enlisted."

"Why would he do that? He was going soon enough anyway." He flashed his stony eyes over me again. "Did you young'uns have a scrap?"

103

"No," I said.

Mrs. Beesom began to cry. She picked up the corner of her gingham apron to wipe her eyes. "My boy's gone. He's the only one I got. He never stayed away over night before."

We seemed to stand there forever, locked in a vise that would not open to free us. I would never tell them about Georgia Lee. They had come to accuse me. If they had come merely asking, I might have told them. I would never tell Mrs. Denny either. I couldn't bear for her to know the truth. And the truth was now very plain to me. I could no longer deny it. Georgia Lee and Floyd *had* run away together. Dimly I heard Mrs. Denny talking to the Beesoms. They weren't looking at me anymore, but around themselves, lost-like, not knowing what to do next. I longed for them to go so that I could run somewhere and hide.

But I did not escape with their leaving. Mrs. Denny kept talking about it after they were gone, not asking me any direct questions, never blaming me, but going over aloud in her own mind what she thought might have happened.

Mr. Denny came home in the midst of it, and she told him the story word for word while I sat numb on a kitchen chair, not even thinking to help with the dinner. I could not eat when we sat down at the table. Mrs. Denny kept pressing food upon me, telling me I should eat, trying to console me one moment that everything would turn out all right, and the next voicing her opinions about the Beesoms, whom she had held in silent disapproval before. Mr. Denny said little.

"I never thought it of him," was his only comment, and I could feel his sympathy flowing out to me in his silence. When dinner was finally over, Mrs. Denny rose and gathered up a handful of dishes. "Don't bother helping,

Keturah," she said with a show of kindness. "You go and lie down for a while. Those Beesoms were enough to take anyone's appetite away."

I made no protest to help. I went up to my room. It was very warm up there in the early afternoon with the sun beating down on the sloping roof. I went over to the window, and crouching beside it, put my head on my arms and stared out at the maple tree wrapped in the hot midday stillness. Beyond the tree rose the barn, its big square opening like a gaping hole through which my happiness had escaped. Slowly the sun moved over behind the tree, but it was no cooler. I was hot with shame, tortured by the memory of Floyd's kisses that he might at that moment be giving to Georgia Lee. I stayed in the sweltering heat of my room all afternoon. If I had cried I am sure I would have felt better. But the tears all stayed inside of me, making a little well of unhappiness that never emptied out for a long time to come. It made a secret, hurting place deep within me. When I went down to dinner that night I was not the same innocent person I had been before. I never would be again.

A week later Mr. Denny came home with the news. I was filling the water glasses at the table when he came up the walk, ignoring Romany who jumped up at him. "Down, Romany," he said roughly, and the dog, mystified at this unusual command, slunk away. Mr. Denny rubbed his forehead as if he had a headache. When he came in the door and saw me, he busied himself dusting off the bottom of his shoes on the scatter rug.

I wanted to ask: "Is something wrong?" but I already knew it was. I stood wretchedly waiting for him to speak. Still brushing off the soles of his shoes, he said: "The Beesoms heard from Floyd."

I held tightly to the water pitcher. After a tormented week of knowing nothing, I was going to hear. Was he back? Was everything going to be all right? I couldn't bear to ask.

"He ran off and got married," Mr. Denny plunged in. "The Beesoms are fit to be tied."

I stared dumbly at the pitcher in my hands.

"They didn't know he had another girl." I sensed Mr. Denny raising his head and looking at me. "Did you?"

Georgia Lee hadn't been his girl. I could honestly say "No."

Mrs. Denny, coming into the dining room with the pine-apple marshmallow salad in a cut-glass bowl, stopped short at sight of us. "Something happen?" she asked.

Mr. Denny told her.

"Who'd he marry?" she demanded, and I was so relieved that she had asked it, that I didn't have to, that I was able to set the water pitcher down on the sideboard.

Mr. Denny scratched his head. "They don't know. All he sent was a postcard. I took it right up to the house, see-ing how important it was, instead of putting it in the box."

"What'd it say?" Mrs. Denny hung on his every word.

"Just, 'Georgia Lee and I got married. We are living in the city. She got a job and I'm going in the Navy since I'm signed up. Please forgive me, Floyd.' That's it, word for word." With that Mr. Denny made a dash for the kitchen to wash up, as if he was glad to have it over with. "I never did give Floyd Beesom much credit in the way of brains," he said on his way. "But I never thought he'd do a trick like that."

"Humpf!" Mrs. Denny bristled as she set the cut-glass bowl on the table. "Trash, I always said. The way

106

they came up here as if it was Keturah's fault and her perfectly innocent. Good riddance, I'd say."

I knew she wanted to comfort me by her words but nothing helped at the moment. I felt ill all over. "I'm going for a walk," I said helplessly.

"Now don't take on about it, Keturah," Mrs. Denny said brusquely. She was always brusque when she wanted to be kind. "You're better off without him. I'm just glad it's not you he's married to." She pulled out her chair and sat down at the table. "I wonder where the girl's from."

But I was out the door. I walked rapidly through the pasture and into the little woods, on down the hill to the creek, dry now at the end of summer, brown leaves crumbled on the flat stones. I stood beside the creek for a long time, as dull as one of the flat stones. After a time I turned back and went up the hill again. In the little grove of trees I stopped, sinking down on the soft moss. My mind became instantly alive. Desperately I went over everything from the beginning: the first time I saw Georgia Lee at the Orphanage. How I had attached myself to her and wanted to be like her, to have for myself that flitting quality, that part of her that could not be defined, that something you couldn't put your finger on and give a name to. It was simply there, looking out from her prettiness. It was like tinsel on a Christmas tree, like the gauzy wings of a butterfly in the sun. It was honest-to-God silk stockings that gave your legs a shine. I thought of her standing at the gate that night in her bare feet, waiting for me, of the cuddly way she had put her head in my lap up in the loft. How she had clung to me; how happy I had been to be with her again. And she had betrayed me. But I could not be sure if she had betrayed me, or if Floyd had simply picked her up and run off with her.

I had to remember everything about Floyd too. The way he had kissed me, the way he caught and held me in his arms, the roughness of him that set me on fire and cooled me a moment later.

The special quality Georgia Lee possessed had been visible that night in the shadowy barn. Floyd had seen it. I remembered how eager he had been to help her. I had been jilted and betrayed but when I got right down to the facts —maybe they couldn't help it. The knowledge didn't ease the hurt.

18

The Dennys never mentioned Floyd Beesom again. For once Mrs. Denny denied herself the chewing over of a piece of real gossip, and it must have been difficult for her at times to hold her tongue, but in my presence she never mentioned his name again. And on Sundays there was no problem. The Beesoms stopped coming to church.

That winter, for lack of anything else to do, I began reading in earnest. I lost myself on those long, winter afternoons in other people's lives, forgetting for a while my own unhappiness. I didn't even go to the store until just before Christmas, not wanting to meet the customers who might nudge each other when I came in, or even Mr. Sims, although I considered him my friend. He might bring up the subject in his kind, blundering way, to sympathize with me.

When I finally did go, it was snowing. Mrs. Denny had

run out of crochet thread again and needed just enough to finish the edge of the dresser scarf for Mrs. Wayburn's Christmas gift. She fussed about it, chiding herself for not having bought enough. I knew she would not ask me to go to the store, nor did she ask Mr. Denny at noontime to get it for her, because of the snow. When he was gone I decided that for her sake I could take whatever I had to meet. I dressed warmly and went out to the kitchen, where Mrs. Denny was reading the paper through a magnifying glass.

"I'm going down to the store for your thread," I announced. "I guess I'd better take a sample."

She looked up from her paper, her eyes small and beady behind her thick glasses. "In all this snow?"

"I like the snow."

She immediately got up and found her thread, and gave me the empty spool to match the number on the seal. "The airing will do you good." It was as if she said: "I'm glad you're getting yourself out at last."

The snow had stopped falling. It lay thick on the ground, banked deep along the road, clinging to the trees and fence posts. Even the wires stretched from pole to pole had a coating of snow. At once I was enveloped in a white world. As if I had stepped out of a dark room, as if I had been released from shadows to light. I trudged down the snow-packed road, the cold tingling my face, and felt alive again. I had been reading a long, sad story in which almost everyone had died. Now, even the sadness of the story was lifted from me, and I felt better step by step. I loved the hills again, the white hills with their thin tracery of black trees, the river dull as a piece of old metal, the railroad tracks stretching up and down as far as I could see, the sagging barns shut against the cold, the silos with the bright yellow and red ears of corn peeking through the open seams, the white farmhouses blinded against the winter, the blackbirds lighting on the wire and sending down a spray of snow, or swooping down to the barnyards for a bit of feed they had spied.

I breathed in the cold air and the fresh, clean smell of everything, and most of all I loved the silence. It was as quiet as the first day on earth must have been before there were any people. It was so beautiful and still, and I was as still on the inside, as if all the upset in me had suddenly dropped away and left only my heart beating and my lungs noiselessly taking in and giving back the good air. I was at home again in the world: I walked in rhythm with an invisible pulse. In a moment I will be able to hear the earth's heart beating, I thought with wonder, and it will tick in time with mine. And I saw myself no longer standing still but moving forward, and I was never again that winter as unhappy as I had been before.

There was no one in the store but Mr. Sims. He was resting against the counter. When he saw me he moved his arms from the elbows, clapping his hands together. "Well I'll be," he greeted me. "If it isn't my old friend Keturah, in all this weather."

He had a cold and his long nose was almost as red as his plaid wool shirt. His loose pants were doubtfully held up by red suspenders. He was genuinely glad to see me. "Where have you been keeping yourself?" he wanted to know. He held out his big, hairy hand, and I put my mittened one into it. He pumped my arm up and down. "I've missed you."

"It was wonderful walking down in the snow," I told him.

He looked at me thoughtfully. "You look mighty fine with your rosy cheeks."

I smiled gratefully. It was good to have someone tell me so. I caught a glimpse of myself in a tin baking sheet hanging on the wall. There was such a glow in my face I scarcely recognized myself.

I stayed for half an hour, too happy to leave. I looked at all the new things that had come in for the holidays—the sweaters and scarfs, the silver bells, the rows of powder cans, the beads. Mr. Sims kept up a lively chatter. No one came into the store; we had it all to ourselves, and we had a wonderful time. When I was ready to go, Mr. Sims gave me a little bottle of lilac perfume. "Just a little token," he said without any fuss. "Something for the season."

I almost forgot to get the crochet thread I had come after. I had started to leave when I thought of it. We both laughed. The door opened, the sleigh bells ringing, as a customer came in. Mr. Sims matched the thread and wrapped it for me as if there was a secret conspiracy between us. He came to the door as I went out. He put his mouth around the edge of it. "Remember, it's always a struggle on the way up."

I never used the lilac perfume. I opened the bottle often and sniffed the strong scent of lilacs, and every time I did I was flooded with the memory of that snowy day. By summer all the smell had escaped from the bottle but it remained on my dresser, a signifying memento.

It was spring again, and I was carrying a cake or a pie over to Miss Cordelia's once a week. Miss Cordelia was more crippled than ever from the long, cold winter. Sometimes she could not come to the door, and when she did not answer my knock, I let myself in. Often as not Miss Cordelia would be lying in a little knot on the couch in the curtainless living room, the light coming in dimly around the lowered shades, her thin body making scarcely a hump under the old patchwork quilt. She was always grateful that I had come, and would ask me to set what I had brought on the marble-topped table that had a carved lamb on a lower shelf, saying she would enjoy it later. I wondered how she was able to help herself at all, but she never complained. Jack, she said, was able to do what was needed. I shivered at the thought of his dark unfriendliness in the house with her. We chatted for a while, then I would get up to go, hating to leave her to the loneliness of the house and Jack, but glad to get away from the gloom and musty smell and out into the fresh air again. Before I left I had to go out to the kitchen for the dozen eggs she always sent to Mrs. Denny. The kitchen was cluttered with unwashed dishes, buckets of spoiling milk spotted with dead flies, and garden vegetables wilting on the table. I was glad the eggs had shells around them to protect them from the mess. I offered to wash up the dishes for Miss Cordelia, but she would not hear of it; even in her helplessness she was still too proud to have an outsider do for her.

Jack would be somewhere about when I left, if he had not been when I came, a patch of black shadow in the garden, in the fields, or around the barn, eying me stolidly for a long moment, then turning back to whatever he had been doing. If he was in the field with the horse, he slapped the reins roughly and the horse would jerk forward, pulling Jack along with him.

One afternoon while I was on my way to Miss Cordelia's a sudden shower came up, and I just made it to the shed when the rain came pouring down, and would have ruined the angel food cake Mrs. Denny had so carefully iced. Out beyond the edge of the rain the sun still shone, and I knew the shower would be over quickly. Behind me the shed was dark and full of cobwebs, the dirt floor strewn with rusty nails, pitchforks and rakes carelessly dropped. The shed was as disheveled as the kitchen. I watched the rain from the open doorway. In the rain Miss Cordelia's house, from which most of the paint had peeled, looked as if no one lived in it. The lightning rods all listed in one direction as if the wind had blown against them too many years.

A faint spray misted in as the water spilled over the roof edge. I stepped back to avoid it. As I did so, I had the eerie sensation that something moved behind me in the shed. I hesitated to turn around to see what it was, some warning fear taking possession of me. It might only be the horse, I thought with a surge of relief, that had wandered into the shed. I turned my head and looked squarely into the face of Jack. He was not two feet away from me. Under his dirty felt hat his unkempt face glistened with sweat, his black eyes pierced with a desperate cunning. I screamed. I heard my voice cry out and mingle with the downpour of the rain, and knew there was no one to hear me but the helpless Miss Cordelia. There was only one thing to do. Clinging to my basket, I made a dash for the outside. Just as I would clear the door, Jack's hands caught me from behind. I dropped the basket with the angel food cake, and struggled to free myself. But Jack was a strong man; although shorter than myself, he was stoutly built. He pulled me back into the darkness of the shed. "Let go!" I screamed. "Let go of me!"

He never uttered a sound. I felt his heavy breathing on my neck. With a desperate effort I kicked back and hit him in the shin with my heel. At the same moment I was able to wrench one hand free. A real tussle began now, and then Jack suddenly caught my throat. His fingers dug into my neck. I gasped and choked as I stumbled against him. Suddenly a wild, inhuman noise broke from Jack. At the same moment I found I was miraculously breathing again. As I clutched my throat I saw what had happened. Jack had stepped on an ill-flung pitchfork, and the tine had gone through his foot. As he danced wildly backwards, the handle flew up and hit him on the back of the head. He toppled over, striking his temple on the rough baseboard of the shed. He lay there, his foot pinned by the pitchfork, his matted hair on his forehead, the perspiration running down his face, his wild eyes fading. His head rolled forward and a flow of blood spurted down into his neck. He lay as still as a stone. I fled. I ran through the pouring rain to the highway, stopping a car that was fortunately passing by. There were two men in it. I recognized Omar Keene, a deacon at the church.

"Jack," I gasped. "Down in Miss Cordelia's shed. He's hurt bad."

Omar threw the car into reverse, backed up, and drove

rapidly down Miss Cordelia's road. All my strength gone, I sat down on a culvert beside the road. I shook until my teeth chattered, drenched as a water rat. I was still sitting there when the car came back down the road. When it stopped I looked first to see if they had Jack on the back seat, but it was empty. Omar leaned out the window and handed me the basket with the angel food cake still in it. "I guess you dropped this. . . ."

Dazedly I reached for it. "Is he . . . ?"

"He's dead all right." There was no sympathy in Omar's voice. "Always said he'd come to no good end. Stepped on his own pitchfork. Must have given you an awful fright."

"I just stopped in to get out of the rain," I began, but Omar had too much on his mind to listen to me. I was saved from giving an explanation that might have needed a lot more explaining when the story got around. "Going home to get my wife to see after Miss Cordelia." He pressed on the gas. "Want a lift home?"

I shook my head. "I'll get your car all wet."

He drove off. So Jack was dead. And the awful thought swept over me that I was partly responsible for his death. No. I refused to believe that. If he hadn't died, I would have. I would be lying there now. . . . I began to run again. I ran the rest of the way to the Dennys'. I would never tell anyone what had happened. They might not believe me. They might think . . . And running on, I realized that it had stopped raining.

The next day they took Miss Cordelia to the County Home. Her house and things were put up for auction. Jack was buried on the place in the little walled cemetery where Miss Cordelia's folks were buried, and no one went to the funeral except the undertaker. No one cared at all that he had died. Everyone had been a little bit afraid of him. They talked of his death until after the auction, and then it was forgotten. But if I had told the true story of what had happened, his name would have been forever linked with mine, there might always have remained some question about how he had happened to step on the pitchfork, and finally a finger of guilt might have been pointed at me.

But before the summer was over I had to tell Mr. Denny. He carried the secret with him where it could never be revealed.

Mrs. Wayburn had an attack of pleurisy, and Mrs. Denny went over to stay with her. She was gone for two weeks. Every evening Mr. Denny and I rode over to see them, and left as dark closed the long evenings. Back home we sat on the lawn and waited for the Flyer to go up. I'll never forget those evenings. Mr. Denny, unhampered by Mrs. Denny's "Humphs!" or the gossip she was wont to interrupt with, held forth under the stars as if time were running out.

"The best thing Mrs. Denny and I ever did," he told me, "was bringing you home that day from the picnic." He paused. "I'll never forget how forlorn you looked up on that platform."

"I wonder what would have happened to me if you hadn't taken me," I mused.

"It's more important to think about what is going to happen to you after you leave us," he replied.

His remark brought me up sharply. I looked up at the stars spread across the summer night. In some future time I supposed I would have to leave the Dennys. I hoped it was still a long way off. "I can't do much but housework," I said idly.

"There's nothing wrong with that." Mr. Denny took

the remark more seriously than I had. "It's a fine thing to go into someone's home and make a better place of it than it was before you came. No work need be beneath you. Do the job well, and you can always hold up your head and look the world squarely in the eye. Carrying the mail didn't amount to as much, in some people's minds, as if I had been a lawyer, but I've always been happy doing it. Carrying a long-looked-for letter to its destination is as important in its way as getting a fellow a right decision in a trial."

"I'll always try to do my best whatever I do," I promised him.

He sucked on his pipe. In the light from the stars I could see him quietly rocking back and forth, soothing his tired bones. He took the pipe from his mouth and rested his arm on the chair. "You're going to be a fine lady one of these days, Keturah."

The sudden tears sprang to my eyes, blurring the stars. For such a long time there had been the unhappiness about Floyd; then the terror of that day in Miss Cordelia's shed. There were nights when I had not been able to sleep remembering Jack lying there with the blood running down his neck, his dimming eyes. And here was Mr. Denny recalling me to what I had once wanted to be, and from which I had wandered so far. His words hung between us as the Flyer came zooming out of the night, whistling as it went through the village, the chain of lights rushing on up the valley and out of sight. Mr. Denny knocked the ashes from his pipe, picked up his rocker, and carried it up on the porch. I followed him. If I had had a moment longer I would have told him one of my secrets.

But the opportunity came again, the last evening before Mrs. Denny came home. We had come back early, as it was hot and stuffy in Mrs. Wayburn's parlor where the shades were kept down all day against the sun, and up only a trifle in the evenings for fear the night air would bring back the pleurisy. The room had a musty smell as if it had not been aired out thoroughly in years. I felt faintly smothered sitting there in the dimness and heat, and after I'd exhausted the pictures on the walls, I always found myself back at the photograph on the mantel of Mr. Wayburn in his coffin. But now when I looked at it I saw, instead of Mr. Wayburn, Jack, although they had buried him in a plain pine box. I was glad when Mr. Denny suggested we get along home where it was cooler.

We reached the top of the hill just as the evening star popped out. "There she is, Keturah," Mr. Denny announced, as pleased about it as the first time he showed it to me.

Romany came running out to meet us. As we came around to the front yard a steamboat whistled as it floated around the bend of the river and came into view. Like a great white palace, lighted on its prow by a single, green light, it sailed up the river, graceful and quiet as a swan. We sat down on the porch steps and watched until it was out of sight.

"There's something I ought to tell you, Mr. Denny," I plunged in, gathering up my courage as the stars popped out fast and furiously.

He took his pipe and tobacco can out of his pocket and carefully filled his pipe. He lit a match, holding it to the pipe. "Are you speaking about Jack, Keturah?"

I gasped. "You mean you know?"

"I always felt there was more to it than you told us. You were so shook up. You weren't the same for a good while after."

"I didn't mean to kill him," I blurted out. "But he was trying to kill me. He had his hands around my neck."

"Why don't you tell me the whole thing from the beginning," he calmly suggested, "and we'll see how guilty you are."

With relief I told him what had happened. When I finished, he waited before he spoke.

"Looking at it from the standpoint of the law," he weighed his words, "any jury would acquit you."

"You mean I'd be sent to jail?"

He snorted. "I mean they wouldn't find you guilty. Any farmer around here would be willing to testify to the surly darkness of Jack's character. They would all have been afraid to meet him after dark. I think sooner or later he would have killed Miss Cordelia. He had that blackness in him." He sucked on his pipe, and the bowl flared as he drew the air through it. "Jack laid the trap for his own death. No farmer worth his salt lets a pitchfork lie around on the floor. Nor a rake. It's too dangerous. How Miss Cordelia put up with him I don't know. Some folks claimed he was her illegitimate son, but that was only gossip. Miss Cordelia never left the place long enough for anything like that to happen." He paused. "No wonder you were shaken up, girl."

I heaved a great, relieved sigh.

"It should strengthen your faith, Keturah, seeing how the Lord's been on your side."

"On my side!"

"Keeping you from being choked. Keeping you from marrying Floyd Beesom."

It was the first time he had mentioned his name since that long-ago day the postcard arrived.

"It wouldn't have been any good for you to marry Floyd. After I got over being mad at what he did to you, I was glad he was gone."

"Maybe I don't believe in God enough," I admitted.

"Faith grows, Keturah. I guess mine is a simple sort of faith, but it's always been satisfactory for me." The katydids and crickets hummed around us. The fireflies flicked on and off over the grass. I slapped at a mosquito settling on my arm.

"Look up there at the stars," Mr. Denny bade me. "All in their appointed places. After a while the moon will come up just where it always comes up this time of the year. At a certain moment in the morning it will be light again. A wonderful pattern the world has. Wonderful to consider." He paused again. "The Creator who fashioned it made us too. He also watches over us."

After a time he said: "I've never been very far from this place. Never seen the mountains, never been to the ocean. Never seen the Great Lakes, or Niagara Falls, or the Mississippi River. But this is enough for me, this hilltop where I can see enough of what my Creator made to satisfy my soul."

I sat staring out into the night, drinking in Mr. Denny's words. Back to my mind came that day last winter when I had walked down to the store in the snow. I remembered the peace and quiet that had taken possession of me. How I had fairly run up the hill going home, happy again. It was something of the same sort of feeling I had sitting there beside Mr. Denny on the porch steps.

"I wish I knew who I was," I said.

Romany came and laid his head on Mr. Denny's knee. He smoothed back the dog's ears. Romany switched his tail against my legs.

"Now that is something I would not be prevailed upon

to worry about if I were you, Keturah." He continued to flatten the dog's ears. "No man knows who he is until he recognizes his Maker."

⋅§ 20 §⋅

The evening I come to now was like most of the other midsummer evenings, warm, humid, gold-lined clouds hanging above the hills with no breeze to blow them away. Mr. Denny came home each day with his blue shirt soaked with perspiration, mopping his face with a crumpled handkerchief as he came up the walk.

Mrs. Denny and I were in the kitchen after supper, frying chicken and making potato salad and deviled eggs for the church picnic the next day.

"Get kind of tired this time of year eating cold fried chicken," Mrs. Denny fussed.

"I never do," I said. "I never had a piece of fried chicken until I came here, and I guess I'll never get enough to make up."

"Cyrus always enjoys it too," she remarked fondly, pleasure coming into her voice whenever she mentioned his name. "So I suppose I'll go right on frying it the rest of my life." She went over to the sink. "Cyrus was tired this evening. Didn't eat much supper, did he?"

I sliced the boiled eggs in half and slipped the yellows into a bowl. I was only half hearing what Mrs. Denny was saying. When Mr. Denny came home that afternoon he had handed me a postcard. "Here's a piece of mail for you,

121

Keturah," he had said simply, as if it was no extraordinary occurrence. I held it in my hands staring at my name. Slowly I turned it over and read the uphill scrawl.

DEAR KETURAH:

I been meaning to write you a long time and tell you I was sorry about everything. I didn't mean you no harm. My baby is two months old. I named her K, short for you because you are my best friend. I am working at the five and ten. Floyd is in the Navy.

Your loving friend,
GEORGIA LEE

The postcard was in my apron pocket. I had read and re-read it, and I did not know how I felt toward Georgia Lee. I knew I could not have signed "Your loving friend," if I had written to her. I didn't think it was a very good idea to give a baby the letter K for a name, especially a girl, even if it was in my honor. I wondered if Georgia Lee was happy about her baby. Floyd had probably never seen it. I wondered if the Beesoms knew they had a grandchild. So far as I knew they had never heard from Floyd again.

But what really troubled me was that Mr. Denny had read the postcard. My cheeks flamed as I bent over the eggs. He had found out that I knew Georgia Lee, that she had been my best friend. I decided that I had better make a clean breast of it to him. The only chance I would have was while Mrs. Denny was busy in the kitchen. I carried the eggshells out to the garbage and hurried around to the front of the house. Mr. Denny's chair was not on the lawn. I glanced up at the porch. There sat Mr. Denny slumped over in his rocker, his arms dangling over the arms of the chair, his pipe on the floor. I ran up on the porch. "Mr. Denny," I cried. "Mr. Denny!" But he did not hear me.

I flew back to the kitchen and flung open the screen door. "Mrs. Denny, come quick. Something's terribly wrong with Mr. Denny." She turned from the stove, all color draining from her face. She dropped whatever she was doing and came hurrying after me.

"Cyrus," she gasped, climbing the porch steps. "Cyrus!" She gathered his hands in hers. She held them in her tight grip as if she would put life back into them. Uttering a long wail, she let go of them. "He's dead!" She threw her apron over her face and great sobs shook her.

I hurried inside and rang up the doctor, hoping against hope that Mrs. Denny was wrong. When Dr. Marble came, he put a stethoscope to Mr. Denny's heart and felt for his pulse. He straightened up, his kindly eyes revealing all he felt. "Cyrus is gone," he said quietly.

Dr. Marble did his best to console Mrs. Denny. But she scarcely heard him. "Cyrus never had a strong heart," he told her. "Ever since that touch of lung trouble years ago. He came in to see me a few weeks ago. I told him he was going to have to slow down."

"He never told me." Mrs. Denny wept.

"There was no use worrying you, Martha. He was bound to go sudden like this sometime or other. I didn't expect it to be so soon. Now come, let's carry him into the house."

But Mrs. Denny was too upset to be of any help. Dr. Marble took Mr. Denny under the shoulders and I lifted his legs. Together we carried him in and laid him on the bed. Mrs. Denny sat on a chair beside him, alternately patting his hand and throwing her apron over her face. I stood at the foot of the bed. Dr. Marble had put coins on Mr. Denny's eyelids, and now that he lay stretched out straight, his face had become peaceful. I fervently hoped Mrs. Denny wouldn't have his picture taken. Because my Mr.

Denny was gone. He would never talk to me again. There would never again be that twinkle behind the steel-rimmed glasses, the quick turn of a smile on his lips, the familiar pipe clamped between his teeth. And suddenly I realized why he had talked to me so much those two weeks. He knew. . . . He knew. . . .

"Oh Mr. Denny," I cried wordlessly. "I wanted to tell you about the postcard. Now you'll never know. I hope you didn't think it was wrong of me not to tell you about Georgia Lee. It was locked up in me. I was going to tell you tonight."

Mr. Denny was buried in the little cemetery beside the church. On Sunday mornings I took flowers over to his grave before I went in to the service. And when the flowers were gone, I took colored leaves, and then branches from the fir trees that had little cones attached. They lasted from week to week during the coldest weather, and there was no need to bring fresh ones. But I always went over and stood a moment beside his grave before I went into the church. All during the sermon I would think of Mr. Denny lying out there in the churchyard, in the rain, in the cold, in the snow, under the shade of the pine trees, and he seemed less far away from me at those times.

Mrs. Denny refused to have his picture taken in his coffin. She told me privately that Mr. Denny had made her promise never to have it taken if he went first. Mrs. Wayburn wanted to bring the same photographer over that had taken Mr. Wayburn's, but Mrs. Denny was firm with her, the only time she was firm after Mr. Denny's death. She seemed to fold up after he was gone. The creases in her face deepened, her eyes sank back in her head, even her large body appeared to shrivel as she ate less and less, and nothing interested her. As her marriage had been cut in half she seemed to be half alive, as if she had always been the weaker partner, sustaining herself from Mr. Denny's strength. And now that she no longer had it to draw upon, she was unable to subsist alone. If I had not been there I don't know what would have happened to her. She never went anywhere except to church, and upon the slightest excuse—the weather, a premonition of a cold coming on, a touch of indigestion—she stayed home from that.

Fortunately Mr. Denny had taught me to drive the spring before, although I never drove the car alone until after he died. But it was a one-man car. It had all sorts of balking habits and constantly made queer grunting noises that Mr. Denny had been able to cope with, but it never ran smoothly for me. I used it only to go for the weekly groceries and to take us to church on Sundays.

❧ 21 ☙

Mrs. Denny's health failed rapidly. Until her sister spoke about it, I did not realize that her mind was going too. She lived almost completely in the past. Once when Mrs. Wayburn was there, she spoke of Mr. Denny as if he were present. Mrs. Wayburn took me aside in the kitchen.

"Her mind's affected, Keturah. She's talking just as if Cyrus Denny was right there in the room with her." Her sharp black eyes widened with fright. "She hears voices!" She stood perfectly still. A tear coursed slowly down her thickly powdered cheek. "I knew Martha would take it hard if anything happened to Cyrus. I think she's just following him to the grave."

125

Her words startled me. I had heard them talk about sending people off to the asylum. "Don't tell anyone about her mind, Mrs. Wayburn," I begged. "I don't want her ever to go to the asylum."

She placed her hand over her heart. "I give you my word. I don't want to see a sister of mine sent there ever." She gripped my shoulders. "Promise you'll stay with her, Keturah. Promise you won't leave her now."

I often wondered how secret Mrs. Wayburn kept Mrs. Denny's illness. No one ever came to see us. Only Dr. Marble coming up two or three times a month bringing his bag of pills. Mrs. Wayburn came each week with some delicacy she thought might tempt her sister, but when the fall rains set in she stretched her visits farther apart. "I can't bear to see my own flesh and blood this way," she would excuse herself. "My own sister." The tears would well up in her eyes, that darted at what she saw in the way a bird's did, and she would push up her glasses and dab at her eyes with a clean white handkerchief.

At night Mrs. Denny slept fitfully, often getting up in the wee hours of the morning and beginning to dress for some event that had taken place in her girlhood. I would have to coax her to take her clothes off again and get back into bed, telling her the weather was too bad to go. As the dining room was the warmest room in the house, she slept on the daybed in there, and I brought a little cot that had been stored away in the barn and slept beside her. She would talk for hours during the night, going far back into the past, and lying there, weary from sleep but afraid to doze off, I learned things about Mrs. Denny that I had never known. It was almost as if I knew her when she was young.

Christmas came and went with little interruption to our

routine. Mrs. Wayburn came over for dinner and afterwards I went for a walk, the first time I had been free in many weeks. It was a cold, cheerless day, the river as gray and flat as the sky, the hills groping forlornly along the horizon, a dampness in the air that penetrated to the bones. I found the spot where Mr. Denny had cut the little fir tree for my first Christmas with them. The stump of it was still there in the ground.

I could see Mr. Denny chopping it down and tying it neatly on the sled. I remembered our walk home through the snow and how he had told me that cream always rises to the top. I looked up at the ragged gray sky. "Mr. Denny," I said aloud. "I'll never rise with you gone." I began to cry. The tears came rapidly and I sank down on the hard ground, holding on to the stump of the fir tree, and wept bitterly. When it was over I felt as empty and cheerless as the earth about me.

Stopping by the barn, I gave the cows and Nellie yellow ears of corn to celebrate the day. The warm, dank smell of hay and animals rose to my nostrils. A soft, shadowy light reflected from the whitewashed walls. As I stood there beside old Nellie, I suddenly felt that Mr. Denny was close by, that he knew everything that was happening, that he was keenly aware of the trouble at the house. It almost seemed as if he placed his hands on my shoulders, and a surge of feeling passed through me as if the knowledge were given to me from him, that I could carry on.

After that it was somehow easier. Mr. Denny was still on my side helping me in some way. So many of the things he had told me came floating back, like messages on little wings to offer comfort.

In February the heavy snows came. It was so cold I covered Nellie with a blanket at night and often left it on during the sunless days. I shoveled a path from the house to the barn, and every day I had to shovel it again as the snow kept coming down. It was dark in the mornings when I went down to milk, Mrs. Denny finally asleep from exhaustion, and it was dark when I went down again in the evenings. I would hurry back up to the house and stir up the fire in the kitchen stove, and fix myself a hot breakfast. It was the only meal I really ate, sitting alone in the warm kitchen with the fire humming in the range, Mrs. Denny quietly sleeping in the next room. The snow slowly blotted out the darkness as there was no sun to light the sky. I felt as if I were isolated on a sea of snow.

The snow began to melt in March. When it was only in patches on the northern slopes, I let the cows out and led old Nellie out into the sunshine. She stood there blinking, scarcely able to move her ancient bones. She gently nudged her head up and down but she did not stray very far from the barn. The weather warmed until a hint of spring came flitting over the hills on a soft breeze. It was a false little wind that set the birds to singing and looking for mates. Winter gathered herself together once more, and we had the worst blizzard of all.

It began snowing before daybreak and by noon the drifts were piled high. The wind howled, swirling the snow into a veil beyond the windows. The curtains moved continuously with the draft. It was a task to keep the fires going against the cold.

Mrs. Denny had a strange, gray look that morning. She would take nothing to eat and one side of her mouth was drawn. She lay quiet until noon, then becoming restless, flung her arms from under the covers and grasped at the air. Strange sounds came from her throat when she tried to talk. As the afternoon wore on and the blizzard continued she grew more restless, as if the weather itself were tormenting her and she must fight against it. A fierce energy would take possession of her; she was at once so strong it was all I could do to hold her down; then suddenly she was so weak she fell back exhausted and sank into a deep, disturbed slumber. I could not leave her to go down and milk. It was dark very early, and with the darkness the wind howled the louder. The snow piled up on the sills; the windows frosted over. It would have been impossible for the doctor to come in the storm. Nor could I call him. When I had tried to reach Mrs. Wayburn earlier, the telephone was dead. I was snowbound in the house with a possessed woman. For the first time I was frightened.

I lit the lamps. The clock on the mantel ticked as slowly as water dripping from an old leak. Each hour seemed to be a whole night long. Mrs. Denny became determined to get out of bed. In desperation I pulled the covers as far under the mattress on one side as I could, stretched them tightly across her body, and sat on the other side to hold them down. I prayed that someone would come but I knew no one would. I prayed that the night would end but the minutes only seemed to lengthen.

Three o'clock in the morning is the loneliest time in the world. The hour belongs neither to the night nor the morning, stranded in an eerie timelessness. Time stood still while the earth, weary of the night and not ready yet for the dawn, rested. It is a time to die. But Mrs. Denny did not die. Nor did the earth's weariness overtake her. She became wild. With all my strength I held her against the thing she fought. I realized, finally, it was Death. And I fought against it with her. I did not want her to die. I did not want to let her go. She was all I had, pitiful though she had become. Together we struggled through the endless hour from three to four, and then, when time began to move forward again, the enemy receded victorious. Mrs. Denny sank back on her pillows, her face ashen, a rattling in her throat. And thus she lay until she grew as cold as the room had become. With one last gasp that shook her from head to foot, she lay still. I waited to see if she would move again. Slowly her features set, the lines in her face dissolved, shadows stained the corners of her mouth and eyes. I stood up and screamed. I made one last effort to call her back. But I did not rouse Mrs. Denny from the sleep of death.

I pressed my face against the window, and the chill of the glass brought me to my senses. One thing had to be done. Quickly getting into my coat and boots and tying a wool scarf over my head, I opened the door. The snow fell inside. Crawling, creeping, sliding, I made my way down to the barn in the swirling snow. Twice I fell into deep drifts, but renewed energy carried me on. When I finally reached the barn, the snow was piled so high against the door I could not open it. I made my way around to the side and found the little ladder up to the loft door buried under the snow. I had to clean off each rung as I went up. At the top I lifted the iron hook, swung back the door, and crept in on the hay. The unmilked cows stomped restlessly in their stalls. I lit the lantern, hung it back up on the nail, and emptied the swollen udders of their milk.

Daylight finally crept under the door and through the windows. It was a strange light, coming both from the snow and the sky. I wiped the steam from one of the little windowpanes and saw that it had stopped snowing. I could no longer put off going for the undertaker.

I had to climb back up in the hay and go out through the loft door and down the ladder again, leaving the full milk pails in the barn. The cats would no doubt have a fine time. The tracks I had made coming down were still there. Like Mrs. Denny, the blizzard had at last spent itself and moved on, leaving behind a world so empty and hushed, I might have been the only person walking out in it. I hoped the Kolbs on the next farm would help me.

⋖§ 22 §⋗

There was no sign of life at the Kolbs'. The narrow, two-storied frame house in which the German family lived looked as if it were frozen in the snow. I went around to the back. With a stiff hand I knocked on the solid wooden door. No one answered, and I knocked again, my hand aching inside the heavy woolen mitten. There was a movement at the window beside the door, someone wiping the steam away, making a little circle for an eye to peer out. I doubt if anyone came to their door all year long, so unfriendly had they always been, and to have it knocked upon on such a bitter morning must have caused them some astonishment. Cautiously the door opened and Mr. Kolb's face, crossed by a heavy, black mustache, appeared around the edge.

"Mr. Kolb," I said quickly, before he could close the door again. "I'm the girl up at the Dennys'. Mrs. Denny is dead."

He opened the door a trifle wider as Mrs. Kolb peered over his shoulder. "What is it?" she asked. "Who is there?"

"The girl from up at the Dennys'," he told her in his broken English. "Mrs. Denny is dead."

131

"In such a storm? Let the girl in, Jacob. Let her come in." He held the door wide enough for me to enter.

The warmth of the steamy kitchen made me giddy. The fire crackled in the big, iron range. I wanted to run over and put my hands over it. The daughter, a widow of middle age and almost as gray as her mother, stood at the sink. She eyed me kindly. "Girl, you must be frozen. Take off your things and warm yourself."

I tried to pull off my gloves but my fingers were stiff. She came over and took off my coat, hanging it over a chair. "Sit down and let me take your boots," she offered, and when I sat down she knelt and pulled off my boots and took them over to the sink and shook the snow out of them. She poured a cup of black coffee and set it on the table in front of me.

"Tell us what happened," she said, her long, sad face unsmiling, as if she had known a lot of trouble herself.

I sat drinking the coffee, telling them of the night, of Mrs. Denny's long illness which they had heard of, but even living in the nearest house for many years, had never bothered themselves about.

"We do not mix with people," Mrs. Kolb excused their keeping to themselves. "We work our farm, we tend to our own business. Mr. Denny was a good man."

"Can you help me get the undertaker?" I asked, half afraid they would say no and I would have to walk to the next house, a quarter of a mile away.

The Kolbs visibly withdrew into their aloofness. Finally the daughter turned to her parents. "Who else will help her in such weather?" She looked at me. "Papa can take us on the sled. Then he can go for the undertaker."

Mr. Kolb took his heavy coat and fur-lined hat from a

hook on the wall, drew on his boots, and went down to the barn. He brought the horse-drawn sled up to the house, and the three of us climbed on. The horse moved slowly through the deep snow, yet we had to hold tightly going up the hill so as not to slide off.

While I stirred up the fires, got fresh wood and coal, the two women heated water. I found Mrs. Denny's best clothes, and the women washed and dressed her, scarcely speaking to each other all the while. They were a strange, cold family; yet they performed a duty that day that made me forever grateful to them.

By the time Mr. Kolb came back, the snow plow had been over the main highway, and the undertaker was able to drive as far as our road. He came up on the sled with his long box. I stayed in the kitchen while they laid Mrs. Denny inside and took her away. The moment the door closed on them, I felt the awful loneliness of the house. The two silent women in the other room might not have been there. A desolation settled on me. I pressed my face against the roller towel on the kitchen door, the towel that Mr. Denny had always dried his hands on. I clung to the roller towel, desperately wanting the Dennys back again. I did not hear the daughter come into the kitchen.

"What are you going to do, girl?" she asked. "You cannot stay here alone."

"But the animals . . . I will have to stay with them."

"You come over to our house and eat dinner first. You need food and sleep."

So the three of us sat on the sled again, the sled that had taken Mrs. Denny down the hill for the last time, Mr. Kolb standing at the front holding the reins. Back in the Kolbs' warm kitchen, when dinner was on the table, I found I was able to eat. Afterwards I lay down in the cold bedroom and fell fast asleep under a feather comforter. While I slept Mr. Kolb went for Mrs. Denny's sister.

❧ 23 ☙

Together, Mrs. Wayburn and I sorted out Mrs. Denny's clothes and possessions, Mrs. Wayburn taking what she wanted. We also had to go through all of Mr. Denny's things, as Mrs. Denny had never touched them. I felt queer about opening his bureau drawers and poking into them, but Mrs. Wayburn went about it all in her brisk way, evidently having done it for many others before. She asked me if there was anything I would like for a keepsake. There was: a little milk-glass vase with pink rosebuds painted on it, which Mrs. Denny had kept on her dresser and I had always admired. I asked if I might have that and Mr. Denny's books. "I've no use for the books," she said. "Take the vase to remember Martha, and the books are yours." I packed the books in two big wooden packing boxes and wrapped the vase, fragile as a shell, in tissue paper. Mrs. Wayburn came into the dining room as I finished.

"I'm real glad you're going to have them. Cyrus was fond of his books." She stood arms akimbo, the front of her covered by a blue and white checked apron. "But where, may I ask, do you intend taking them?"

I tried to close the lid on the box but it would not go down. I took the books out again and rearranged them. Mrs. Wayburn had broached a subject that had been on my mind,

134

as I suppose it had been on hers, but neither of us had dared to bring it out into the open. What she was saying in reality was: "What is going to become of you, Keturah?"

"Someone has to stay here and take care of the cows and Nelly," I suggested hopefully.

"We'll sell them as soon as the place is appraised. You can't live here alone. It wouldn't be right for a girl your age."

"We can't sell Nellie," I protested.

"I'll take her over to my place. She can stay in the barn. She's old enough to be done away with but Cyrus Denny would turn over in his grave and come back to haunt me if I had that horse destroyed." She dusted off the company dishes that she had set out on the table, a hand-painted set that she was going to take with her. "Besides, you don't have any money to live on."

I hadn't thought about that.

"You're going to have to find work," she said matter-of-factly. "I'll give you a recommendation."

"I don't know anyone who needs a girl."

"Maybe you'll have to go to the city. We'll look in the paper and see if there is anything suitable advertised. Of course we'll have to be careful. Things can happen to a girl in the city."

In the meantime I was to stay at her house at night, riding back and forth on the milk truck that delivered the full cans at the station in the morning and brought the empty ones back at night. Thus I could milk and feed the animals. Mr. Denny's old Model T had stopped running.

Old Nellie did not survive the spring. I brushed her and fed her lumps of sugar and handfuls of corn. I knew she would feel strange over at Mrs. Wayburn's, and I half wished she would drop dead before she had to be moved.

She very nicely obliged by doing that very thing. I found her one morning stretched out in her stall, already stiff. Again I went for Mr. Kolb, and he hauled her away on the sled that rang on the rocks as it went down the hill. I watched him haul Nellie away with more relief than sadness.

Occasionally I walked down to the store. Mr. Sims was interested in helping me find a "situation," as he called it. He leaned across the counter, his long nose jutting toward me. "City's not for you." He shook his head. "We'll watch out for something roundabout. Something's sure to show up." And he gave me a wink from one of his small eyes, bright as a chipmunk's.

Mrs. Wayburn answered two ads in the city paper but neither reply was satisfactory to her and she did not pursue them further. She decided we would wait until the cows were sold and make a trip to the city and visit a reliable employment agency. "That way," she said, "we're sure to be protected."

The appraiser finally came in May. The cows were sold and the farm put in the hands of an agent. It was difficult to part with Delia. She had grown into a fine, fawn-colored cow, still a pet, nuzzling her wet nose against my arm, her swimming brown eyes pleading for a rub on the forehead or an extra ear of corn. But at last she went with her mother. After the cows were gone I went down to see Mr. Sims for the last time. Once I was over at Mrs. Wayburn's, it would be too far. Mr. Sims was at the meat block cutting up a side of beef. He laid down his cleaver, wiped his bloody hands on a towel hanging above him and again on his apron for good measure, and came hurrying over to me. "I was hoping you'd come."

"I came down to say good-bye."

He passed over my words. "I've got a situation for you, I think," he announced. "Comes highly recommended by my niece's sister-in-law."

It was the first good news I'd had. "Where?"

" 'Bout fifty miles from here. Country place." He nodded his big head on which the long, black hairs still tried to conceal the bald spot. "My niece was up Sunday. Her sister-in-law gave notice she's leaving. Getting married in June."

I hung on his every word. "Do you think I'd do, Mr. Sims?"

He planted his big hands down on the counter, his hairy arms rising from them like sturdy tree trunks. "Of course you'll do. Just hold your head up and act like you know about everything they ask you. You'll learn if you don't know immediately. This place don't have just a hired girl. They have servants."

He whipped out his billfold from his pants pocket and taking a card from it, handed it to me. One corner had a tiny smear of blood on it. I read the name on the card: *Miss Hawthorne*. Even scrawled in pencil it looked important. "Now if they didn't have someone hired before my niece got word to them, you should be hearing from this Miss . . . Miss . . ."

"Miss Hawthorne," I supplied. The name sounded even more important when I said it aloud.

"Miss Hawthorne." Mr. Sims classed it with all other names. "She'll write you."

"But I'm going over to Mrs. Wayburn's. I may never get the letter."

"Go over to the post office and get them to forward it."

Two customers came in and Mr. Sims went over to wait on them. When they left he opened the candy case and began filling a bag with two of each. He went from one end of each row of glass dishes to the other, slid the door shut, and handed me the bulging paper bag. Two licorice sticks stuck out of the top. "A farewell present," he said.

I thanked him. "I'll always remember you, Mr. Sims." He nodded. "Write to me if you get the situation."

I went out of the store clutching the bag of candy with the licorice sticks poking out the top, not able to bear another word from him. Over at the post office I had my address changed.

Before I left I had gone up to my little room under the eaves. The curtains were gone from the windows, the bed stripped; it looked as if no one had ever lived in it. I remembered the first night I had come up there with Mrs. Denny carrying the lamp, and I had thought it the prettiest room in the world. I went over to the window and looked out at the maple tree, all motionless and green in the May afternoon, the sun behind it. I had told the tree my secrets, kneeling there at the window, sometimes when it was so dark I could barely see its outline against the sky. I felt the tree would miss me too. As I stood there, suddenly way up in the top of the tree one leaf began to twirl. The whole tree was caught in stillness save for one twirling leaf. It flapped as if a strong breeze blew, but none of the other leaves moved. I thought it would spin itself right off the tree. But the stem held it until it was still again, and it became a part of all the leaves. I could not pick out which one it had been.

I thought about the leaf maybe wanting to break loose but unable to snap the tiny stem that held it. Or maybe some small bird or insect had been nibbling at its stem, but God had tied it to the tree good and tight and the leaf was safe. And it came to me that no matter how hard life hit against me, I would always be tied by the roots I had here at the Dennys, and I would find them strong enough to hold me. Whatever was to become of me, I was a part of the Dennys, as the leaf was a part of the tree. I went back downstairs and left the house, never to go back into it again.

❦ 24 ❧

The next week the letter came for me at Mrs. Wayburn's. I hurriedly tore it open. It was written in ink, on fine white paper, the lines flowing gracefully across the page.

"Dear Miss Brown," I read aloud. Mrs. Wayburn was at my elbow, as excited as I was. "She calls me Miss Brown." I laughed.

"And isn't that your name?" she demanded. "Folks you don't know shouldn't be too familiar."

"I'm not used to hearing it. It sounds important, doesn't it?"

"Get on with the letter and we'll see."

"Dear Miss Brown," I read again just to hear it. "You have been recommended to me by Miss Pembroke, who says she does not know you personally, but that you have been well spoken of by her relatives. Kindly be here next Monday at two for an interview. Cordially, Alice A. Hawthorne— She wants me to come!" I cried. "Next Monday."

The next day I packed. I was going to work for Miss

Hawthorne. Nor did Mrs. Wayburn, in our excitement, re-member it was to be an interview. She promised to send the boxes of books as soon as I was settled, but I squeezed Mr. Denny's Bible and *Tale of Two Cities* in my suitcase to have something to read until they came.

The problem was how to get there. It worried Mrs. Way-burn that I would have to go clear to the city and change buses and have a long wait in between. Then fortunately, her eavesdropping on the party line paid off. She learned from a crisscross of conversation that Mr. Dorn was going in that direction Monday morning, to look at some cattle. No sooner was the line free than Mrs. Wayburn rang the Dorns and asked if Mr. Dorn would give me a lift. He told her he would be glad to pick me up at eight o'clock. This would bring me to my destination long before two o'clock, but I hoped Miss Hawthorne wouldn't mind.

On Sunday morning after church, the people I knew came over and shook hands. The Campbells were there with the Drury twins, who were now the Campbell twins, having been legally adopted. A year after they took the twins, Mrs. Campbell had had a baby of her own and an-other one the past February. She hovered over all four chil-dren, showing no partiality. The twins were fat and docile and no longer sucked their thumbs. They put up their round little faces for me to print a kiss on.

Mr. Palmer came back a second time to shake hands. Be-hind the freckles a flame of color stained his cheeks. "I will miss your singing," he said again, his teeth clicking. "Al-ways enjoyed singing with you." A white-gloved hand slipped over his shoulder, and one of his sisters caught him away. He looked back as he went down the aisle behind her. I waved and he grinned broadly. I could almost hear Mr. Denny's chuckle.

I waited at the gate for Mr. Dorn. Mrs. Wayburn sat on the porch rocking. Already the sun was warm and my long-sleeved, dark cotton dress was going to be too hot. I had combed my hair with a great deal of care, catching it together in the back with a big bone barrette. I wore my only summer hat, a wide-brimmed black straw, similar to the one I had worn the day I left the Orphanage. Mrs. Wayburn had given me a new pair of tan lisle stockings which I ordinarily would have saved for Sunday, but which I wore that day to make a good appearance. They were almost as thin as silk. My black Oxfords were polished and shined.

At one minute to eight Mr. Dorn came around the bend in his big, rattling cattle truck. He slammed on the brakes and came to an abrupt stop in front of the gate. I picked up my heavy suitcase. Mrs. Wayburn stood up on the porch, a handkerchief in her hand. I set the suitcase down, ran up and kissed her, and ran back down, picked up my suitcase again, and climbed up in the truck beside Mr. Dorn. I waved to Mrs. Wayburn as we drove away. Thus I parted with my girlhood.

~§ PART II §~

Hawthorne

I WALKED slowly up the long, tree-lined road to the house. Overhead, giant oaks laced leafy arms to shut out the sun. My suitcase, tied securely with a rope, was heavy. Hawthorne. I had seen it spelled out in brass letters on the stone gatepost. Although the big iron gate was open, I had the strange feeling that it swung to behind me, enclosing me in Hawthorne. In a few steps I walked from one world into another.

It was only ten thirty. I was not expected until two. At the bend in the road I took Mr. Denny's silver watch out of my purse and looked at it again. Five minutes had passed. Mrs. Wayburn had given me the watch the night before. "You've nothing to tell time by, and Cyrus would like for you to have this, I'm sure." She had laid the watch, worn from slipping in and out of Mr. Denny's pocket, in my hands. It had been Mr. Denny's most prized possession. His mother had given it to him when he went to the city to study law. I ran my fingers over the back he had smoothed so many times. There was nothing that could have given me more pleasure than to have Mr. Denny's silver watch, although I would never have dared ask for it. Just to hold it in my hand gave me confidence. I picked up my suitcase, that grew heavier each time I lifted it, and rounded the bend in the road.

I will never forget my first sight of the house. It rode on the top of the long, green lawn like one of the big, spanking white boats that went up and down the river. Across the front, long, green shutters framed the windows. I counted them, twelve, six up and six down. Flowers spilled from beds and borders—petunias, geraniums, phlox, delphiniums. I had never seen such a beautiful place. I moved toward it as in a dream.

The road wound past the lawn and on around a tree-shaded terrace set out with fresh white yard chairs and tables. I went up the path of stepping-stones leading to the front door. I hesitated before the heavy brass knocker. If I lift it, I thought, I will be inside my new world. My hand trembled as I raised it. The knocker banged against the door. No one answered. I tried again. Still no one came. I spied a bell beside the door and pressed my finger on it. I could hear it ring inside the house. After a moment the door opened and a blond girl in a green uniform, with a bit of white apron tied around her, looked out at me.

"Yes?" she inquired. She was scarcely older than myself, and quite pretty. She looked me up and down, then her light blue eyes came to rest on my suitcase that had seen its days. I realized she thought I had something to sell.

"I would like to see Miss Hawthorne," I managed to say under her forbidding glance.

"What for?"

"I've come to work for her."

The girl's pale blue eyes widened. "You mean you're the one with the appointment?"

I nodded. "Yes."

"It was for this afternoon. At two, if I remember right. Miss Hawthorne likes things at the time she sets."

I gathered my courage at her rebuff. It was a holdover from contending with Mrs. Atwood. When Mrs. Atwood tried to put me in my place it always made me want to fight back, as if I must show her that I was a human being with rights too. "I've come early," I said. "I had to catch a ride to get here."

The maid looked me up and down again, her glance appraising me as an awkward country girl. I could see she didn't think I'd suit Miss Hawthorne.

"Then you might as well come in," she said abruptly, "and wait." With this welcome, I stepped into the hall.

"I'll go tell Miss Hawthorne," she said, still curt. "Have a chair if you like." She went off down the hall and disappeared through a door at the end of it.

The inside of the house was more beautiful than the outside. There was a long, white stairway with a dark bannister curling over it, white walls and woodwork. The color came from the gold-framed paintings on the walls, and the deep, soft rugs. The dark furniture gleamed with a high polish. On either side the hall opened into a large room. In the one, the white curtains hung to the floor, there was a grand piano; in the other, the walls were lined with books. I had never seen so many books.

The maid finally came back, her hips swinging slightly. She was no friendlier than before. "Miss Hawthorne will see you," she announced, as if she didn't approve of the state of affairs.

I picked up my suitcase and followed her down the hall. At the door she stood aside to let me pass, then turned and closed it behind her. I found myself in a small sitting room or study. Thin white curtains hung at the windows, sway-

147

ing slightly with the breeze. Miss Hawthorne was sitting at a desk in the center of the room. She was older than I had expected. Her steel-gray hair was wound in a roll over each ear. Her thin white dress was severely tailored, and around her neck was a heavy silver chain on which hung a large silver cross. Her gray eyes under her steel-gray brows reminded me of the glint of the railroad tracks. She looked right through me.

"I believe your appointment was for two this afternoon?" she said without greeting me at all.

"It was the only time I could come," I explained. "Mr. Dorn brought me in his truck since he had to come this way."

She only raised and lowered her thick eyebrows. "I'm quite busy this morning." She hesitated a moment. "I suppose we might as well go ahead now you're here."

She motioned me to a straight chair in front of her desk that seemed to be waiting for me. "Sit down, please." I sat carefully on the edge of it and settled my suitcase beside my feet. Miss Hawthorne's glance lingered on the suitcase.

"Why did you bring that?" she asked.

"I want to work here," I told her.

She looked at me more sharply. "Why?"

"I haven't any place else to go." I couldn't tell her that I already belonged there, that the gate had seemed to swing shut behind me to keep me there, that the house had already taken me in.

She sat very still. "Tell me about yourself."

I wet my lips that had become dry. "There isn't much to tell. The Dennys took me from the Orphanage when I was sixteen. First Mr. Denny died, then Mrs. Denny. I can work hard," I assured her.

"How old are you?"

"Nineteen."

"Your parents?"

"My mother died when I was born."

"Your father?"

"I don't know who he was."

"Did you like it at the Orphanage?"

"No."

"Did you like it at the . . ."

"The Dennys'," I supplied. "I loved the Dennys. I would have stayed there forever if they hadn't died."

"Do you have any money?"

"Two dollars. Mrs. Wayburn gave them to me when I left, in case of an emergency. And Mr. Denny's silver watch; and she let me have his books. She's going to send them to me."

This disturbed her. "How many are there?"

"Only two boxes. He didn't have many books. He kept reading the same ones over."

"How much schooling have you had?"

I told her.

"But you like to read?" she pressed.

"I don't read too well," I confessed. "After Mr. Denny read the books aloud I managed to get through them."

She spread her hands out on the desk. They were beautiful, ringless hands, the fingers long and slim with scarcely a sign of knuckles. You could tell she'd never done any housework. Her hands looked as graceful as birds perched on the edge of the desk.

"I need someone to take care of a child," she said slowly. "Do you know anything about taking care of children?"

"Oh, I do. I helped with the young ones at the Orphanage."

She sat quiet for a moment. "This is not exactly an easy

position," she said. "Adrianne is not difficult but there are other things . . ." She seemed to be waiting for my reaction.

"I'm not afraid," I assured her.

She gave me another penetrating look. "I don't believe you are." She sighed. "It's not easy to find someone competent out here. It's board and room and five dollars a week. Do you want to stay?"

I caught my breath. "Yes!"

She immediately became brisk again. "You must understand that you are not to ask questions here. I don't like people prying into things. You will have your duties. Your free time may be spent in your room or walking out of doors, or helping with anything Mrs. Woeste asks you to. Mrs. Woeste is the housekeeper. You will be with Adrianne except when she is sleeping. She is a queer little thing, having no mother. But perhaps you will understand her, as you didn't either."

Miss Hawthorne stood up. She was not very tall. She stood as straight as she sat. It gave her the appearance of height and dignity. She seemed very thin in her plain white dress and silver chain and cross. At one time, I thought, she must have been beautiful.

"Marie will show you to your room. It adjoins Adrianne's. The girl you're replacing had to leave early. Marie has had to look after Adrianne as well as her other work. She'll be glad to be relieved." Miss Hawthorne pressed a button on her desk and Marie came back. "You may show Keturah to her room," she told Marie. "I hope you two girls will get on together."

"Yes, ma'am." Marie answered as crisply as Miss Hawthorne had spoken, and I doubted if we would get on together.

Marie led the way up the backstairs. Her hips swayed slightly under the bow of her white apron. "So you're going to stay," she observed. "That was quick enough. Keturah. What an odd name."

I could tell she didn't think much of it. I did not reply. She opened the second door on the long hall. "Here's your room. I'll be back soon as you unpack. I haven't finished dusting up front."

I walked to the center of the room, holding on to my suitcase. It was like the first time I had gone into my room at the Dennys'. There was something similar about the two rooms—bare white walls, a single bed, a small dresser, white curtains at the window. But here lovely pictures splashed color on the walls, there was a little desk on spindly legs with a lamp beside it, a big, flowered chair, and two braided rugs on the polished floor, one beside the bed, the other in front of the dresser. And the ceiling didn't slope. The room seemed to be all light and air. I set my suitcase down and clasped my hands together. "Here I am, Mr. Denny," I whispered. "I'm here!"

Between my room and Adrianne's was a white-tiled bathroom with hot and cold running water and a real bathtub. I doubted if Mrs. Wayburn would believe it all when I wrote to her.

I unpacked my clothes and hung them in the closet, put my Bible and *Tale of Two Cities* on the desk, the little hand-painted milk-glass vase with pink rosebuds and Mr. Denny's silver watch on the dresser, and went over to the window. Just beyond it was a tree, a great, old oak tree with gnarled branches stretching up over the top of the house. In its leaves birds twittered, and as I watched, a gray squirrel ran up the trunk and was lost in the green. I put my nose to the screen and sniffed the summer smells mixed up in the tree, smells the wind had blown into it and the leaves had caught and held. It was like my maple tree.

There was a small sound behind me. I straightened up, thinking Marie had come back. The room was empty. The bathroom door moved. Crack by crack it opened wider. A live doll appeared around the edge of it, one hand clinging to the doorknob. Under her straight black hair, cut in bangs across her low forehead, her eyes were as black and round and shiny as two buttons. The tiny mouth was no bigger than a tight rosebud. The little legs hanging out of the blue smocked dress looked too fragile to carry her far.

"You're Adrianne," I said gently, so as not to frighten her.

She kept her black eyes intently upon me. She might have been a little chipmunk watching me cautiously at the edge of its hole, deciding not to move until it knew what I was going to do.

I slipped down on my knees. "I'm Keturah," I said softly. "I've come to take care of you."

Still she kept her distance. I was afraid she might go back through the door again and be lost in the storybook she had slipped from. I held out my hands but she did not stir.

"Come here," I urged. "I'll show you a squirrel. I just saw him run up the tree. Don't you want to see him?"

She let go of the doorknob and walked past me to the window. "Where?" She pressed her face against the screen.

I stooped beside her. "He's out there in the leaves. Maybe he'll come down the tree again to find some food for his babies."

The door opened and Marie came in. She was annoyed when she saw Adrianne. "How did she get in here?"

"She walked in," I said.

She looked crossly at Adrianne. "You're supposed to stay in your room. How can I go off and leave you a moment if you're not going to mind?" She shrugged. "Well, you're off my hands now. I had enough looking after my sister's kids at home. That's why I went to work, to get away from kids." She stuck her head in the closet. "Well, I see you've got your things hung up. Come along and I'll show you the rest."

In Adrianne's room everything was white except the blue walls and blue ruffles at the top of the windows. A low shelf along one wall held dolls and toys of every shape and size. "There's enough to play with," Marie said, "but she hardly touches anything. Just this old rabbit." She picked up a stuffed gray rabbit with long, floppy pink ears from the small bed. "She won't eat or sleep without this. All the other stuff they could send over to my sister's kids. They'd have a time. But catch anyone here giving anything away."

Adrianne put her hands up. "I want my rabbit." Marie gave it to her. Adrianne hugged the battered rabbit in her arms and sat down on a little red chair and watched us.

There was a row of tiny dresses in the closet, hung on tiny hangers. "How can she ever wear them all?" I marveled.

"She can't. No one ever sees her anyway. When outsiders are here you're to keep her upstairs or in the backyard. Out of sight, out of mind. You'll learn. No one's here now but Miss Hawthorne. The place is dead. Mrs. Drew is coming next month with her kids. Then you'll have your hands full. God, I hate that woman."

Miss Hawthorne had told me not to ask questions, but so much was happening all at once it was all I could do to take in what was right before me. Marie gave me Adrianne's routine. "She has breakfast at eight. You go down to the kitchen and get it and bring it up here. Yours too. You can take her out afterwards if the weather's nice; if not, you stay up here. Lunch is at twelve sharp and dinner at six. You bring all the trays up. You'll get tired eating up here, but that's your job not mine, thank heavens. She takes a nap after lunch and is in bed at seven thirty. I've been bored to death up here the past week." She turned to go. As she opened the door she paused, speaking over her shoulder. "You'll get on with Mrs. Woeste if you're on time."

With these brief instructions, she left. I sat down in the rocking chair to get everything straight in my mind. Adrianne sat hugging her rabbit, never taking her eyes from me. There was something about her that reminded me of the Drury twins, the way they had silently accepted whatever happened to them. I reached out my arms to her. "Come here and let me rock you," I offered. For a moment I thought she wasn't going to, she remained on her chair staring at me, then slowly she slipped off the edge of it and came to me. I gathered her up and held her close. The frail little body was no weight at all in my lap. Adrianne laid her head against me and put her thumb in her mouth.

When time came back to me, I glanced at the clock. It was quarter after twelve. I flew down the backstairs to the kitchen. Mrs. Woeste was at the stove. Above her hung a row of shining pans. "I'm sorry I'm late," I blurted out. "I forgot the time."

It seemed a whole minute before she turned around. She gave me a hard look. "When you're late it makes me late. Miss Hawthorne has her lunch at twelve fifteen. After that the help eat."

"I won't be late again," I promised.

She picked up a tray of dishes from the table and served food into them from the pots on the stove. She had a broad,

154

strong back, a large bun of gray-streaked hair on the back of her head. There wasn't a part of Mrs. Woeste that didn't say: "This is my kitchen. What I say, goes." Even her thick ankles, in black cotton stockings, were like strong stalks growing out of her sturdy shoes. "You're Keturah, I take it."

"Yes."

She carried the tray back to the table and poured out two glasses of milk. Her plain face was lined and weathered. I doubt if she had ever tried to make it any different than it naturally was. She was not the sort of person who would try to improve on what God had given her. "There," she said, the glasses filled. "Adrianne eats like a bird. See that she drinks her milk." She looked at me with a sharp eye. "I daresay you have a healthy appetite."

I nodded, flushing.

"You'll be the only one around here does. Miss Hawthorne scarcely touches her food, Marie's afraid of getting fat, Mr. Hodges has no teeth. If you don't get enough first time, come back for seconds." With this small invitation I felt as if I had received some sort of approval from her. Probably as much as she would ever give.

I carried the tray upstairs and set it on the little table. Adrianne sat on one side in her red chair, I on the other on a footstool. Adrianne picked up her spoon but made no effort to eat.

"It's good," I told her. "You're going to eat your lunch, aren't you?"

She slowly stirred her soup. I ate mine quickly, then taking her spoon, dipped it in the soup and held it to her lips. She opened the little bud of her mouth and let me put the spoon in. She held the spoonful a long time, then slowly chewed the vegetables. I had fed her half the soup when she refused to open her mouth again. The milk was no easier. It took forever for her to finish the glass. She watched me constantly but her gaze was warmer now, as if I were no longer a stranger, as if she were beginning to trust me. I had never met so many appraising glances as I had in the few hours since I'd arrived. I felt as if I were passing from one test to another, being graded, judged. How I was faring I could only wonder, and hope for the best.

"Can you say Keturah?" I asked Adrianne.

She studied a moment, as if the name had to be chewed first, like her food. "Tura," she said finally.

I laughed. "Tura. I like that. Nobody ever called me Tura before."

"Tura," she said again; her lips parted, and she smiled for the first time.

When I took the tray back to the kitchen Mrs. Woeste was waiting for me again. She glanced at the clock. "Dishes should be down by one." It was ten after.

"It took me so long to feed Adrianne."

"She ought to eat by herself. She's three years old. My children ate by themselves before they was two."

"She wouldn't eat alone. She wouldn't eat until I fed her."

She raised an eyebrow. "You're not going to spoil her?"

"She's got such a little mouth, maybe it's hard to get the spoon in by herself," I dodged Mrs. Woeste's question. "Maybe that's why she's so tiny. Nobody ever bothered to feed her and her stomach's shrunk."

Mrs. Woeste's heavy bosom heaved with a sigh. For all her talk I felt she was more gruff than unkind. She was like Mrs. Denny in that respect. Mrs. Denny was gruff so as not to be embarrassed by her own kindness. "She's had the best of attention. Miss Hawthorne wouldn't let it be otherwise."

Back upstairs I put Adrianne down for her nap and went

156

into my room and stretched out on the bed. I was tired from being up so early, the jolting ride in the truck, from all the new things that had been happening to me. I still seemed to be moving in a dream. I closed my eyes. When I opened them again, compelled by something beyond myself to open them, Adrianne was standing beside the bed watching me. I glanced over at Mr. Denny's silver watch propped up on the dresser. It was three thirty. I had fallen asleep. I drew Adrianne up on the bed beside me and we lay looking out at the tree.

The first week passed quietly enough. Adrianne was like a small shadow at my side. As the weather was nice, I took her out after breakfast and again after her nap. We had the yard to ourselves except for Mr. Hodges who was busy in the flower beds or the vegetable garden down near the barn. We sat on the terrace or under the oak tree at the back of the house, or we walked over to the summerhouse that was half smothered in honeysuckle and clematis vines. It always smelled sweet in the little, round summerhouse; the breeze coming through the green lattice sides was thick and sweet as honey. Bees buzzed in the vines, and butterflies flitted in and out, losing their way for a moment until drawn back by the light outside.

Miss Hawthorne might have gone away for all I knew. Marie kept her distance, as if our ways were too different for her to become friendly. She poked her head in Adrianne's room once in a while, but I kept our rooms and bath clean, and there was no need for her to come in if she didn't care to.

I loved the big, spacious yard, the beautifully kept flower beds and borders, the great, old shade trees. And I had Adrianne. I had someone to care for. At the end of the week we were completely devoted to each other.

Miss Hawthorne sent for me while Adrianne was sleeping. She sat at her desk as she had the morning I arrived. She wore a pale blue dress which relieved the whiteness of her skin, the blue calling to the surface whatever color was in her. Her cool gray eyes regarded me from a greater distance than the space between us.

"Sit down, Keturah," she said, immediately I came in. "I wanted to give you time to get yourself situated. I hope everything has gone well?"

I sat down on the same straight chair I had before.

"I love Adrianne, Miss Hawthorne," I told her.

She smiled briefly. It was gone so quickly I wondered if she had really smiled. "I'm glad you do." Her voice was as cool as a little wind that would not pause to catch the warmth of the sun. "She needs someone to love her." She paused. "It's good you have her outdoors so much. She needs the sunshine. She's never been too robust. She has dreadful winters." She sorted some papers as she talked. "If there's anything you need, you are to let me know."

"Yes."

"That will be all, Keturah."

I stood beside my chair, not quite ready to go. "Miss Hawthorne," I ventured. "My books haven't come yet. Do you think something happened to them?"

158

She had already picked up her pen. "I'm sure nothing has. Freight is slow in arriving out here. I'll have Mr. Hodges inquire at the post office."

I thanked her and went back upstairs.

The next day it rained and we had to stay indoors. When I put Adrianne down for her nap, I went back to my room and found myself with nothing to do. I had finished *Tale of Two Cities* again, the day before. I remembered the library downstairs I had glimpsed that first day as I waited in the hall. I wondered if Miss Hawthorne would mind if I went down and borrowed a book. The house was quiet except for the dripping of the summer shower. Everyone seemed to be off napping somewhere. I didn't see how it would do any harm to go down and borrow a book. I would put it back as soon as I finished it. I went down the backstairs and through the long hall to the front of the house. I had not been there since the morning I arrived. I was struck again with its spacious beauty, the delicately patterned rugs, the shining dark furniture. Over the front door was a fan of glass, each pane a different color. Even on that dark day they shone like jewels at the end of the long hall.

In the library, books lined the walls from floor to ceiling. I thought Miss Hawthorne must know everything if she had read them all. I walked past the shelves, admiring the bindings, the gold letters of the titles. I searched for one that might be familiar, but none were. At last I came upon something that sounded interesting. *Country Life* was printed in gold letters on the blue binding of a small book squeezed between two large ones. I took it off the shelf and the two big books moved together as if no space had been between them. No one would ever notice that a book was missing.

Back in my room I curled up in the big flowered chair to read. Mr. Denny's books were all old and worn, but this one was like new, none of the edges had been turned down, the pages as unmarred as if they'd never been read. I would have to be very careful to leave no fingerprints on it. Written on the inside page in bold handwriting were the words: *To Alice A. Hawthorne. This is what it has been to me.* It was signed TCB. The book was easy to read. The words flowed along like a brook, like drops of water slipping musically down to make a little waterfall, creating images I recognized, striking such fond memories that I relived what I read: a walk through winter woods, birdsong calling up the spring, a stream rushing over the rocks and squeezing under fallen logs, swirling into little pools that caught the dry, falling leaves. I was halfway through when Adrianne woke up. That night I finished the book before I went to sleep. The next day I read it again. After I finished it the third time, I decided to take it back and get another book. But someone was always stirring about when I had the opportunity, and after dark there were no lights downstairs except at the back of the house, and I didn't dare go down and turn on a light in the library.

As I was bringing the mail up the road one afternoon, I saw Miss Hawthorne leave the house by a side door where her rooms were, walk swiftly over the grass and disappear behind a row of pointed fir trees. I hurried up on the terrace and peeped into the library. There was no one about. My own books had been delivered and stood on shelves in my room like old friends. But I knew them by heart. And here were so many inviting books I hadn't read. While I looked for another one, I heard footsteps coming down the hall. I took the first book at hand and stuck it inside my blouse. I went out and around the back of the house and up the back-stairs. When I took the book out and read the title, *The Moonstone,* I wondered if I would be able to read it. But it had such fascinating and terrifying pictures, I was caught to struggle through.

I had to read slowly. But I could scarcely bear to stop reading and go to sleep, for want of knowing what was going to happen next. So engrossed was I in the book that I did not hear the storm until the curtains suddenly blew out in the room, the lights flickered, and a crash of thunder shook the house. I rushed into Adrianne's room to close the windows. She was silently sobbing in her bed. The lightning flashed, she held her breath, then broke into her quiet sobbing again. I pulled the blinds down and tried to comfort her. There was a knock at the door. So fresh was I from the pages of *The Moonstone* that I was half afraid to answer. "Yes?" I called weakly. The door opened and Miss Hawthorne appeared in her dressing gown, her hair hanging down her back. She looked like some gray ghost in her flowing sleeves and her long, gray hair streaming down behind her. If she had had a candle in her hand, I think I would have screamed.

"Is everything closed?" she asked. She came across the room and stood by the bed. "I should have warned you. Adrianne's terrified of storms. No one could ever do anything with her." The lights flickered again, followed by a crack of thunder and a low wail from Adrianne.

"I'm glad you're not afraid," Miss Hawthorne noted. "I like a good storm. There is something elemental about a storm. I hope you can comfort Adrianne. Good night." And she went back out of the room, closing the door behind her.

I hovered over Adrianne until the storm was over and she

fell asleep again. Back in my own room I turned out the light and watched the lightning lessen until it came only at long intervals, and was no more than a faint flicker beyond the tree.

I lay there thinking what a strange place I had come to. Beneath the beauty of Hawthorne lay a chill and loneliness as withering as a frost. What had happened to make Miss Hawthorne withdraw into herself, to spend her time here alone with a few servants and a child she had no affection for? Why was Adrianne here? Where had she come from, to whom did she belong? And I vowed to myself that I would stay with her until she grew up and lost her fears. She was such a tiny, fragile thing, like a doll caught into a shape and size she might never escape from. I fell asleep just as the stars were sprinkled back into the sky. I saw them glitter over the oak tree, polished by the rain, proclaiming all was well with the night.

Adrianne was as frightened of horses as she was of storms. A handsome riding horse pranced in his stall in the barn and stuck his long, silky nose out of the high window. At sight of him Adrianne trembled and clung to me, hiding her head, and nothing would induce her to make friends with the horse. To soothe her, I carried her over to the vegetable garden where Mr. Hodges was chopping weeds with a hoe. Shoulders bent, face and hands weathered, an old, sweat-stained felt hat protecting his head, Mr. Hodges tended his garden and flowers as if he had an affection for them. Sometimes I helped him find the cabbage worms, or held the tomato plants while he tied them up. This morning I walked down the rows of sugar corn, Adrianne trailing behind me, to see if any ears were ripe enough to be picked. Mr. Hodges leaned on his hoe, pushed his battered felt hat back on his head. "Reminds me of Mr. Clay as a boy," he said. "Always coming down to see if the corn was ripe enough to eat. Couldn't wait for the first ears."

"Mr. Clay?" I said, and realized I had raised a question. But it was too late to take it back.

"He'll be around one of these days," Mr. Hodges warned. "Comes and goes." Mr. Hodges was for the most part non-committal. We could be beside him a long time before he spoke. "Stays over there when he comes." He nodded in a direction across the fields.

I saw a white cottage almost hidden in the trees. A path across the meadow led to it.

"Been empty about a year now," Mr. Hodges reflected. "Fine view over there."

"Could we go and have a look?"

"Don't see any harm in it. No one there."

The sun was hot as I carried Adrianne across the meadow, but the grove of trees offered a cooling shade. As we rounded the front of the house I stopped short. The land fell abruptly away at the edge of the short lawn. Spread below was a lush, green meadow crossed by a sparkling stream. Beyond the meadow was a woods, and in the far distance a range of high, blue hills. Wild honeysuckle tangled over the steep bank to the meadow, smelling sweetly in the warm sunshine; white butterflies drifted over it. There was something vaguely familiar about the view, as if I had seen it before.

It became a favorite place to go. It reminded me of the Dennys', with the river flowing through the valley, the hills rising on the other side. Here the view was wider but just as lovely. No one ever asked where we had been. As long as we kept out of the yard on Miss Hawthorne's side of the house and I was in the kitchen in time to pick up the trays, no one cared. A month drifted by and I scarcely knew it had passed. I was reading *The Moonstone* for the third time.

⊷§ 3 §⊷

Miss Hawthorne sent for me again. I thought she had forgotten about me, it had been so long since I'd seen her. She seemed less cool when I came into her study. She was walking about and did not ask me to sit down.

"We're having guests," she said at once. "My niece, Mrs. Drew, is coming with her children. Derrick and Wendy aren't as well behaved as Adrianne, I'm sorry to say, but I hope you can look after them when necessary. There will be entertaining, and when we're occupied I'd like you to look after the children."

Having looked after more than one child at a time at the Orphanage, this did not disturb me.

"They'll be here a month if Mrs. Drew doesn't get tired of the country before then. I hope it won't be difficult." She sat down at her desk and put the tips of her long, white fingers together, making a steeple of them. "It should be good for Adrianne to have other children about. Last summer she was too small for them. Perhaps this year it will be better."

She did not look too sure about it. "That will be all, Keturah."

I went back upstairs not quite knowing what to expect.

From the summerhouse we watched the Drews arrive. They came roaring up the road in a long, tan car with the top down, the brakes screeching to a stop on the driveway. The boy jumped out first and ran around the trees, the little girl jumped out and ran after him. Their hair was bleached and straight, their skin deeply tanned. Mrs. Drew lit a cigarette before she opened her door and slid out from under the wheel. She was tall and slender. Her bright golden hair was cut short and curled all over her head. "Anybody here?" she called out.

Marie came to the door. I remembered how she had said she hated Mrs. Drew. But she came down the steps smiling as if she were glad to see her. Miss Hawthorne appeared in the doorway and waited for her niece to come in. While Marie took the bags out of the car, Mrs. Drew went up and kissed Miss Hawthorne on the cheek. I wondered how she dared to.

Adrianne watched with curious eyes. She held on to my skirt, timid of all the sudden noise. Even from our distance, I recognized something wild and uncontrolled in the Drew children. I knew at once they would never play well with Adrianne.

The car unpacked, Mrs. Drew drove it to the garage and came back and sank down in one of the white chairs on the terrace. Miss Hawthorne sat across from her; the children had their hands full of acorns they had quickly gathered. The boy raised an arm and threw an acorn at his sister. She screamed and started after him. He ran and ducked behind a tree. The little girl stomped her foot. "You damned Derrick!" she screamed.

Her mother spoke sharply to her, and she went back to her chair. She sat there pouting. "Spoiled brats," Marie had told me the day before, in one of her rare moments of friendliness. "You'll have your hands full. That boy kicked me in the shins last summer, and I spanked his little behind.

I hope you do the same if it happens to you. His mother—"
She broke off as if she had said more than she should have
and had been warned not to talk about the Drews. She had
gone quickly out of the room and did not come back.

After her nap, I dressed Adrianne in one of her prettiest
dresses, a pale pink smocked at the top. She looked like
a little pink flower with her ruffled petticoat spreading the
skirt. We came around the house and found them all sitting
under the trees again, the children playing a game on the
table. Miss Hawthorne called: "Bring Adrianne over here,
Keturah."

As we came up on the terrace Mrs. Drew said without
enthusiasm: "So here is Adrianne. She's still awfully small,
isn't she? Come here, dear." She reached out a golden hand.
"And let me see you."

Adrianne clung to my hand. I bent down, edging her forward. "Go on, Adrianne. Go see the lady." But I knew
Adrianne wouldn't. I could see her resisting this golden
woman who was even more striking close up, with her long,
green eyes and her long, full lips painted bright pink. Her
skin was fairly dazzling, as if the sun hovered just beneath
it.

"She's a queer one," Mrs. Drew said finally, and leaned
forward and pecked Adrianne on the cheek as she had her
aunt that morning. "There. Now you see I won't bite you."

Derrick and Wendy had merely glanced up and gone
back to their game. Miss Hawthorne introduced me
to Mrs. Drew, who gave me a short scrutiny but said, not
unkindly, "If you've had a snap up to now it's over with
my two Indians here. You're going to have to keep that fragile Adrianne out of their way if they're not to break her like
a china doll."

I picked Adrianne up and carried her off, feeling they had

166

had enough of her, not liking her being talked about as if she wasn't there. Under the oak tree in the backyard, we gathered a little pile of acorns together.

"What are you doing?"

I glanced over my shoulder. It was Derrick Drew poking his head down to see.

"We're gathering acorns for the squirrel," I said.

"Those are old, dead acorns," he said wisely, "from last year."

"We're just pretending," I told him.

He was immediately agreeable. "Can I help?"

I made room for him. His eyes were green like his mother's. His skin had the same golden vitality under the tan. He helped us gather nuts, then he sat down on the bench with us and asked questions. "What's your name?" he asked.

I told him. He said it once, grinned.

"That's a funny name. I never heard anyone called that name."

"I never heard anyone called Derrick," I told him. "I thought a derrick was something you used on an oil well."

He thought this was very funny. He threw back his head and laughed loudly. "She thought I was an oil well," he laughed, and I felt perhaps we were going to get on better than I had been led to expect. He didn't look as if he were going to kick me in the shins.

Everything changed with the arrival of the Drews. Mrs. Drew had breakfast in bed, and Marie grumbled at having to carry trays all hours of the morning. The children badgered Mrs. Woeste with their likes and dislikes of food. Once out of doors they were all over the place with no respect for the flower beds. Mr. Hodges went around mumbling under the brim of his old felt hat, shaking his head. Miss Hawthorne kept to her rooms until late afternoon. Occasionally Derrick and Wendy played with us under the trees, but all at once they would be scrapping with each other, or running off to something else that caught their changeable attention. I seldom could settle their arguments; more often than not they began slapping each other, and one or the other ran off crying to their mother.

The second week Mr. Drew came. He was a large man, his face red from the sun and from other reasons I learned about later. He had small, pale eyes above his puffy cheeks, and his pale blond hair grew thick only on the sides of his head. He was getting bald on top. He sat out in the yard most of the time he was up, a glass in one hand. The only time he seemed to notice his children was when they raced around his chair or crawled under his hammock, giving him a bump. Then he yelled at them, chasing them away.

I began to see that in some ways Wendy and Derrick were as unfortunate as the children in the Orphanage. They had parents and all the food and clothes they needed, but they had no more love and affection than the orphans had. I would feel sorry for them and take them down to the barn to play, or for a hike across the meadows to the brook that ran below the cottage, where we waded barefoot and found snails and bright pebbles.

Other guests came on the weekends, friends of the Drews, and the house was noisy and full of people.

One afternoon when I was on the terrace with the children, Mrs. Drew and Miss Hawthorne came out of the house. The children had color books and crayons spread out on the table, so we did not move away. Mrs. Drew sank into a long chair, lit a cigarette. Her bright hair was caught in a mesh of sunlight drifting through the leaves. "I hope Clay isn't going to be too disturbed," she said. "Of course I'll be glad to see him. But you know how he likes absolute peace and quiet."

"He'll bury himself in the cottage, don't worry," Miss Hawthorne said.

"Isn't it about time Clay snapped out of it?" Mrs. Drew spoke through a thin curl of smoke. "After all, he can't go on like this the rest of his life."

Miss Hawthorne gently lifted her beautiful white hands that always reminded me of fragile birds, and let them fall back into her lap. "Clay isn't free to do as he likes, my dear."

"That doesn't mean he has to live like a hermit." Mrs. Drew's voice had a touch of annoyance in it. "There are a lot of women, I daresay, who would be happy for the chance to amuse him."

"He doesn't need to be amused," Miss Hawthorne said. "He's not like you, Eloise."

She shrugged her golden shoulders cut by the straps of a flowered dress. "Maybe it would be better if he were a little."

"You're both extremes," Miss Hawthorne said. "Clay in his way, you in yours. You are your father and Clay is his mother."

"Oh, Aunt Alice. Clay is you!"

Mr. Clay, as the help referred to him, was coming and no one seemed too pleased. I wondered what sort of man he was that no one was anxious to have him arrive. The people at Hawthorne were a puzzle to me. Educated, traveled, even related, yet scarcely connected by any personal ties. They might all have been strangers to each other.

Adrianne's rabbit caused the first disturbance. I had left Adrianne playing in her room while I went down to the kitchen to empty a dustpan of broken glass from a bottle I had dropped on the bathroom floor. In the kitchen I found Mrs. Woeste banging the pans together in the sink.

"Those children ain't been down to eat yet," she commented dourly. Her glance rested on the wall clock. "Ten o'clock. And they expect me to keep the cereal warmed up." She shook her head. "Don't know why I put up with it every summer. It's all right the rest of the year but summers my kitchen's messed up all day long."

I emptied the broken glass in the trash can. Mrs. Woeste continued her tirade. "Worst is right before dinner when they got to get the ice all chopped up for their drinks. Not that Mr. Drew ain't using ice all day long, but dinnertime they got to empty the box until I hardly have enough for the glasses on the table. And sandwiches no bigger than your finger, but enough of them to take the edge off their appetite, so Miss Eloise can hardly touch her dinner for worrying about her figure."

"It won't last forever," I tried to console her.

Mrs. Woeste sighed, her heavy bosom rising under her

dark calico dress. "That's true enough. They've gone to scrapping so it won't be too long before one of them picks up and leaves and the other will soon follow. I been here a long time, and Miss Eloise never failed to raise a rumpus every time she comes. Before she had a husband it was with Mr. Clay. Mr. Clay always had my sympathies. He was the older but Miss Eloise knew how to twist him till it hurt." She tucked a stray wisp of straight black hair behind her ear before she went back to her pans. "Life ain't been fair to him."

When I returned upstairs the door to Adrianne's room was standing open, and Derrick, still wearing his pajamas, had Adrianne's rabbit and was punching it in the face. She sat silently on the floor, one finger stuck in her mouth, her eyes filled with unshed tears.

"Derrick!" I scolded him. "What are you doing in here? Give that rabbit back to Adrianne."

He thrust it behind his back and eyed me defiantly.

"Give it to her, Derrick," I demanded.

"I don't have to."

I reached for him but he jumped up on the low toy shelf and began running along it. "You can't catch me. You can't catch me," he singsonged.

I finally caught hold of the seat of his pajamas. He swung around, kicking at me, still clutching the rabbit. With one swift movement I lifted him down from the shelf. He was so surprised, his grasp on the rabbit relaxed and I took it away from him. He ran for the door. I slammed it shut behind him. Marie popped in through the bathroom. Her face was flushed, her blue eyes stormy. She was all out of breath.

"Well," she exclaimed, straightening her apron, her back up. "You'd think married people would sleep in the same room with each other. How was I to know he'd moved in that room by himself?"

She started picking things up as if she wanted to use up a bit of time.

I gave Adrianne her rabbit that was a little more battered than it had been before Derrick got hold of it, took her up in my arms. I could feel her trembling. I thought suddenly of Delia, the little calf I had seen born of Daisy, the way it had trembled on its spindly legs and shivered that first morning of its life. As I held Adrianne close she became calm. I talked softly to her while I dressed her. Marie was primping in front of the bathroom mirror. She flitted out as abruptly as she had come in.

Derrick and I stayed in opposite camps for a while after that. He would not mind me at all, and if I tried to correct him he stuck his tongue out. I knew that sooner or later we would come to grips again.

⇛ 5 ⇝

I could not sleep. When I had turned out the light the hands on Mr. Denny's silver watch stood at 12:30. I had been reading another book from the library. I now had three library books, never having had the opportunity to replace the first two on the shelves where they belonged. Fortunately no one had missed them. The heat pressed down in the dark. I wondered if it would be cooler out of doors. I slipped into my robe, tiptoed in to see that Adrianne was sleeping soundly, and went down the back stairs in the dark, out through the kitchen and around to the terrace. No lights burned on the first floor. But lights shone from the second-floor windows where the Drews had their rooms. The shades had not been pulled down and the light reflected in patches on the lawn.

I lay in the long chair with my feet up, the night air stirring gently up from the meadows. Through the open windows I heard a door close upstairs. Immediately there were angry voices. I recognized Mrs. Drew's. "Get out of here, Ralph," she said icily. "I mean it." There was quiet for a moment and then a loud slap. Mr. Drew swore and I was sure Mrs. Drew had hit him. "Not with that little blond maid around will you come in here," Mrs. Drew snapped.

Marie. Did she mean Marie? That morning Marie had popped into our rooms. I had not thought too much about it then. But now . . . Perhaps I should have moved away but I was held there on the terrace by a sordid fascination.

The Drews appeared in the window above me, struggling with each other, Mrs. Drew in a black nightgown, Mr. Drew naked from the windowsill up. "Get out," Mrs. Drew cried, in a frenzy now. "Get out!" And with that she gave Mr. Drew such a shove he went down on the floor. A few moments later the light was turned out and all was quiet. The light continued to burn in the windows of the next room.

I sat huddled in my chair, shaken by the scene I had witnessed. What kind of people were they to be married to each other and hate each other so? How could Mrs. Drew look so beautiful and be so gay when guests were there, and her nights were spent like this? Sometimes when she lay out on the terrace in the very chair I was sitting in, her long, bare legs and sandaled feet stretched out in front of her, her golden head thrown back on a pillow, her pink-nailed hands dangling over the arms, her skin aglow with captured sunlight, she might have been the lady in the picture I had looked at on Sunday afternoons at the Orphanage. Mr. Denny had said a lady was gentle, kind, loving, a good wife and mother. None of these could be applied to Mrs. Drew. And yet she looked like a lady. Could you look like a lady and not be one? I wondered. Or was it like Mr. Denny said—looks weren't the qualification?

I sat there in the dark with the light from the upstairs windows making two pale squares beyond me, and thought about the Dennys. It was the first time I had been homesick since I had come to Hawthorne. Now such a wave of it spread over me that I longed to run all the way back to the Dennys and find comfort.

Out of the darkness a pair of headlights flashed up the road. I gripped the arms of the chair. Whoever could be coming at that time of the night? Perhaps, I reasoned quickly, it was some friends of the Drews who were late in arriving. The headlights whisked over me, and the car drew to a stop beside the terrace. "Hello there," a man's voice called out. "Has everyone gone to bed?"

I walked over to the car, certain now it must be a late guest. From the lights on the dashboard the man at the wheel was plainly visible. "I'm afraid so," I told him. I tried to explain my presence there in the dark. "I was just getting a bit of air. It's so hot in my room."

"Who are you?" he demanded. The voice was stern, unfriendly.

"I'm Keturah. One of the help."

"Clay!" Mrs. Drew called down from the window. "We'd given you up for tonight."

He leaned toward the window beside me, and I stepped aside. "Eloise! You're here?" He didn't sound pleased.

"Is that any way to greet me after a whole year?" She hung out of the window in her black nightgown.

He ignored her remark. "I'll see you tomorrow. I'm going on over to the cottage." He shifted gears and drove off.

So that was Mr. Clay. I had an odd, lasting first impression of him there in the dark. Of a restless, detached person, of someone as cool and unfriendly as Miss Hawthorne.

◄§ 6 §►

Miss Hawthorne called me down to her study the next afternoon. She was at her desk writing letters and did not look up when I came in, nor when she spoke. I wondered if she was going to scold me for being out on the terrace the night before.

"Have the children been playing with the books in the library, Keturah?" she asked abruptly.

I replied that I had no knowledge of it.

She blotted her letter, carefully folded it, and put it in an envelope. "Several of the books are missing," she said after she had sealed the envelope. "One of the books I wanted particularly just now."

"They are in my room," I confessed.

She fastened her gaze on me. "Why would you be taking books from the library?"

"To read."

"But you have your own books."

"I've read all the novels several times."

"You have *Country Life*?"

"Yes."

She waited a moment. "Why did you choose it?"

"I thought I could understand it."

"Did you?" Her cool gray eyes had not left my face.

"Next to *Tale of Two Cities* it's the best book I ever read. Things are just the way they are in the book."

She glanced away for a moment, out the window.

"It was a good book," she admitted. "It's too bad it was the only book." Her eyes came slashing back at me again. "You should have asked for the book, Keturah. *Country Life* is a very special book and I would hate for anything to happen to it."

She fingered a button on her white blouse. "I hope you weren't afraid to ask . . ." Her voice trailed off as if the words went on in her mind, creating a picture that in some way saddened her. Then she lifted her head and said: "My nephew Clay Barton has arrived. He'll be here for some time. He stays at the cottage and he doesn't like to be disturbed. Mr. Clay isn't especially fond of children," she added, and I felt she would rather have left the last sentence unsaid. I knew what she meant. We were to stay away from there.

She stood up. "Would you mind bringing the books back now, please?"

I got the books and brought them back down to her. I was thankful they were in as good condition as they had been when I took them from the library. I laid them on the desk. "Thank you," she murmured. I turned to go. "Keturah," she stopped me. "Since you enjoy reading, I want you to use the library. After the Drews are gone, perhaps I can help you select some books."

"You mean I can read as many as I want?"

For a moment Miss Hawthorne almost slipped out of her narrow cage. We had come upon some mutual point of understanding, a common bond sprang up between us, a love of books drew us together. But she pulled herself quickly back into her rigid pose, as if she must contain herself within it and not give way to impulse. "The right books, if you wish to improve yourself."

It was several days before I saw Mr. Clay again. I came around the house with Adrianne, looking for the Drew children who had disappeared. I stopped when I saw Mr. Clay on the terrace with Miss Hawthorne and the Drews, remembering Miss Hawthorne's cautioning. But she had seen us. "I was looking for Derrick and Wendy," I said quickly.

Mr. Clay turned his head and looked at us. My first impression of him did not change. Even with other people around he seemed set apart, alone within himself. He was dark where Mrs. Drew was light; his skin was sallow without the golden lights, his hair dark and straight; he looked as if he seldom smiled. His long legs stretched out in front of him, he leaned back in his chair as if he were tired.

"They're not here," Miss Hawthorne said shortly, and her look told me to disappear too.

We went back under the oak tree and sat on the edge of the sandbox. Adrianne piled her rain-washed blocks on top of each other. She watched them topple over and began building them up again. I decided not to worry about the Drew children since their parents didn't seem to mind where they'd gone to. Looking up, I saw Mr. Clay standing on the walk. His hands hung loosely at his sides; his mouth was tightly drawn; there was a dull expression on his face. He stood there watching Adrianne. She placed the last block on a teetering stack, sat back to watch it tumble down. "Whee . . ." she exclaimed, clapping her tiny hands together. She raised her eyes and saw him. Slowly she slipped her finger into her mouth. Mr. Clay stood rooted to the spot, as if he couldn't move. Then, with such an anguished look in his dark eyes I could scarcely bear to watch him, he turned and rapidly walked away.

I caught Adrianne up in my lap as if she had been stepped on. Why did they all treat her the way they did? Had she no right to be here? Wasn't this her home? I knew I dared not ask the answers to these questions. Yet I could not but wonder at Mr. Clay's strangeness there on the walk, as if he had come seeking but was stopped as by a door slammed shut in his face. An air of mystery and sadness penetrated the fine day.

A few mornings later I came back from taking the breakfast tray down to the kitchen, delayed by Mrs. Woeste's complaints, and reached the top of the stairs just as Derrick flew out of Adrianne's room, her rabbit under his arm. I ran down the hall after him. As he sped around the corner he stepped on a small rug that slid and threw him. I caught him before he could get up. He kicked me sharply on the shin.

"Give me that rabbit," I demanded, pinning him down. "You've no right taking Adrianne's rabbit away from her."

He squirmed and kicked. "I won't."

I turned him over and smacked him soundly on his bottom. He let out a yell. The door beside us opened, and Mrs. Drew stepped out in a flimsy white nightgown.

"Whatever are you doing to Derrick?" she exclaimed sharply.

"She's killing me!" Derrick screamed.

"Let him go," she ordered. "You've no right to touch my children."

I released my hold on Derrick, and he scrambled to his feet. "Give me that rabbit," I said ignoring his mother.

He clutched it tightly.

I looked at Mrs. Drew. "It's Adrianne's. I think he should give it back."

"You needn't tell me what you think," she snapped. She took the rabbit away from Derrick and tossed it to me. "There. Now be on your way." She led Derrick into her room. I could see right through her nightgown. "For heaven's sake," I heard her scolding him. "Haven't you enough things of your own without taking that poor little thing's?"

In the afternoon, Wendy played with Adrianne in the sand. After a while Derrick edged around the house, keeping his distance. Arms widespread to balance himself, he carefully walked along a strip of bricks bordering the grass, hoping, I suppose, I would take notice. He slipped off and got back on again. He walked the bricks until he was beside the sandbox. Before long he was playing quietly, dipping sand up in the bucket, pouring it onto a growing mountain. He found a shell in the sand and carried it over to me.

"Want to see a shell?" he asked, head down, not going to meet my eyes. He held out his hand, the shell on his palm. I picked it up and admired it.

"You can have it if you want," he offered.

I took it for what it was, a token of truce. "Thank you," I said, and slipped it into my pocket. After that Derrick and I remained on good terms. I had no more trouble with him, and he never tried to get the rabbit away from Adrianne again.

The next week the Drews left and quiet settled on

179

the place again. Marie moped through the house, the complaints coming from her now instead of from Mrs. Woeste, who was relieved at being able to serve meals on time. Mr. Clay began to come up to the house for dinner (Mrs. Woeste saw that there was food at the cottage for his breakfast and lunch). She and Marie went down several times a week to clean and change the linens.

Sometimes from a distance I saw Mr. Clay out walking, or riding off on his horse, or sitting with Miss Hawthorne on the terrace. But we kept out of his way when he was about, and he didn't come seeking Adrianne again.

<§ 7 §>

I had never strayed far beyond the barn. But one morning was so clear and blue and the air so bouncy, I walked on and on with Adrianne, following a path that led down through the pasture and on through a little thicket, leading out into a grassy patch where cows grazed, then, dipping suddenly, wound into a little glen thick with blackberry bushes. Beyond the bushes a barbed-wire fence marked the boundary of Hawthorne. On the other side of the fence, on a ledge of the hill, was a small pond choked with water lilies. An old rowboat was caught in the lily pads. Above it, on top of the hill, was a white house with blue shutters, not as large as Hawthorne but quite as lovely. A row of white columns rose from the ground to the high porch roof. Under its shade, a woman dressed in white sat in a rocking chair, reading.

A little girl was sitting under one of the trees near the house playing with a doll. She would hold the doll up in front of her, put it back in her lap, and hold it up in front of her again. There was something oddly studied about the way she lifted the doll, put it down and lifted it again. She looked to be about twelve years old, almost too old to be playing with dolls. I wondered if we moved over to the fence she might come down the hill. Something cautioned me not to move closer, to remain behind the screen of bushes, as if the presence of the woman on the porch who, I decided, must be the girl's nurse, would forbid our intrusion. But every few days afterward we walked as far as the blackberry bushes and, from their protection, watched the girl. Sometimes she was under the tree with her doll, or she was up on the porch sitting perfectly still in a chair beside her nurse. I wondered if she were ill that she was not more active.

Shortly after the Drews left, Miss Hawthorne called me into the library. She greeted me formally, standing beside a table on which a pile of books had been stacked. "I've selected some things for you to read," she said. "Once a week you will come to my study and we'll discuss what you have read that week. If there are words you don't understand, write them down and bring the list along." She picked up the stack of books and handed them to me.

I counted them. There were seven. "These ought to stretch my brains," I said.

She gave me a piercing look from her gray eyes. "Reading is as good a way to get an education as any. I had little formal education. You may not like all the books I chose for you but read them. They'll take you to new places and new people."

Mrs. Woeste made a sudden show of friendliness. She asked if Adrianne and I wouldn't prefer eating our lunch in the kitchen rather than upstairs.

"I don't mind some people in my kitchen," she said. "Some I do. If you want to eat your lunch here at the table you're welcome."

As Marie had said, it was boring at times to have three meals a day with only a small child who had to be coaxed to eat each bite. I was glad to sit in the kitchen with Mrs. Woeste bustling about the stove, fretting over her corns, the weather, or the way the meal was turning out. At least someone was talking. Sometimes Mr. Hodges ate with us. Occasionally he spoke but usually he was anxious to get back to work; he ate as fast as his toothless gums would allow him. He only grunted when Mrs. Woeste asked him if he wanted seconds. She always took his grunts for yes, putting another helping on his plate. Marie waited to eat with Mrs. Woeste.

One day after lunch, Mrs. Woeste asked me to take a piece of apple pie down to Mr. Clay. She had just finished baking it, the apples steamed as she cut into the flaky crust. She had not been able to get it baked in time to take it down herself.

"I'll look after Adrianne till you get back," she offered. "Mr. Clay likes his pie hot." She put the pie on a plate, covered it with a clean, white towel, and urged me to hurry before the pie turned cold.

Mr. Clay was sitting on the porch steps smoking a pipe.

"Mrs. Woeste sent a piece of apple pie," I said, not quite knowing how to meet his long, sad face and lack of greeting. "She wanted you to have it hot."

He made no move to take the plate from me. "You take care of Adrianne," he said.

I nodded. And I saw him again as he had stood there that day behind the house watching Adrianne, and walking quickly away. There was some of the same intenseness about him now.

"I trust it's not too difficult."

"She couldn't be more easy to take care of," I assured him. "Right from the first we loved each other."

He looked out over the valley. I had learned from Miss Hawthorne that when she looked away, she was through speaking to me. Mr. Clay seemed to have the same habit. I held the plate out to him so that he had to take it. "You'd better eat your pie."

"Thanks." He took the plate from me. I left him there holding it. I wondered if he would bring himself around to eating the pie before it got cold.

I had read *Tess of the D'Urbervilles* twice by the time the first week was up and Miss Hawthorne sent for me. I intended to read it again. A kinship had been established between Tess and myself; her troubles were as overwhelming as mine once had been. I wept through many of the pages.

I think I astonished Miss Hawthorne. She began asking questions but soon stopped as I poured out the story. "You've lived it," she remarked, when I'd finished.

"It's just the same as if it happened to me," I told her.

"Who is the author?" she asked.

I hesitated. "You mean who wrote the book?"

She nodded.

"I never thought to look," I admitted.

"One of the reasons I chose these books for you," she said, "was because of their authors. They are all well-known and famous writers. When you read one book by an author you like, you usually want to read more of his work. Thomas Hardy wrote the book." She told me about him. She asked if I ever read the Bible.

"Every morning I read a chapter."

"Where are you now?"

"I just skip around. The way Mr. Denny did."

"Do you get much from it that way?"

"When I come to something Mr. Denny read a lot, I do. Mr. Denny read the Twenty-third Psalm about every other morning. So do I."

Miss Hawthorne made no comment. She handed my book back and told me to come again the next Thursday at two, with another book read.

In six months I had read and discussed two dozen books. One or two I did not like but Miss Hawthorne said they were good for me. After twenty-four sessions with Miss Hawthorne I felt no closer to her than before. She lived in a private place I would never be able to invade no matter how educated I became.

Mr. Clay stayed through the fall. When the weather turned cooler he would be off in the mornings on his horse, sometimes not coming back until dinnertime. Or he drove off in the car and would be gone for two or three days at a time. The first of November, he packed his bags and left. I didn't know he was gone until Mrs. Woeste told me at lunch. I had met him only once after I took the pie down. Adrianne and I were coming up the path behind the barn, having been down to watch the little girl at the house on the hill. It had been a rewarding trip. That morning the little girl had strayed halfway down the hill with her doll. The nurse was on the porch, reading as usual. I could not resist moving over to the fence, hoping the girl would see us and come on down the hill. She spied us for the first time. She came very slowly on down the hill as if drawn on a string I held. I hoped she would not turn and run away. She stared at us as if we had come from another world. She held her doll by the hand, its battered feet dragging the ground. Her black hair hung straight to her shoulders. Her round black eyes seemed not quite to establish us. When she reached the fence she put one hand up on the wire, her bare arm extending from the loose white sleeve of her dress. Her arm was pale and flabby, like the arm of a person who had been ill a long time. There were faint creases at the corners of her eyes. I realized with a start that she wasn't a child at all.

"Hello," I said, trying to hide my shock.

There was no change whatsoever in her expression. She made no attempt to speak. She merely stared at us from her black, diffused eyes.

"Laura!" The nurse's voice rang out. I saw her coming rapidly down the hill. "Come back here, Laura. Immediately."

But Laura did not move. She did not even flick an eyelash. The nurse had to come all the way down and take her by the hand and lead her away. She gave us not so much as a glance.

It was a great temptation to ask Mrs. Woeste about the girl at lunchtime. But I did not dare. I had been told not to ask questions. Nor did I want to be forbidden to go back and learn more about the strange little girl who was not a little girl at all.

As I came up the path carrying Adrianne, Mr. Clay was brushing his horse beside the barn. I felt it only polite to speak to him as we passed by. "Good morning," I ventured. He went on brushing his horse as if I hadn't spoken. We were almost past him when he raised his head as if he'd just heard me. He glanced at us from the corner of his eye. "Good morning," he acknowledged shortly, as if whether the morning was good or bad made no difference to him, and went back to grooming his horse.

In a moment he called out: "Perhaps Adrianne would like to see the horse."

I looked back over my shoulder. "She doesn't like horses. They frighten her."

"Bring her here," he ordered.

I could only obey his command. I carried Adrianne over beside the horse, feeling her grow tense in my arms. She clung to my neck, her small body trembling.

"There's nothing to be afraid of," Mr. Clay said, suddenly gentle, and as gently stroking the glistening side of the chestnut horse. "Look. He's not going to bite you."

Adrianne only clung more tightly to me. "She's the same with storms," I warned him.

His eyes, that I saw now were not black as I had supposed, but pure brown, were suddenly shot through with a glint of hardness. "Are you going to coddle her too?"

I met his look. I was not afraid to protect Adrianne. "It's not good to frighten her like this."

I think he realized that I meant to hold out against him. But he did not give in at once. "Are you sure you know what is good for her?"

"I should," I answered calmly. "I'm with her all the time."

His jaw set. The rebuke hit him. A vein throbbed at his temple. Without another word he went back to brushing his horse.

I did not see Mr. Clay again, nor did I want to. Evidently

186

he did not speak to Miss Hawthorne about our encounter, as she never mentioned it to me.

Nor did I see the strange girl Laura again for a long time after that day. The weather closed in. On the heels of the languid Indian summer days I loved so much, with the trees all turned inside out with color, the heavy rains began, followed by cold, and later, snow. The weather didn't open up again for long walks with Adrianne until spring.

∝§ 8 §∝

Adrianne, as Miss Hawthorne had predicted, was like a delicate flower in the winter. She caught cold easily; there were nights when she could scarcely breathe. I would have to go down to the kitchen and heat the teakettle, and make a croup tent over her bed. Often I would be up with her all night long, and in the morning Miss Hawthorne, who must have heard me on the stairs, would come out to the kitchen when I went down to get the breakfast tray, and inquire about Adrianne. She seldom came up to her room. She saw to it that Adrianne didn't lack for anything but she showed no affection at all toward her. I felt that in some way Miss Hawthorne resented Adrianne being in her house but she could do nothing about it. Why, I wondered without ever finding any answer, was Adrianne there? And who did she belong to, this little mite who struggled so to breathe during the cold winter months?

About once a month I wrote to Mrs. Wayburn. She answered in pencil on lined tablet paper. She wrote that the Dennys' place had been sold, but brought less than she had expected. She sent me ten dollars, saying after everything was settled she had it to spare. I told Miss Hawthorne about it one Thursday afternoon.

Miss Hawthorne, in a gray wool suit, was all one color—her eyes, her hair, her clothes. "What do you do with your money?" she asked me.

I had bought writing paper, stamps, a few postcards, and on the few times I had ridden to the village with Mr. Hodges, a ten-cent bag of candy. I had most of my earnings left. I told her that I kept it in my dresser drawer. She suggested that I put it in a savings account in the bank.

On her return from a trip to the city, she gave me a little black book with my savings noted in it. I think that little black book, in which was written how much money I had to my name, set me up more than anything had in a long time. It was another step up the ladder. I was no longer dependent on other people. The book said so. I was Keturah Brown, Savings Account.

I sent several postcards to Mr. Sims, letting him know how I was getting along. I had one back from him, written uphill with a blunt pencil, a faint pink stain on one corner that I was sure came from the meat block. *Dear Keturah,* he wrote. *Enjoyed hearing from you. Glad to know you like your situation. Remember to keep your chin up. Business is good but could be better due to weather. Rsptfly. yrs., J.P. Sims, Esq.*

On an afternoon in late spring Miss Hawthorne called me down to her study while Adrianne was having her nap.

"I'm going for a walk," she announced. "I thought perhaps you would like to come with me."

It was the first time she had asked me to accompany her anywhere and I went along, pleased at the prospect. We left her rooms from a side door, went around a large flower bed bursting with tulips, and over a flagstone path to the row of pointed fir trees I had seen her disappear through the day I was bringing up the mail. She had once warned me that that part of the grounds was private and we were not to invade it. We passed through an opening in the trees, hidden to anyone who didn't know it was there. I caught my breath. Spread out before us was a small, formal garden walled on four sides by dark, green firs. In the center, a fountain rose from a small pool in which goldfish flashed in the sunlight. At either end of the garden a dogwood tree bloomed, as pure and white as angels' robes. A thick border of yellow tulips ran all around the garden.

"This is my sanctuary," Miss Hawthorne said, after we had stood a moment in silent admiration. She sat down on a white iron bench, leaving room for me beside her. There was no need to talk. It was the loveliest spot I had ever seen, the peace of it flowed right down inside of me. "I need this," Miss Hawthorne said after a long silence.

I thought I knew what she meant. That here in her garden the trouble of the house disappeared. That she could contend with anything as long as she could come here to escape from it once in a while.

We sat on for a spell, then she suddenly stood up, and I followed her back to the house. In her study she spoke again. "Since you liked it so much, I trust you'll come with me again."

I felt a sudden sympathy toward her as she stood there in

the center of the room, thin as paper, growing old, yet fortified by some inner strength that carried her through her life. For a brief moment I felt almost close to her. But her gray eyes had moved away. The signal was given. I left her standing there, thinking I don't know what.

❧ 9 ❧

Mr. Clay came unexpectedly before the dogwood finished blooming.

Adrianne and I were sitting on the porch steps of the cottage. He walked around the house and found us before I knew he had arrived. He stopped short at sight of us, hanging on to his suitcase. He looked just as he had in the fall, dark and moody and tense. I remembered with a pang how I had defied him the last time I saw him.

"I didn't expect to find anyone here," he acknowledged our presence. The tone of his voice implied he remembered, too.

"We come down here for the view," I stammered. "It reminds me of my other home."

He opened his mouth to say something, closed it. He seemed to be waiting for us to get out of his way. I stood up, pulling Adrianne up with me. "I didn't know you were coming—"

"Never mind," he said, as I lifted Adrianne from the steps. "You might as well enjoy it when I'm not here."

He looked sharply at Adrianne. "She doesn't grow. Does she eat enough?"

"She's been sick all winter," I told him.

"Do you think she will grow up?"

I was shocked at the cold question, yet underneath I sensed it somehow mattered. "Of course," I assured him. "I give her the best of care."

For a brief moment his eyes were not cold, but sad. "I'm sure you do." And he went up the steps and unlocked the door.

I knew Mr. Clay had not been expected. There had been no cleaning, nor any word about it in the kitchen. When we appeared for lunch, Mrs. Woeste was in a flurry.

"Just like the man to come without notice." She lifted her shoulders that were broad enough to hold her troubles. "He'll just have to take what he finds. Since Marie's off, I'll need you to help me clean up this afternoon."

Mr. Clay was out when we arrived. We saw him walking along the creek. "Now we can raise a little dust," Mrs. Woeste said, relieved.

Everything was in order except for a light coating of dust. I wiped it away while Mrs. Woeste put clean linens on the bed. Dusting the desk, I glanced at the titles of the books standing between a pair of gray elephant bookends. One on Iceland caught my fancy, and I picked it up and thumbed through it, looking at the pictures. A photograph fell out and fluttered to the floor. I picked it up and looked at it. Against a dark background was the face of a very pretty young girl with dark hair and eyes, a faint smile at the corners of her lips. She wore a single strand of pearls above her low-necked white dress. Her hair was cut short and fell in soft curls. She must have been about twenty. There was something in the face looking back at me that was oddly familiar. But before I could pursue it further,

Mrs. Woeste came back into the room and I hurriedly stuck the photograph between the pages and put the book back in place.

"Mr. Clay's busy writing," she informed me. "You'll have to carry his dinner down tonight. I'll take care of it afterwards but I'll be late getting dinner as it is this evening."

When we left, the house was ready for Mr. Clay to live in comfortably and undisturbed.

I carried the basket of food down with a bit of anxiety. Mrs. Woeste had told me exactly what to do, but I wasn't sure how Mr. Clay was going to like it being me. Mrs. Woeste had warned me not to disturb his "moods" as she called them.

I needn't have worried. Mr. Clay was writing at his desk and scarcely noticed I'd come in after my timid knock at the door. I set the dropleaf table at the end of the living room and put the food on it.

"I thought you took care of Adrianne," Mr. Clay said, bent over his papers.

"Mrs. Woeste couldn't come tonight," I hurriedly explained. "She didn't expect you and it threw her off schedule."

He put down his pen, leaned back in his chair, sighed. "I didn't know I was coming until the last minute myself," he said, with something of an apology.

"You'd better eat before your food gets cold," I urged.

He sat studying me. I squirmed inwardly under his direct gaze. "You look like a good, strong girl," he said, evidently thinking he was paying me a compliment. "Are you satisfied here?"

"Yes." After a moment, I added, "It's a beautiful place."

His gaze drifted off. "Yes," he murmured. He rose from his desk and went over to the window, his back to me.

"You won't forget to eat?"

"No."

I left him standing there. All the way up to the house I thought of how Mr. Clay was like Miss Hawthorne, lonely, unfriendly, as if some great sadness hung over him. I remembered the picture that had fallen from the book. I wondered if the girl in the picture was someone he had once cared about. There he was in his lonely house, and Miss Hawthorne up in her big, lonely house. If only they would put their loneliness together, I thought, some of it might go away. But they were like trees that would not bend with the wind. The gale cut through them, breaking off all the little twigs that might have leafed out into some sort of happiness.

Mr. Clay stayed for two months. He was busy writing; he seldom came up to the house. He rode in the early morning and sometimes around evening, but our paths never crossed again. He left as unexpectedly as he had come, and no one missed him when he was gone except Mrs. Woeste, whose work was lighter.

Occasionally Miss Hawthorne took me to her garden. Sometimes we sat quietly on the bench. Other times she walked up and down over the flagstone path. Sometimes she talked; sometimes she didn't say anything. The dogwood trees leafed out, the tulips faded, the lilacs bloomed and scented the garden; and then it was time for the roses. There was a hedge of red roses, large and fragrant, opening into a blaze of color. I was amazed to learn that Miss Hawthorne tended them herself, coming out early in the mornings to spray and prune. She gave the roses the tender care she might have given children. With more abandon than I had seen her express, she bent over the roses, sniffing their perfume, caressing a crimson petal, plucking off a brown leaf.

Only once did she mention Mr. Clay after he left. She seldom spoke of anything personal to me, as if she were forbidden by some inner compulsion to reveal the secrets of her family. She told me that he had gone to Europe to gather material for his work.

"He has a brilliant mind. It used to gather in everything he saw or did, and gave back as much. Now it all runs . . . " She rose and walked swiftly up and down beside the roses, as if she would run away with what she was about to reveal. As suddenly she came back and sat beside me and asked if I had been accustomed to going to church before I came to Hawthorne. I told her I had.

"Do you miss it?"

I thought about it a moment. My life had changed so, the old life had really slipped away from me. For the first time in a long while I remembered the Sugar Creek Baptist Church and Mr. Palmer coming over every Sunday morning to sing with me. "I'd forgotten about it," I said honestly.

"Would you like to go with me on Sunday mornings?"

I turned to her in surprise. "I didn't know you went."

She told me about the little Episcopal church she attended in the village. There was an early prayer service. She was back before I came down for the breakfast tray, breakfast being served a half hour later on Sunday morning.

"I wouldn't know what to do about Adrianne if I went," I said.

Miss Hawthorne had already solved that problem. Mrs. Woeste, having extra time on Sunday morning, could look after Adrianne until we came back. Miss Hawthorne had made up her mind to have me attend church with her and nothing would prevent it. As she always did when she wanted me to do something, she asked first if I were agreeable. I was sure that if I had not been, I would still find myself doing what she had decided upon. Miss Hawthorne was used to having her own way.

The church was small and gray, built of old stone, and had room for less than a hundred people. The early morning light fell through the blue and red stained-glass windows upon the simple walnut altar, creeping along the vaulted, dark beamed ceiling. It was as peaceful as Miss Hawthorne's garden. Even the singing was hushed and slow, and I wondered if Mr. Palmer would have enjoyed it at all. The rector, an old man with a few wisps of white hair above his pink ears, had a warm smile and a lingering handshake for me that first morning. I liked him at once. As he read the prayers in his soft voice that somehow reached into all the corners of the church, I felt as if he were saying them especially for me. I knelt when Miss Hawthorne knelt and sat and stood when she did. In a few Sundays I no longer had to watch her, the ritual became familiar. I liked the kneeling part. I could keep my mind on my prayers better when I was on my knees. And I found that I was happy to be going to church again. The lack had been there but I had not been conscious of it on the surface. It put the weeks back into a familiar pattern.

In July Mrs. Drew came again with the children. This time Mr. Drew arrived with them, and Marie was given a month's vacation at the same time. This meant I had to help with the upstairs work in the mornings. However, the Drews got up so late I often could not make the beds and tidy up until after eleven o'clock. Adrianne would follow me around as I did the children's rooms, but I put her to coloring or looking at a book in her own room while I did the parents' rooms, as Mrs. Drew was often about and I knew she did not care for Adrianne. I came and went with no more than a brief "Good morning" from her.

Derrick and Wendy were as wild as ever. Several times I heard Miss Hawthorne speak sharply to them. She took the matter up with Mrs. Drew in my presence. "Isn't it time Derrick and Wendy learned their manners, Eloise?" she asked. Mrs. Drew had just sat down in a white wicker chair on the terrace. Miss Hawthorne had come up from the flower beds around which the children had raced, carelessly stepping on the petunias. Mrs. Drew took a long sip from the tall glass she had carried out with her.

She shrugged. "I'm afraid they take after their father."

"You should have thought of that before you married him," Miss Hawthorne replied, annoyed.

"I know. I know it too late," Mrs. Drew said, as if the blame were all his. She was still beautiful and golden, her hair a shade lighter than the year before, her skin a shade darker, but her eyes had lost some of their luster. "At least they're healthy," she added, almost as an afterthought, as if that excused them some for their wildness. She glanced over at Adrianne sitting beside me looking at the pictures in a book. I had been on the terrace watching the children when Mrs. Drew came out. They had been busy with a game when, suddenly tired of it, they had rushed off around the house. "Adrianne is as puny as ever," she noted. "Clay should have considered that."

I looked up quickly. What did she mean? The question must have shown clearly on my face.

"What's the matter, Keturah?" she asked. "Didn't you know he's her father?"

"Hush," Miss Hawthorne said quickly. She looked to see if Adrianne had heard but she was engrossed in the pictures, her finger pressing a flower on the page.

"Why all this hush-hush?" Mrs. Drew exclaimed, exasperated. "Is the child going to go all through life—"

"I don't want you to speak about it further," Miss Hawthorne ordered. "Things will be here the way I decide."

"Oh, Aunt Alice!" Mrs. Drew obeyed her reluctantly. "You're living in the dark ages."

They went on talking but I was no longer listening. Mr. Clay was Adrianne's father! I could not believe it. There was no resemblance between them. He was a tall, strong man; she was so tiny and small-boned. He did not even like children. He paid no attention to her at all. My head spun. And I remembered the time Mr. Clay had come around the corner of the house and found us under the tree, Adrianne playing with her blocks: how he had stared at her, how he had seemed to want to reach toward her, the misery in his eyes, how he had turned away. How every time he came upon us something seemed to tear at him, torturing him. If it was true, then Mr. Clay must have been married. But where was Adrianne's mother? I decided she must be dead. That was what Mrs. Drew had meant about Adrianne being so puny. But if she was Mr. Clay's child, why did he reject her? Why didn't Miss Hawthorne care about her? Why did they all treat her as if she didn't belong?

When I rose to go, taking Adrianne by the hand, Miss Hawthorne cautioned me. "You are not to speak to anyone of this, Keturah."

I nodded, too confused to answer.

"The door's been closed a long time."

I carried Adrianne upstairs and held her while she ate the cookie I gave her. If I had loved her before, I cared for her even more deeply now. The fact that she had a father who ignored her made her more of a friendless waif than ever. "I love you, Adrianne," I crooned, hugging her to me. "I love you more than anything." She fell asleep in my arms, and I laid her gently down on her bed and watched her as she slept. The dark fringe of her lashes were two little crescents on her white cheeks. The little rosebud mouth was slightly open with her breathing. The tiny fingers were softly curled, like doll fingers that never opened out straight. She seemed scarcely sturdy enough to grow up, yet I would do all in my power to help her.

◄§ 11 §►

Mr. Drew's room was a shambles. There were broken glasses on the floor, a puddle from a spilled drink, one pillow was tossed on the dresser, another had been flung over the foot of the bed. I noticed the suitcases were gone. When I went out to the hall closet for the broom and dustpan, I heard Mrs. Drew speaking in a loud voice over the downstairs telephone. She reached the party she wanted just as I opened the closet door. I overheard her without intentionally eavesdropping.

"Teddy," she said, her voice hard, the way it was after she had been drinking. "This is Eloise. I'm down here at Hawthorne. Can you hear me?" She waited a moment. "This time I've had it. I want you to start proceedings immediately.

"No, this is final," she said after listening to the other end. "I want a divorce and the children. He's not to have them at any time. He's not a fit father for them."

Again there was a pause, time enough for me to move on, but I waited now to hear the rest. Then: "He left this morning, bag and baggage. I told him to take his clothes and get out. No, I don't intend to see him again, ever, I hope."

All day she was irritable and drank a great deal of whiskey, and about five o'clock she disappeared. Miss Hawthorne asked me to look after the children and see that they had their dinner. Out in the kitchen Mrs. Woeste banged the pots and pans. Derrick and Wendy had been in and out of her way all day.

"Sleeping it off, I suppose she is." She tossed her head as if she would toss the Drews out of her kitchen for good. "A divorce ain't going to solve anything." (I wondered if she had listened to the telephone conversation too.) "Miss Eloise needs to grow up and shoulder her responsibilities. I wonder when they're leaving."

Mrs. Woeste did not have to wait long to find out. The next day Mrs. Drew packed and drove off at noon with Derrick and Wendy. She had a fierce headache and she looked all of her age, frowning and squinting at the sun as she started off in her high-powered car with the top down. As they sped away the sun glinted on her golden head and the two blond heads of her children.

There was peace only in Miss Hawthorne's sanctuary. After the Drews were gone she took me along with her two afternoons in a row. She sat and read while I looked. White butterflies hovered over the flowers; a golden bee bumbled in and out of the cup of a red rose. As always when we were there, we seemed removed from the rest of the world, as if we had stepped into a little boat and sailed far away from shore, where the dark rumblings of the house could not be heard. Some people do not believe that houses take on the climate of the people who live in them, but I know they do. The Dennys' house had an open friendliness, like Mr. Denny himself. After he died it went away as Mrs. Denny's sorrow cast a shadow in the rooms. There was a feeling inside the house at Hawthorne that I could never put my finger on and say what it was. But the house lacked happiness. The shadows that fell into the big rooms on dark days were the kind you steered clear of, as if there lurked in them something to be afraid of. They must have been made up of Miss Hawthorne's loneliness, Mr. Clay's restlessness, the fighting of Mr. and Mrs. Drew, the lack of affection for Adrianne, and all the other things I didn't know about. And yet there was something beneath it all; buried under the gloom there was a leftover of gayer days, the sound of long-ago laughter, the echo of love, the noises of a family growing up. When the sun streamed in the rooms I often wondered what it had been like when Miss Hawthorne was a girl, or when Mr. Clay and Mrs. Drew were children and came to spend the summers. Faint chimes of a past, spent happiness were picked up by the streaming sunshine. But on rainy days I would shiver in the library that had a faintly musty smell in the dampness, or in the formal dining room with the dark, heavy furniture and old oil paintings, although the air itself was not cold. The house was without a warmth of its own.

Miss Hawthorne stopped reading and sat with her book closed over her finger. She sighed. "When Mrs. Drew . . ." she began, "when Miss Eloise was a little girl she was such a gay, bright child, so full of promise." There was a sadness in her voice, and I felt she was speaking more to herself than to me. "She was very well brought up. Private schools, travel abroad. After her parents were killed in an auto accident she was never quite as stable. Then she met Ralph Drew and married him. It was never the thing she should have done." She sat gazing at the summer flowers that had joined the roses, the blue and purple larkspur, the glossy Shasta daisies, the trembling coral bells, the yellow marigolds. "I came back and reopened Hawthorne after the accident. I had been living abroad a good many years. But I felt Eloise and Clay had always looked upon this place as a second home." She was no longer speaking to me at all; she was using their first names; she had forgotten to say Miss and Mister. "I'm afraid I wasn't of very much help to them. I've never been really close to either of them. Clay I always understood better. He was more like myself."

This was the most Miss Hawthorne had ever disclosed about the family. This was all there was to be for a time. I wanted to ask about Adrianne's mother but I remembered in time that I was not to ask questions. Even at this moment I dared not ask one. Miss Hawthorne had said that door was closed. It was all like some giant puzzle that could never be worked to the end. A piece fitted in now and then, and the puzzle put aside again. But as I learned little by little about the family, I felt myself becoming more drawn into it, as if a web were being spun in which I was to become more and more entangled. Having no family of my own I clung to each thread as it was woven.

❧ 12 ❧

It was in August that the first real tragedy happened. Or was it the first? Some might have said that Mrs. Drew's getting a divorce was a tragedy but I didn't see how it could be when they fought so terribly when they were together. If they hated each other so, it seemed better to me that they didn't live with each other. And I didn't think the children were losing much in the way of a father. Maybe now Mrs. Drew could go back to being the person she had been before she met Mr. Drew. I don't think Miss Hawthorne felt badly about it at all. I'm sure she was relieved to have Mr. Drew gone from her house forever.

In late August you can catch summer slipping away but you can't pen it up. The locust trees turned brown from the blight that came with the hot, rainless days. A sigh of the wind, and a shower of leaves would swirl down from the locust trees, covering the grass below like so many tiny, curled bacon crisps. In the woods the leaves on a dying sugar maple were bright red, as if the tree's blood were running out. The golden glow began to bloom; farewell summer and purple ironweed. A light film of dust covered the weeds along the road, there was a faint haze in the air, and the hum of insects rose in wave upon wave of strident prediction of more dryness and heat. Everything green was dimmed.

Before the hazy, midmorning August sun became too hot, I took Adrianne down the path behind the barn, through the pasture where the weeds on either side were now taller than her head. To her, it must have been like walking through a forest. She could see only the watery blue sky overhead. Under the shade trees the cows already rested. From behind the blackberry bushes I saw that the yard and porch of the white house up on the hill were empty. The water was so low in the pond, one end of the boat was on dry land. I noticed a white flower blooming beside the boat. A water lily, I thought. But at once I was aware that it wasn't a flower; it was the skirt of a white dress. In sudden horror I realized it was Laura's skirt. Laura was floating upside down beside the boat, caught in a tangle of lily pads.

I tried to climb the meshed fence but the wire was too thin to hold my weight. And there was a barbed wire strung across the top. I could only scream, hoping someone would hear. But no one came.

"Help! Help!" I shrieked again, and at last the screen door on the porch flew open, and the nurse came running out.

"Down in the pond," I shouted. "She's down in the pond!"

The nurse came flying down the hill. When she reached the pond, she waded into the water in her white shoes. It was not deep, only up to her knees. As she picked Laura up, the girl's black hair dripped over her face like a black veil. She carried her to the grass and tried frantically to revive her, moving her arms and breathing into her mouth. She must have worked with her ten minutes, while I stood helplessly on the other side of the fence. At last she looked over at us. "I only went into the house for a moment to answer the phone!" she cried. "I wasn't gone five minutes. She never went near the pond before."

She picked the small, lifeless body up in her arms and carried it up the hill. The arms that were not the arms of a child dangled from the loose, white sleeves as if they no longer belonged to the body. Something white was still caught in the lily pads. It must have been the doll Laura always carried.

Adrianne had watched without a word, clinging to the fence with her tiny hands. "Why did she go in the water?" she asked after the nurse disappeared into the house.

"She must have wanted to get in the boat," I said, coming out of my shock. And gathering Adrianne up in my arms, I fairly ran back up to the house. Mrs. Woeste was polishing the bottom of her pans. At sight of my face, she exclaimed: "Are you ill, Keturah? Have you had a sunstroke?"

"The little girl," I cried. "The little girl drowned in the pond. I saw her floating there and I couldn't get over the fence."

Mrs. Woeste's face tightened up. "What girl?"

I told her where I had been and what had happened.

She put her hand, with the steel wool in it, up to her forehead. "God in Heaven, she's dead at last." She untied her apron. "I'll go tell Miss Hawthorne. She'll be wanting to know." She hurried out of the kitchen without giving me any explanation.

I waited until she came back. I could tell from her set look that she wasn't going to tell me anything more.

"Miss Hawthorne wants to see you in her study," she said briefly. "You can leave Adrianne here." She sat down and lifted Adrianne onto her lap. "Poor little mite," she crooned, smoothing Adrianne's hair. "Poor little mite."

For the first time I went into Miss Hawthorne's study without knocking on the door. I was still too shaken by what had happened to think clearly. Miss Hawthorne was standing beside her desk, obviously upset by the news Mrs. Woeste had brought her.

"Keturah," she began at once, "tell me exactly what happened."

As I told her she stood with her hands clasped together, head bent. "Her face was in the water all the time," I finished. "Down in the lily pads."

"Sit down, Keturah," Miss Hawthorne said gently. "I know this has upset you." She waited a moment, still standing beside her desk. Then she asked: "How did you happen to be down there?"

I admitted that we had often walked down there after we had discovered the girl playing in the yard. "She only came down to the fence once. I thought she was a child but when I saw her close up I wasn't sure."

"Why did you never ask about her?"

I looked directly into her cool, gray eyes. "You told me not to ask questions here."

She had no answer to that. After what seemed a long time, she said, "She was Adrianne's mother."

If she had told me she herself was Adrianne's mother, I could not have been more shocked. I sat stunned as if she had struck me a physical blow. Adrianne's mother! They hadn't even known each other. Adrianne had stood behind the fence and watched her drowned mother lifted from the pond. . . . I covered my face with my hands. "Poor little mite," Mrs. Woeste had crooned. How true. How true.

Miss Hawthorne waited until I became calm again.

When I looked up she was at the window, staring out. How frail she looked in the strong light falling over her. How suddenly old. No wonder she looks old, I thought, with all the trouble she has to bear.

"I might as well tell you about it, now it's over." She spoke in a voice as tired as she looked. "Laura was a beautiful young girl. Clay was madly in love with her all his life. She had a great passion for riding. She was an expert rider. She had no business riding when she was carrying a child but she wouldn't give it up." A trace of bitterness crept into her voice. "She was out alone one day and was caught in a storm. The lightning struck a tree nearby and her horse bolted, throwing her. Adrianne was born prematurely. We never thought she'd live, and no one cared if she did or not. All the attention was focused on Laura. When she came out of the coma, her mind was gone." She paused. "Clay wouldn't give up. He spent two years taking her to the best doctors in the country. Finally he brought her back to her old home, with a nurse and servants to look after her, hoping against hope that being in a familiar place would bring her mind back. It's cost him a fortune but he's never said one way or the other about it." She looked suddenly, directly at me, her gray eyes dimmed by tears lying too deep to be shed. "He could never accept Adrianne. She was too much a reminder of Laura."

Nothing, nothing, I thought, will ever shock me again. So this was in the shadows, this had lurked in the gloom. This was the ghost that haunted Hawthorne. I remembered the picture that had dropped out of Mr. Clay's book that day down at the cottage when Mrs. Woeste and I were cleaning. It must have been Laura. I remembered the dark hair and eyes. But those eyes had been young and dancing, not black marbles through which no light pierced.

Miss Hawthorne came back to the present with a quick movement away from the window. "I'll have to call Mr. Clay." As she said "Mister" she removed the closeness we had reached, it abruptly established our former relationship. "I hope he's in New York."

"I wonder if he'll come," I said, scarcely realizing I spoke aloud.

Mr. Clay did come. He never spoke to anyone, and I kept Adrianne out of his sight. The funeral was held at the little Episcopal church where Miss Hawthorne and I went on Sunday mornings. Only Miss Hawthorne and Mr. Clay went from the house. I kept Adrianne upstairs all afternoon, as if I were keeping her away from something that might harm her. She played contentedly in her room, unaware that the thread which had tied her into life had snapped. If I merely shut my eyes I could see her clutching the thin wire fence, her round, solemn eyes watching the lifeless figure being carried up the hill. Those arms that dangled like a rag doll's had never held her. A fence with a barbed wire strung across the top had separated her from her mother. It would remain between them forever.

◄§ 13 §►

In the winter that followed I sometimes wondered whether Adrianne's mother, in Heaven and in her right mind again, wanted the baby she had never had a chance to care for in this life. With the first damp days in the fall, Adrianne began to take cold. It was like the previous winter over again. Many a night I had no sleep at all as she tossed under the croup tent I made for her. It had always been difficult to get her to eat. Now I was lucky to get a custard or a soft-boiled egg or a bit of warm milk past her lips. I was completely confined to the upstairs, going down only for our trays. Occasionally Miss Hawthorne inquired about Adrianne but only once did she come upstairs to see her.

"I don't know anything about children," she confessed helplessly, standing beside the bed where Adrianne was peacefully sleeping for a change. "Much less a sick child. We're fortunate to have you here, Keturah. I'm sure you're as good as any nurse."

I assured her that I tried to be. I didn't want her to get a nurse for Adrianne. The doctor came two or three times a week, and I followed his directions carefully. Once he remarked: "I believe it is only your love for her that is keeping her alive, Keturah." No one ever tried harder to keep someone alive. She was all I had. No matter how much her mother wanted her, I wanted her too. And yet, I constantly was aware of the pull away from me. She would be better for a week or so, then the wheezing would begin again, the little chest become congested, and the little lips turn blue.

Just after Christmas, Miss Hawthorne unexpectedly went away for three months. She had been very considerate while Adrianne was ill, excusing me from reading or going to church. But the last, cold morning of December she sent for me to tell me she was going away. She was wearing a pale blue wool suit I had never seen before. Around her neck was the silver cross she wore on Sunday mornings. She looked nicer than I had ever seen her look. Coming into the room, I thought for the moment that she was beautiful, in a way that a painting is beautiful, not warm and close, but cool and set apart, so that it was only to look at from a distance. If you got too close something happened to it, you saw the brushstrokes.

"You look tired, Keturah," she said kindly. "I suppose I shouldn't be going away and leaving you now, but I want to go back to the South of France once more. I haven't been for years. I lived there once." I could hear the longing for it in her voice, the way she had loved it, how she had missed it. "I have a chance to go with a cousin in the East. If I pass it up, I may never get to go again."

I thought of how lonely the house would be without her, but then I remembered how little I had seen her the past few months. She might not have been there at all most of the time, for all I knew.

"Mrs. Woeste will be here with you," she went on. "Marie will come in twice a week. I'm sure you won't need me."

"I hope Adrianne's better when you come back," I said, not knowing what else to say.

"Keturah." Her eyes, that looked almost blue above her blue suit, turned their gaze to the window. "If something unforeseen should happen while I'm gone . . . if you really need someone, I want you to get in touch with Mr. Clay. I'll give you his address in New York. But don't send for him unless it's absolutely necessary."

I wondered what good that would do since he had not been back since the funeral.

"I'm leaving tomorrow."

I caught my breath.

She gave me a quick look. "You're not going to mind being here alone with Adrianne and Mrs. Woeste?"

"No," I murmured, not knowing truly how I felt about it, knowing it would do no good to say I didn't want all the

209

responsibility, but not wanting, either, to do anything to spoil her trip. For her, I was glad she was going away. She had never been away from the house for more than a few hours since I had been there. It would be wonderful for her to go back to some place she had liked so much. "We'll make out," I assured her.

She smiled slowly. "You're such a substantial person, Keturah. I could never have gone off without someone as trustworthy as you here."

One would have thought I wouldn't have liked Miss Hawthorne for the way she treated Adrianne, never paying any attention to her, never coming up to see her, not even treating her as one of the family. But in some way I understood that it wasn't in Miss Hawthorne to be close to anyone, that it was impossible for her to step into another person's world. Yet there was something in each of us that met at some halfway point, some place of mutual agreeing. And I would never dare intrude on her privacy. I think Miss Hawthorne recognized this and it gave her what confidence she had in me.

No sooner had Miss Hawthorne left than the house seemed as empty as an August rain barrel. The downstairs was dark in the evenings except for the night-light in the kitchen. Mrs. Woeste slept with her door bolted, and I locked our doors into the hall at dark and didn't stir out of them until breakfast time. Miss Hawthorne had bought an electric plate on which the kettle could be heated in the bedroom, so there was no need to go to the kitchen during the night. Occasionally I stopped by the library for a book and with Miss Hawthorne gone, I chose books to suit my fancy, not caring what they did for my mind.

Sometimes in the long afternoons Mrs. Woeste came upstairs and sat with us, as it was lonely for her, too, down in the kitchen. On the days Marie was there they gossiped over hot cups of coffee. Once in a while Marie looked in on us, but in a short time we ran out of things to say to each other. The doctor's visits marked the passing of time.

I thought if I could keep Adrianne alive until spring she would get well. She had before. She was as sensitive to the seasons as a plant. She folded up in the cold and opened up to the warmth of the sun. She lay in my arms as pale and fragile as an uncurled bud, and she smiled only when I told her an amusing story. There was a favorite one that I had made up for her, about a little mouse that wore a red jacket and a little fur hat. When, instead of his nose, he stuck his little fur hat out of the mousehole to fool the cat, the smile would begin in her eyes and creep down to her lips until they finally parted, revealing her small, white, even teeth. Sometimes little Tommy Mouse lost his hat to the cat but when the cat found out he had been fooled, he would drop the fur hat in disgust, and Tommy Mouse would run out and get it when the cat wasn't about. I think I told her this same story every night. She always asked for it when she was trying to go to sleep.

Miss Hawthorne sent lovely postcards with pictures of pink houses, or delicate blue oceans, or of large churches with steeple-crowded roofs. The description of the picture in the upper-left-hand corner of the card was always in French, so I couldn't read it, but she wrote a few words to explain the scene. I could tell from her postcards that Miss Hawthorne was happy to be back in the South of France.

The winter was almost over. Spring was coming. The first days of March were lamb soft. The sun shone brightly. I held Adrianne up to the window so the sun would shine on her. She seemed suddenly brighter than she had been in months. She walked around the room, touching her toys. She sat on the tricycle Miss Hawthorne had ordered for her for Christmas. Her feet barely touching the pedals, she held tightly to the rubber handlebars as I pushed her back and forth until she was tired. But at the end of the week the cold returned. The wind crept under the windows, and I stuffed the sills with paper and pulled the blinds tightly down. The weather did not have to touch Adrianne for her to feel it. The first night of the cold I had to put up the croup tent again. It was the worst attack she had had. I called the doctor in the morning but he could not get out to Hawthorne because of the sleet that had iced the roads. It was two days before he could make the trip. When he saw Adrianne he shook his head. He took me out in the hall after he finished examining her. He was a kindly old man, having doctored the Hawthornes for many years. He never said very much but his hands were always gentle and he had a sixth sense about illness, and I knew if anyone could help Adrianne to be well, he could. He placed his hands gently on my shoulders.

"I'm afraid she isn't going to be with us very much longer," he said. "I think you had better write to her father."

I had learned from him that he had delivered Adrianne after her mother was thrown from the horse, when she couldn't be moved to a hospital before her child was born. He had told me what a tiny mite Adrianne had been, how he had despaired for a time of saving her life, and that it was a miracle that she had ever lived at all. He knew Mr. Clay and how he was, and when he told me to write to him, I felt I must, although I didn't know how I could persuade him to come, or of what use he would be. When I hesitated, he pressed his hands tightly on my shoulders. "After all, he is her father, Keturah."

He must have told Mrs. Woeste about Adrianne down in the kitchen. She came bustling up the steps, holding her skirts to her knees, her calico apron covering the ample front of her. She stood beside the bed shaking her head. With a corner of her apron she dabbed at her eyes and sniffed. "They've all run off and left her. It's a shame, is what it is. Poor little thing. But maybe she'll be better off with her mother in Heaven. You've got to look at it that way, Keturah. I'm sure that poor girl's in her right mind now, and longing to have her baby in her arms."

"I can't let her go, Mrs. Woeste," I protested.

"It's the good Lord Himself says what's what. And we have to abide. And what has the poor child to look forward to on this earth but being sick to death every winter, and a father who never looks at her?" She straightened up. "You go ahead and write to him like the doctor said, Keturah. Mr. Clay's warped with sorrow but somewhere inside of him is a heart. Maybe something you say will touch him to come when he's needed here to make arrangements. He won't come before, I doubt." She dropped her heavy body onto a chair. "I'll stay here while you write the letter."

I sat at the desk in my room, a sheet of paper spread out

213

before me, the pen Miss Hawthorne had given me in my fingers, but I didn't know how to begin. Adrianne coughed in the next room and suddenly I knew I had to write the letter no matter what Mr. Clay thought. I prayed to put it the way it should be said. When I finished writing, I called Mrs. Woeste and read it aloud to her.

DEAR MR. CLAY:

I am writing to tell you that Adrianne has been sick all winter. I hoped I could keep her alive until spring came because then I was sure she would get well. But Dr. Fry came this morning and said she was not going to make it. He told me to write to you. Mr. Clay, if I were you, I would come. I am sure you would feel better about it afterwards. I know to see Adrianne makes you very unhappy but you would just have to be unhappy one more time. It would make things right to have her father here when she died.

Respectfully, KETURAH BROWN

P.S. You will have to come as soon as possible if you are coming.

Mrs. Woeste said it sounded all right to her. I carefully copied it over on a clean sheet of paper as tears had fallen on the first one. Then I folded it, put it in an envelope, sealed it, wrote the address Miss Hawthorne had given me, and gave it to Mrs. Woeste to give to Mr. Hodges to post.

"He can drop what he's doing and take it down right now," she said, and I could see her giving him his orders when she went down to the barn to look for him.

Adrianne stayed about the same for the next few days. But the fourth night later she had a convulsion. I was so frightened I ran out into the hall and pounded on the floor above Mrs. Woeste's room as she had told me to do if I needed her. She came up at once in her long, white nightgown, a white crocheted cap on her head, a blanket over her shoulders, as the halls were cold. When she saw Adrianne's eyes rolled back in her head, she picked her up, rushed into the bathroom, and as quickly as I could run hot water in the tub, put her in it. In a few moments Adrianne relaxed but she was almost lifeless, wrapped in the big towel in Mrs. Woeste's lap. Back in the bedroom she opened her eyes and called "Tura," searching for me with her black eyes. Mrs. Woeste handed me the bundle of her, and I sat down in the rocker and held her close against me. Mrs. Woeste put the blanket around her shoulders again; now that the emergency was over she was conscious of being only in her nightgown. We sat there with the overhead light on, waiting, waiting, the sound of the rocker creaking over the floor, the only sound in the lonely house.

Mrs. Woeste suddenly sat bolt upright.

"There's someone downstairs," she whispered hoarsely. She became almost as pale as Adrianne.

I heard the noise too. And almost at once footsteps coming up the stairs. Mrs. Woeste ran over and locked the door. She leaned against it as if her weight would prevent its being opened. There was a knock on the door. "Keturah?"

Mrs. Woeste crossed her hands on her chest. "It's Mr. Clay!" She gave a great sigh of relief. She unlocked the door, unaware that she had left the blanket on the chair again. She let him in before she realized she had nothing on but her nightgown.

"God in Heaven, Mr. Clay," she cried at sight of him. "You gave us a fright." At the same moment she discovered that the blanket was gone and dashed back to get it. She flung it tightly about her, flustered at her predicament.

Mr. Clay stood just inside the door, still in his overcoat,

his eyes searching at the same time they seemed to be afraid to see what he had come for. Mechanically he pulled off his gloves and took a few steps into the room. I lifted the blanket from Adrianne. She slept deathly pale, the black fringe crescents of her lashes closed on the blue shadows under her eyes.

"She's just had a convulsion," Mrs. Woeste said, collected again.

He raised his eyes from Adrianne to me. I could scarcely bear to meet his stricken look. "I'm so glad you got here," I said, thankful from the bottom of my heart that he had come.

"Can't we get her to the hospital?" he asked.

"It's thirty miles away," Mrs. Woeste reminded him.

"We could drive there in an hour."

"Oh, if we could," I breathed. "Maybe they could save her."

I had not undressed. Mrs. Woeste wrapped more blankets around Adrianne while I got into my wraps. Mr. Clay went to get the car. "I'll have it warm," he called back as he disappeared through the door. At once everything was settled. There were no further questions as to whether it was the right thing to do. Mr. Clay had come out of the night with a solution when we had none. It was the one thing we needed to give us hope.

"Hurry," Mrs. Woeste called as I went out the kitchen door to the car with Adrianne in my arms. "Hurry."

We sped down the long avenue of trees. Once on the highway I felt the speed of the car increasing but I had no fear with Mr. Clay at the wheel. Adrianne whimpered lightly.

"Maybe she's frightened of the dark." I spoke for the first time since getting in the car. "I'll tell her her favorite story so she won't be." I put my face down to the edge of the blankets.

"Little Tommy Mouse lost a button on his red coat. Did you know that, Adrianne?" I began. "He was all ready to go out. He had put on his little fur hat first and his little red coat last, and when he went to button it up he saw one of the bright gold buttons his father had brought him from Chicago was missing. He went over and showed his mother. 'It was sewed on very tightly,' his mother said, being quite put out about it. 'You must have twisted it to have it come off. How careless of you not to have heard it fall.' 'Maybe it fell on a soft rug,' Tommy said, 'and no one but a cat could hear.' 'Well, young man, you just go out and look for it and don't come back until you find it,' she scolded him." I went on to tell how he hunted in the grass and in the attic and in the cellar and all the places he'd been. And of how he saw it hanging on the cat's collar and he had to wait until the cat was asleep to go and cut it off. How he reached home safely and his mother sewed the button back on his little red coat.

We had reached the edge of the city by the time I finished. We had gone through the long darkness, and now there were streetlights at the corners, a light here and there in a store window, but the town was asleep and deserted. Mr. Clay scarcely slowed down for the cross streets. Luckily there were no other cars about. Adrianne lay very still in my arms, and I knew the story had soothed her and she had fallen asleep.

Mr. Clay had no trouble finding his way to the hospital. I wondered if it was the one he had taken his wife to after Adrianne had been born, and they had moved her to the hospital. He drew up at the Admittance door and switched off the engine. Jumping out, he came around to open the door for us. I held Adrianne as close as I could, the March wind howling around the building as if it would snatch her from my arms. It was only a few steps to the warm inside. An intern came out in the hallway as the door closed behind us. He must have seen our headlights through a window. "Emergency?" he asked briskly.

"The child is dying," Mr. Clay told him. "We hoped you could do something for her here."

The intern was very young. His black hair glistened under the bright lights. His strong, white hands reached out for Adrianne. He turned back the blanket and his eyes became alert. He swung around and carried her into a small, white room and laid her on the waiting table. We stood behind him while he unwrapped her, raised her eyelids. He opened her mouth and breathed into it. He remained bent over her for several minutes. When he straightened up he did not turn around. "I'm afraid it's too late," he said, his hands hanging helplessly at his sides.

A cry escaped me. "You mean she's dead?"

He nodded. "She must have died fifteen or twenty minutes ago."

Numbly I walked over to the window and stared out at the bleak, cement driveway. My hands were clenched inside my coat sleeves. I felt chilled to the bone. I don't know how long I stood there. I was conscious at last of a pair of strong hands on my shoulders. I remembered Dr. Fry's hands on my shoulders a few mornings ago, gentle hands that had sought to give me courage. A sob that seemed to come from somewhere else than inside of me broke from my throat. While I wept the hands tightly held me. Someone was with me. It mattered a great deal. I wiped my face on my coat sleeve, having no handkerchief, and, turning around, I looked into the face of Mr. Clay. There was no expression

218

there at all. I felt myself falling against him, and his hands that had been on my shoulders kept me from sinking to the floor.

On the ride back Mr. Clay drove as rapidly as he had on the way in. When we reached the gate, the first streaks of daylight were visible at the edges of the sky. Hawthorne looked white and lonely, like a ship way out in the middle of the sea with nothing around it but water and sky. As we stopped at the side of the house, Mrs. Woeste opened the kitchen door, fully dressed now. The smell of coffee came floating out on the warm air released from the kitchen. She knew, without us telling her, what had happened. "She didn't make it," she said, and there was no need to answer.

We sat at the kitchen table in our heavy coats, and drank her hot coffee. I was too tired to take mine off; I was still cold. I went upstairs to my room and fell across the bed. I was thankful that the door to Adrianne's room had been closed.

◆§ 15 §◆

On Sunday mornings when I went to the small gray stone church, I always took a bouquet of flowers along that I had picked from the garden, the dew still on them, and put them on Adrianne's little grave that stretched, half as long, beside her mother's. In the cemetery behind the church, other Hawthornes were buried. There was a tall monument in the center of the plot with the name HAWTHORNE boldly carved on it, and surrounding it, a host of graves, each with its own little marker. There was a tiny one for Adrianne, with a stone lamb carved on the top of it. I always gave the lamb a little pat and breathed a prayer that Adrianne was happy in Heaven. It gave me some comfort to think that she was with her own mother.

Mr. Clay stayed for a week after the funeral. The two of us, along with Mrs. Woeste and Mr. Hodges, attended the service at the church. The casket was closed when it arrived, and Mr. Clay would not let it be opened. It rested at the front of the church under a spray of lilies. The minister's soft voice spoke comforting words but I could not remember them five minutes after the service. Numbly the four of us stood beside the minister in the cold cemetery. Mrs. Woeste was the only one alive enough to wipe a tear from her eye. Nothing was real; nothing was true. In a few minutes, I kept telling myself, we will go back to the house, and I will go upstairs, and Adrianne will be there in her room.

Mr. Clay shut himself up in the cottage, and I carried his dinner down to him each evening. Mrs. Woeste claimed she had a touch of rheumatism and it was too far for her to walk, but sometimes I thought it was an excuse to get me out of the house. I put the food out on the table for Mr. Clay, but often the next evening I found it standing there untouched and I carried it back up to the house again. Mr. Clay did little more than acknowledge my presence while I was there. He seemed to grow thinner during the week, and the shadows under his eyes deepened. In my grief I felt a kinship with his sorrow. I also knew that nothing I could say would ever reach down into the depths of it.

I ate little myself. The weather was dreary, and the time

hung heavily on my hands. I moved in a gray mist that nothing penetrated. Even my favorite books failed me. I sat by the hour staring out at the bare March trees.

The last evening Mr. Clay was to be there, Mrs. Woeste cooked him a specially tempting dinner of all the things he liked best: rare roast beef, homemade noodles, rich, brown gravy, string beans cooked long with ham, and an apple pie that she proudly held up in her hands before cutting his half.

"If he doesn't eat this," she said, "he'll never care to eat anything. He's got to come out of it sometime." She gave me a sharp glance. "The both of you have."

Mr. Clay was sitting in front of the open fire when I let myself into the cottage. He had a book in his hands but he was not reading. He was gazing absently at the fire. He went on staring as if I hadn't come in. Knowing that he was leaving in the morning and hating to see him go away as unhappy as he was, I made an effort to be cheerful.

"Mrs. Woeste cooked your favorite dinner tonight, Mr. Clay," I told him as I unpacked the basket. "She'll be terribly disappointed if you don't eat all of it."

The day was already gathering to a close. The shadows stretched out in the room but the light from the fireplace flickering through them, gave the place a certain coziness. Mr. Clay closed his book and looked at me for the first time that week.

"Will you stay while I eat?"

It was the last thing I expected him to say. He had never asked me to do anything. But I heard beneath his asking the fact that he could not bear the loneliness any longer. I remembered how he had held me at the hospital until I became calm. Behind his coldness I knew now there was

221

something else, something he had buried within himself all these years. I wondered what we would talk about. It didn't matter: I would stay.

"If you'll come and eat."

As he sat down at the table I went to the fire and held my hands out to it. My eyes fell on the book he had left in the chair. I read the title, *Country Life*. I picked it up, opened it, and read a few lines at the beginning. "This is my favorite book," I said. "I read it when I first came here and I think I know it by heart."

He had served his plate and taken a first mouthful of food.

"You do?" His voice held a note of interest. "Why did you like it?" he asked after a moment.

"Because it's the way the country really is. The way it was at the Dennys'. I felt I was back there while I was reading it."

"It was the first book I wrote," Mr. Clay confessed.

I gazed at him in astonishment. "You mean you wrote it?"

He gave me a look from his place at the table. "Then you weren't saying it just to flatter me?"

I shook my head. "I found it one day in the library. I took it because I thought I would be able to understand it, it being about the country. I never looked to see who wrote it. It was before I knew about authors."

He took another bite of food. "Sit down," he said. "You don't have to stand up like a servant."

I sat down in his chair. Although his words had a sharpness behind them, they did not bother me. I was not thinking about what he said. I was thinking that he had written *Country Life*. That if he had written the book he loved the country as much as I did. It was a part of him too. I wasn't afraid of him anymore. I knew I never would be again.

I browsed through the book while he went on eating. He must have realized how hungry he was. He ate everything I had brought. He was too busy eating to speak to me again. When he finished, he came over and stood by the fire, his back to me.

"You can tell Mrs. Woeste her dinner was excellent. It's the first food I've enjoyed this week."

"She'll be glad to know," I assured him.

After a moment he said: "You must miss Adrianne very much."

I couldn't answer at once. Then as his back was to me and he couldn't see the sudden tears at mention of her name, I managed to murmur, "She was everything I had." And suddenly I was weeping, the first time since that night she died. But this time the tears fell silently, and I had a handkerchief in my pocket. I wiped them away as they fell. When I finally looked up I saw Mr. Clay had turned around and was watching me.

"I'm sorry," I apologized. "I do feel better now."

"I want to thank you for all you did for her."

It did not sound like Mr. Clay's voice. I had never heard him speak so gently before. All the harshness was, for the moment, gone from him.

"I was no father to her. I never felt that she was my child. You must hate me for the way I ignored her."

I sat staring at him. How could I hate him when I knew what he was like inside? How could I hate him when he stood there in front of me, his face drawn, weary, his eyes dark and lost? I realized I had never hated him even after I learned he was Adrianne's father. I couldn't hate him any more than I could hate Miss Hawthorne for being the way she was. "No," I said. Then the words I sought for rose to my lips. "You came when I wrote to you. You came that night when we needed you the most."

He wet his lips as if he were going to speak again, then he turned back to the fire and stared into it.

"I keep remembering that little story you told her on the way to the hospital," he said after a while.

"It was her favorite story. I made it up for her. She wouldn't go to sleep until I told it." A memory surged over me. "All the time I was telling it to her she was dying in my arms."

Neither of us spoke for a time. "I imagined one something like it when I was a boy," he broke the silence. "But I had to tell it to myself before I went to sleep at night."

I smiled slowly, feeling for the first time as if the gray mist had lifted.

"What do you plan to do now?" Mr. Clay asked, abruptly changing the subject.

A long time ago Mrs. Wayburn had asked me that question. When we were packing up the dishes after Mrs. Denny died. I had been as unprepared for it then as I was now. When I didn't have an answer, Mr. Clay continued: "You don't want to just stay here and do housework. You're quite above that, I should think."

I sighed. "That's all I know how to do. And take care of children. I've never done anything else. Mr. Denny said it didn't matter what you did so long as you did it well. Wouldn't it be better for me to do housework than stagger around with something I didn't know about?"

He reached for the poker and began stirring up the logs. "You don't know what you can do until you try." The fire fell apart and he threw another log on it and waited for it to catch. "Who is Mr. Denny?"

To talk about Mr. Denny . . . to tell who Mr. Denny was . . . The words rolled off my lips. Mr. Clay never interrupted me but sat quietly watching the fire. I don't know how much of what I said he heard. I was content to talk about Mr. Denny if no one but myself listened. Suddenly I realized it was dark outside. I jumped to my feet.

"I must get your dishes back up," I said quickly. "Mrs. Woeste will be wondering, I've been gone so long." As I gathered up the dishes and put them in the basket, I apologized for talking so much. "Once I get started on Mr. Denny I can't stop. He meant more to me than anyone else ever has except Adrianne."

Mr. Clay merely glanced at his watch and remained by the fire while I put on my coat and hung the basket over my arm. "I hope you feel better, Mr. Clay," I said, ready to leave.

I thought a faint smile touched his lips, or maybe it was only a shadow cast by the firelight.

"Good night," I bade him as I stepped out the door.

The night was full of bright stars, the air frosty cold. Mr. Clay's shadow fell across the porch. "Can you see your way up?" he wanted to know.

"The stars will light me," I assured him. I went down the steps and started up the path. "Good night," I called again, and as I went around the house I heard his "Good night" ring out on the clear, sharp air.

I did not see him again before he left early the next morning.

It was like a new morning to me. I stepped back into life.

I took up living in the lonely house, spending the long hours with Mrs. Woeste in the kitchen, doing a bit of embroidery I had stuck away in my dresser, or I went into the library and curled up in a chair and read until the hours of the day shrank to a few minutes of time. And underneath it all I waited for Miss Hawthorne to come home. Miss Hawthorne would settle my future. I supposed she would tell me to leave. And yet I felt I belonged somehow to Hawthorne. I couldn't bear to think of life away from there. But Mr. Denny's cheery optimism had become deeply ingrained in me. Something would pop up for me when the time came, I was sure.

❧ 16 ☙

Miss Hawthorne arrived home the first of April. We had spent the week turning the house inside out. The weather had been warm enough to open the windows, and the old, winter dust flew out, the pillows were aired, the blankets washed and sunned: the little scatter rugs were taken out on the terrace and thoroughly shaken. The trees were showing a first bit of green, and the tulips were pushing their heads between the daffodils in the flower beds. I was constantly reminded that Adrianne had failed to make the spring, as I had so hoped for her, but when I placed a bunch of pale pink hyacinths on her grave, I had a sudden, warm feeling that she was skipping up and down in spring somewhere else, that her little feet never tired now, her small chest no longer heaved with her breathing, her black eyes danced with laughter. I went into the church with this feeling and I drifted back to Hawthorne containing it, and I believe some of it has stayed with me ever since. I never grieved as deeply for Adrianne again.

I met Miss Hawthorne in the hall the day she came home. It was as if I were the family, greeting her back. She took my hand and gripped it firmly. There was a faint flush in her cheeks, her eyes had a tinge of blue in their grayness, and she moved with more vitality than I had thought possible of her. But she seemed to have left some of herself in the South of France. She spoke of her trip with warmth, as if she still lingered where she had been, as if all of her had not returned. Gradually this wore off, but she was never quite as content at Hawthorne as she had been before she went away.

She sent for me the afternoon after her return. She was at her usual place, her desk, in a pale gray dress the color of her hair. The flush was still in her cheeks and she no longer looked as fragile as paper. There was a lovely blue vase on her desk.

"I know you've been through a great deal, Keturah," she began briskly, "so I won't bring it all up again. I'm sorry you had to be here alone, but if I had to do it over again, I wouldn't give up my trip."

She touched the vase. "I brought this for you. I thought you might like it for your room."

There were sailboats painted on the side of it, the sails tinged with the colors of the sunset behind them. "For me?" I exclaimed.

"I saw it one day in a shop and it struck my fancy. I could see it belonging to you." Before I could properly thank her, she changed the subject. "Now I want to talk about you."

So here it was. The time had arrived for her to tell me.

But the thought of owning the vase took the blight off it.

"I've been wondering what you will do now," she plunged in. When I didn't answer because I had no answer, she said: "I hope you don't want to leave here."

She had reached into my mind and taken my thoughts and put them into words. I could not speak for a moment. "You mean you want me to stay?" I said finally. On top of the vase it was more good fortune than I could accept. Yet there it was, hanging on the end of a limb I could reach.

"I've grown accustomed to your being here," she went on. "Nor do I think you should stop your education when you have so much promise. You shouldn't go all your life working servant class." She leaned forward on her arms crossed on the desk, and I could see clearly the dark pupils of her eyes swimming in their gray seas. "Keturah, if I were to tutor you more intensively now that you have the time, you could go out and do anything you wanted to do."

I felt compelled by some strong force in her that would reach out and take something from within me and mold and shape it the way it should be. I was dazzled by the image that flashed through my reeling brain.

"You mean I could be an honest-to-God lady?"

I could have bitten my tongue off. But it had slipped out and there was no taking it back. Miss Hawthorne's eyebrows shot up and came down to hover above her eyes again. "I would like to make a lady out of you," she said, studying me as if it were a challenge she was inclined to accept. "Are you willing to study hard?"

"Yes," I breathed.

"Then it's settled. You'll stay on as my companion, for want of a better title. You will still receive a salary. I want you to be independent, not to feel that you are beholden in any way. There will be enough for you to do to earn it." She rose and handed me the vase. I was in the hall when she called me back.

"Mr. Clay wrote me that you were a real soldier." She tapped her fingers on the desk. "I think he's beginning to let go of the past. I sensed the change in his letter."

I left without telling her that I, too, thought he had. I had not yet come to the place where I could discuss Miss Hawthorne's family with her. Too long I had not been allowed to give an opinion. But Mr. Clay's compliment hung in my ears as I climbed the stairs. I could not bear all the kindness that had burst upon me in one afternoon. The compliment, the knowledge that I was to stay at Hawthorne, the blue vase, Miss Hawthorne wanting to make a lady of me. I wept quietly in my room. The tears finally dried up for a long time to come.

∽§ 17 ই∾

The effects of Miss Hawthorne's trip lingered on. She began to go out more. She bought a beautiful new gray high-powered car, and taught me to drive it. The first time I sat behind the wheel I was petrified of all the gadgets. Mr. Denny's old car had taken all my effort to drive. This one slid easily along the road, there was no coughing in the engine, nothing rattled. By the time we returned I had mastered the gadgets and was enjoying the sense of power that driving the new car gave me.

Miss Hawthorne also sent for a book of etiquette, and under her watchful eye I practiced the lessons. I learned all

229

the things that seemed to come naturally to Miss Hawthorne. One day while I was practicing how to rise from a chair without bolting out of it, Miss Hawthorne said abruptly: "I think you ought to reduce, Keturah."

So she bought a book on dieting and chose a diet for me to follow. This was the hardest thing I had to do. Always partial to meat and potatoes and bread, I had to concentrate on vegetables and salads. As I now ate dinner in the evenings with Miss Hawthorne, and she ate very sparingly herself and saw to it that I had little more than she did, I often left the table still hungry but my stomach must have shrunk, because gradually I didn't care to eat so much anymore.

Now that the shadows and mystery of Hawthorne were dissolved, guests were invited occasionally. I listened attentively at the dinner table to the chatter of a world I knew little about, careful to speak only when I was spoken to.

Mrs. Drew did not come that year. She was busy getting married again. Instead she sent Derrick and Wendy to Hawthorne for a month, and while they were there I looked after them. They were still wild. But it was good to have children about again. We played croquet on the lawn, went for picnics in the woods, and waded in the stream down below the cottage. By the time they left they were less wild than when they had come. And they didn't want to leave. They begged to stay on, not anxious to be with their new father. But Miss Hawthorne felt they had been there long enough; she sent them home with the promise they could come back the next summer.

Mr. Clay was abroad again. His letters came more frequently, and occasionally Miss Hawthorne read parts of them to me. Once something slipped out before she realized she was reading it aloud. I guess she didn't expect it to follow the paragraph she had been reading. "I feel free again," he had written. "I am actually interested in what I am doing for the first time in a long, long while." She sat with the open letter in her hand, a wistful expression on her face. She did not continue reading aloud.

In the fall there were new lessons . . . history, geography, English. I kept a notebook in which I wrote compositions. At the beginning of each week Miss Hawthorne gave me assignments and on Friday I brought them to her completed. We spent the whole day together as she heard my lessons. If my education had been limited before, it was most abundant now. Miss Hawthorne was a good teacher. She made the lessons interesting, especially the geography. She had been to many of the places I studied about and her firsthand knowledge painted the scenes vividly.

We often went out to the little formal garden in the late afternoons. Sometimes Miss Hawthorne took a book of poetry from which she would read to me. She had a quiet, measured reading voice. I liked to listen to her although I did not always understand what she was reading. Other times she would walk slowly around the garden admiring the flowers, or speaking her thoughts aloud. Once, walking slowly back and forth over the thick grass, she said: "It is good to be acquainted with solitude, Keturah. It can become a friend. Solitude is not loneliness. It is being with yourself. The self of you that bears the real issues of life—joy, pain, sorrow. Even death."

The coils of gray hair were wound tightly over her ears, her hair pulled smoothly down into them so that in the sunlight she seemed to wear a silver cap. If anyone knew about being alone, Miss Hawthorne did. She not only wore a silver cap, she lived in a silver case that was seldom opened. There was always a reserve about her, even with her guests.

Perhaps I was allowed as close to her as anyone ever had been. Yet when she was through talking to me or teaching me, she dismissed me abruptly and went back to being by herself. I couldn't think of how she might have been when she was young. She seemed to have been born old and solitary. I wondered if any man had ever kissed her. It seemed fairly impossible. But then one bright October day, when the whole countryside was riotous with autumn, the sky blue enough to reach out and stroke it, something happened to make me realize she had been young once, as young as I was.

From behind the curtains in the library I saw the long, black car nose up the drive, stop at the front of the house, and the chauffeur step out. He opened the back door for a slightly stooped, gray-haired man in a gray suit and hat. The man leaned on his cane for a moment but he scarcely used it as he came up the steps. I waited until the bell rang, then hurried out into the hall to answer it. I was most curious to know who it might be.

A pair of keen blue eyes greeted me from a deeply tanned face. A brisk, small, gray mustache graced the full upper lip.

"I've come to see Miss Alice Hawthorne," the man announced, pronouncing his words distinctly, an old-fashioned air about him as if he had stepped out of the past. "Is she at home?"

Miss Hawthorne had gone to spend the day in town. I told him so. Disappointment clouded his blue eyes. He inquired when she would be back, and I told him not until evening.

"Who are you?" he asked.

I told him, feeling a surge of pride in announcing myself as Miss Hawthorne's companion.

"Will you kindly tell her Henry Judson came to call?" He reached in his pocket and brought out a calling card which he handed to me. He lingered on the step as if he were reluctant to leave. He looked up at the house and down at the late marigolds still blooming in the borders, and then around at the Jack Frost colors of the trees. He looked every inch a gentleman. I wondered if I should ask him in. "Everything is just the same," he said. "In forty years I doubt if a blade of grass is different."

"Are you kin to the Hawthornes?" I asked him.

He shook his head. "No. I might have been but I'm not."

While I was trying to figure this out, he asked if the formal garden was still over behind the fir trees. I told him it was.

"I wonder if I might go and have a look at it again."

I saw no reason why he shouldn't. To be on the safe side, I offered to go with him.

"That will be most kind of you," he consented.

While the chauffeur waited at the car, we walked over to the garden. Mr. Judson tapped each stepping-stone with his slim cane, murmuring to himself as if recalling memories. When we entered through the screen of fir trees, he stopped and looked around him. "Nothing is changed here either," he noted.

He sat down on the white iron bench, his cane between his legs as if he were going to stay a while. After a moment I sat down beside him. He seemed content just to sit and look. The dahlias were putting on a fine show. Some of them would have covered dinner plates. Finally Mr. Judson sighed and twirled his cane, the rubber tip flattening down a spot in the grass. His neatly manicured hands, wrapped around the crook of his cane, were as tanned as his face.

"It was here," he told me, "I asked Alice Hawthorne to marry me."

"Miss Hawthorne!" I exclaimed.

"Yes. Why does that startle you so?"

"I don't know . . ." I stammered. "I thought nobody ever asked her."

He put his head back and laughed, the laughter catching in the creases beside his eyes. "My dear girl. I must have asked her a dozen times myself."

I forgot about not asking questions. "You mean other people did too?"

"I suppose so. Alice was a very attractive girl." He sat smiling to himself. "What is she like now? Tell me, how does she look?"

I tried to describe her to him. I said only the best things about her. "She looks like a lady," I said, feeling that was the finest compliment I could pay her.

He dug his cane down in the grass. "She was always that. And too damned scared of having anyone discover the real girl."

After a moment I offered: "She's very much alone."

"Serves her right. She didn't need to be."

I looked up quickly and saw that a shadow had crept into his blue eyes, a dash of stubbornness had set itself upon his face, his jaw was set, his lips pressed together. He remained lost in thought, and I did not disturb him. Abruptly he took one hand off the cane, reached over and pushed my chin up with his fist.

"Don't you dare tell Alice Hawthorne I exposed her. She'd never let me come back tomorrow. Promise you'll see that she's here."

On the way back to the house Mr. Judson explained that he was stopping over in the city on his way across the country, just to see Miss Hawthorne again. "Maybe it was foolish of me to come," he said. "But I wanted to see her once more."

I promised him Miss Hawthorne would be there the next afternoon. I liked him. I wondered why Miss Hawthorne hadn't.

But when Miss Hawthorne came back, and I told her Mr. Judson had been to see her, she did not take it at all as I had expected. She froze up like a pond in winter. She went immediately to her room.

After dinner, as we strolled outside, she asked me what he had said while he was there. I told her that we had gone to the garden, that he wanted to see it again, that he had looked at it and left.

"I thought Henry Judson was dead." Her voice was as cool as the breeze blowing through the blue October evening.

A flock of dark birds appeared in the sky. They flew high above us with no seeming sense of direction, whirling aimlessly as snow. Once the whole flock tumbled toward us, then suddenly swirled and soared into a V formation, rising upward and out of sight. They swooped right out of the sky. How did they know, I marveled, when to stop falling earthward and soar upward? How did the word get to each one when to turn, when to glide, when to flap a wing? How was it that not one of them ever bumped into the other? Where they came from and where they went I could not tell. I turned to speak to Miss Hawthorne. But she was looking at the vacant sky, her mind as far away as the birds. She was as pale and remote as she had been in the hall when I had told her of Mr. Judson's visit.

18

After Adrianne's things had been sent away to Marie's sister's children, the room had been made into a study for me. The morning after Mr. Judson's visit I was studying at my desk when I heard Miss Hawthorne's bell in the hall. She was waiting for me at the foot of the steps.

"Keturah," she said quickly, when I reached her. "I want you to do something for me this afternoon."

I sensed at once it was not going to be easy.

"When Mr. Judson comes I want you to tell him I'm not at home. You won't have to lie. I am going out."

"But Miss Hawthorne . . ." I had promised Mr. Judson.

"I wish you to do as I say," she said sternly.

She turned and walked away, through the library and out onto the terrace. I tried desperately to think of something I could do to save the situation. I followed her to the terrace. She was standing in the center of it looking completely desolate, as if she were on a boat that was sinking.

"Miss Hawthorne . . ." I began, my perspiring hands clenched at my sides. "Miss Hawthorne, Mr. Judson stayed over just to see you. He'll be terribly disappointed."

She gave me a cold look. "Keturah! Are you trying to tell me what to do?"

It was the first time since I had become her companion that she had spoken to me as she would to a servant. It sobered me for only a moment. I couldn't let her drown there in front of my eyes.

"I promised Mr. Judson you'd be here."

She looked at me queerly. "You mean he made you promise?"

"Yes."

As she stood there her back straightened, her head lifted, then her chin. You could see the old Miss Hawthorne slipping back into herself again.

"I'll see him," she said firmly. "You may answer the door, since you know him so well. I'll be in the living room."

Fifteen minutes before Mr. Judson was due, I was in the library watching the road. I heard Miss Hawthorne come out of her room down the hall and go into the living room. At five after two, the long, black car came up the road. From behind the curtains I watched the scene repeated from the day before, the chauffeur getting out, opening the door, Mr. Judson leaning on his cane a moment before he started up the steps. He wore the same gray suit. When he rang the bell I hurried to answer it. He asked at once: "Is she here?"

"Miss Hawthorne's waiting in the living room," I announced formally, and stood aside to let him pass.

He gave me a pat on the shoulder. "Good girl," he whispered. "I bet you had to bridle her."

I leaned toward his ear. "Almost."

I went upstairs so Miss Hawthorne would not think I was eavesdropping, stepping hard on the stairs for her to hear. I lay on my bed and looked up into the tree turning from green to brown in the October afternoon. The leaves were as still as the golden weather. The whole tree was caught in stillness, as if snared in a golden net. Way up in the tree one leaf began to stir. It flapped as if a strong breeze blew, but none of the other leaves moved. I thought it would drop off, but it hung on, until finally it was still again and could not be picked out from the other leaves. Once the same thing had happened to a leaf on the maple tree at the Dennys'. I remembered how it had come to me, then, that no matter how hard life hit against me, I was tied strongly by my roots there. Transplanted I had been, but I had been able to survive and grow. I felt somehow it would always be that way whatever happened.

Voices drifted up from the yard. Leaning close to the screen, I saw Miss Hawthorne and Mr. Judson walking toward the garden. She wore a printed silk dress I had never seen. She must have brought it from France; it was brighter than anything she had ever worn, bright flecks of blue and yellow. Around her neck was a string of large yellow beads. I could see them on the back of her neck. As they disappeared behind the fir trees, I wondered if they would finally marry. But how terribly old to marry, I thought.

Mr. Judson came for four straight afternoons. The last day he stayed for dinner, entertaining us with tales of his travels in various places around the world. Miss Hawthorne had the printed silk dress on again and the yellow beads, but she was her usual cool self, although she laughed lightly when Mr. Judson made a joke. As we were finishing our dessert, a cherry pie baked to perfection, Mr. Judson paused before he took his last bite. He looked directly across the table at me.

"I've seen about everything, Keturah," he said. "And I must say I've enjoyed it. I suppose that's as much as anyone can ask from life."

I did not know what sort of reply he expected from me. I smiled across the table at him. Miss Hawthorne did not look up from her pie.

"Money has never been an essential," he continued. "I was poor until I was fifty. Then a remote uncle died and left me enough to go traveling on. It was an unexpected windfall." He shrugged his shoulders. "I was as happy before I had it as after I got it. It merely opened up opportunities I could have gone on living quite contentedly without."

Miss Hawthorne still did not look up. I felt he was saying all this for her benefit, that behind his words was a meaning I knew nothing about. It might have belonged to a conversation they had had sometime together.

Mr. Judson carefully ate his last piece of pie, took a sip of coffee from the fragile china cup, and set it gently back on its saucer. He whisked his napkin across his little gray mustache and laid it beside his plate. He took a cigar out of his pocket and went through the process of getting it lit. The smoke curled from his lips. He slid his eyes around to Miss Hawthorne.

"Why so quiet, Alice? Can't I raise an argument out of you? Or do you agree?"

There was a bit more pie on her plate, but Miss Hawthorne believed it was a mark of etiquette to leave a little bit on your plate, to show you had not been piggish in your eating. She had tried to teach me the habit, but I always forgot about it until the last bite was gone. She lifted her head and met his look casually. "Perfectly," she said, pushing back her chair and rising. Mr. Judson was immediately on his feet. I watched them walk into the living room, Miss Hawthorne's back straight, Mr. Judson limping slightly on his cane. I began to clear the table.

Out in the kitchen Mrs. Woeste asked me about the dinner. "Did he enjoy it?" she wanted to know.

"He ate every bite." I scraped the plates for her, an apron

239

tied over my best dress. I asked one of the few questions I had dared to ask at Hawthorne. "Do you think they will marry?"

She was putting the leftover food into little china bowls to be stored away in the icebox. She took a deep breath.

"It'll be a miracle if they do," she said bluntly. "What would Miss Hawthorne want with a man this time of her life when she's done without one all these years?"

If Mrs. Woeste knew Mr. Judson had once been in love with Miss Hawthorne, she gave no clue. She had never discussed them with me and she wasn't going to begin. "Don't go around getting ideas in your head anything romantic is going to happen around here," she warned. "This isn't a place for happiness."

I thought about what she had said afterwards. It was true, I supposed; at least none of the Hawthornes was happy. They had everything to make it with but they weren't. Perhaps they just didn't know how to be. I would have to be careful not to catch their unhappiness from them.

19

Mr. Judson went off to California, and Miss Hawthorne did not mention him again. He had slipped in and out of her life for four days without leaving a visible mark. I had nothing to think about but my lessons. In November, when the weather began to turn cold, I found that my winter clothes that had been stored away in the cedar closet were too big for me. I had lost twenty pounds. Even my winter coat hung loose on my shoulders. Miss Hawthorne took me to the city to shop.

In the dress department of the largest store in the city, the saleslady brought out an armful of dresses to show us. My head spun. I used to spend months poring over the pages of the catalogues before I bought anything. How was I going to choose on a moment's notice? But when I went into the little dressing room and slipped on the first dress, I found it fitted me perfectly. All the agony of losing weight was suddenly worth while. I stood entranced before the long mirror, gazing at the girl looking back at me as if I had never met her before. Her dark eyes shone, her hands were as white as her arms, her dark hair neatly done on the back of her neck. I had changed. I slipped into each dress sure it was the one I wanted. We ended up buying a gray wool, a brown wool, two ginghams, and a lovely yellow silk for dinner when there would be company.

We were ready to leave the store with all our bundles, when Miss Hawthorne remembered we hadn't bought a hat. We rushed over to a hat counter on the first floor. I tried on brown ones to go with the coat we had bought, but they were all too small. Finally Miss Hawthorne picked up a yellow felt with a high crown and a wide brim. A tiny pheasant feather was fitted into the brown ribbon that circled the crown. I put it on at the mirror.

"It fits you perfectly," the clerk said. "And it lights up your face."

"It's *your* hat," Miss Hawthorne agreed. "It's most becoming.

Back at Hawthorne with all my new clothes, I wished that company was coming so that I might dress up, but no one came to Hawthorne at that time of the year. I sat in church on Thanksgiving morning, much more conscious of my yellow hat than with any thought of what I might be thankful for. After the service, while Miss Hawthorne spoke to the rector at the door, I went around to the little cemetery. It looked bleak and desolate under the gray skies, the little marble lamb seemed to be shivering in the cold. "But Adrianne is not here," I reminded myself. I looked up at the thick sky. "I wish you could see my new hat, Adrianne," I said softly.

When I went around to the front of the church, Miss Hawthorne was waiting for me. She did not like cemeteries. Even when we brought flowers I had to take them in alone. She only looked in once a year to see that everything was being taken care of. Once she had pointed out to me her parents' graves and the graves of Mr. Clay's parents, but she had only paused a moment. Seeing everything in order, she hurried out. Miss Hawthorne resisted death as she resisted life.

❧ 20 ☙

But company did come. On his way back from California, Mr. Judson stopped by again. Miss Hawthorne had not mentioned his coming back; whether she had heard from him or not, I didn't know, but she was out again when he came.

In the bright winter day the sun came into the rooms, searching out the dark corners. I had a sudden, fanciful desire to try on my yellow silk dress to see how it looked in the sunshine. I put the yellow hat on too, and had just stepped to the mirror when the doorbell rang. Mrs. Woeste would be napping. I ran down to answer it. Opening the door I found Mr. Judson on the steps.

"Well, well," he declared at sight of me. "Where are we off to?"

"I was just trying on my new clothes," I hastened to explain.

He admired them. "You should stay out of those drab colors. I remember you as a country mouse. And here you are . . . a butterfly."

"Oh, Mr. Judson," I murmured. Then remembering why he was there, I hastily told him, "Miss Hawthorne is out again."

He was crestfallen for only a moment. He looked up hopefully. "Do you think she might be back?"

Miss Hawthorne had gone to a meeting at the rector's. There was a chance she would be back early. I invited him to come into the living room and wait. "But your chauffeur can't stay out in the cold."

"Perhaps he could wait in the kitchen," Mr. Judson suggested.

I opened the door again and called to the chauffeur to come in out of the cold. I led him back to the kitchen and gave him the paper to read. "When Mrs. Woeste gets up she'll give you a cup of coffee," I told him.

Mr. Judson was just as brown as he had been six weeks ago. The California sunshine had gone on tanning him. He sat in an easy chair, and I chose a straight one with yellow needlepoint that matched the color of my dress, sitting as I had often practiced, feet crossed at the ankles, hands crossed in my lap. I felt as stiff as a picture and wondered if I looked like one. Mr. Judson told me about his trip.

"Now I'm headed for the South of France for the winter," he said. "I much prefer it to California."

"That's Miss Hawthorne's favorite place," I told him. "Yes." There was a twinkle in his blue eyes. "I just missed her there last winter. By a day or two. It was too much of a coincidence. An earlier train, a later boat. It created the urge to see her again."

There are times I can't think of anything to say. This was one of them. It usually happened I wasn't expected to answer. This was also true.

"As one gets older," Mr. Judson went on, as if he preferred having an audience, "one's friends slip away. One by one I find their names in the obituary columns. And I find old friends are best at my time of life. There is much to remember with them. Good and bad perhaps, but much to remember."

He asked if he might smoke, and I fetched an ashtray on a marble stand and brought it over to his chair. He took a cigar out of his pocket, bit off the end, lit it, and puffed until the end glowed. Through a curl of smoke he regarded me. "Isn't it a bit lonesome for you around here?"

I told him that Miss Hawthorne was teaching me. I found myself telling him about Adrianne, how I had been afraid I would have to leave after she died. How glad I had been to stay on.

"I never thought I'd like to live here," he said. "I always had the feeling the place might smother me."

I laughed.

"It was true," he said, leaning toward me. "But I never had the chance to find out. Alice never forgave me for being too poor to support her. She lacked the daring to try life on a shoestring."

"But you could . . ." A door opened and closed down the hall, footsteps came rapidly toward us. I had just been about to say: "But you could support her now." Miss Hawthorne stood in the doorway.

"Well, Henry Judson!" she said, catching her breath. "This is a surprise." She caught sight of me, sitting on the best antique chair in my yellow silk dress. "Keturah," she demanded. "Did you know Mr. Judson was coming? You're all dressed up."

I stood up quickly, explaining that I had been trying on my dress when the doorbell rang.

"Perhaps you had better go and change it," she dismissed me crossly. She took off her coat and hat as I left the room. I was angry with her for the first time. I thought she had been rude. She had treated me as a disobedient child in front of Mr. Judson. She had broken the lovely bubble I had been existing in as he sat and talked to me. Defiantly I took off the yellow dress and hung it in the closet. I put on a blouse and skirt and marched down the backstairs and into the kitchen, where Mrs. Woeste and the chauffeur were having coffee. I poured a cup for myself and sat down at the table with them.

The chauffeur eyed me. "I could have sworn you had on a yellow dress when I came in."

I put up my chin. "Really?"

"Miss Hawthorne chased you out," Mrs. Woeste guessed.

I slowly stirred the hot coffee. I looked across at the chauffeur. He seemed upset at my rebuff. "I did have on a yellow dress. A lovely yellow dress. But I changed it."

Mrs. Woeste looked at me queerly. "What's got into you, Keturah?"

"Nothing," I said. I was still rankled. But the hot coffee, the warm kitchen, the friendliness of the two of them, slowly moved the feeling away from me. I sat chatting with

245

them for half an hour, then glancing at the clock, decided I'd better go back upstairs before Miss Hawthorne found me again.

The next day Miss Hawthorne left for town early, telling Mrs. Woeste she would not be back for dinner. It was a rare thing for Miss Hawthorne to do, as she did not like to drive after dark. I supposed she was meeting Mr. Judson in town. The day following her trip to town, he came again in the afternoon and stayed for dinner. They chatted pleasantly at the table but beneath the talk I sensed an air of tension. At the end of the meal, Mr. Judson said he was leaving for New York in the morning, catching a boat in a few days for the South of France.

"Don't you envy me a bit?" he slyly asked Miss Hawthorne.

But she ignored it. "How long do you expect to be there this time?"

"Until I have the urge to leave."

"You are a fortunate man."

He eyed her narrowly, the creases pressing deeply beside his eyes. "In some ways, yes." He waited, but she did not reply. "You could do the same. If you wouldn't let this place trap you." He leaned toward her. "It's caught you all your life, Alice."

She slowly turned her long-stemmed water glass around on the tablecloth. "Perhaps."

She spoke lightly but I think she spoke the truth. I got over being angry with her in that moment. Once again I felt a bit sorry for her. She looked a lonely figure sitting there at the head of the table. And yet she could easily have dispelled her loneliness with a single look or word. I truly believe that if she had given Mr. Judson any encouragement at all, he would have taken her with him.

We spent a quiet Christmas, a large, untrimmed pine tree in the library the only decoration. Miss Hawthorne liked the smell of pine, but she thought the tree shouldn't be spoiled with ornaments or lights. I remembered longingly the trees we had had at the Dennys', what fun it had been trimming them, the magical moment when the candles were lit.

In the morning we went to church. When we came home Miss Hawthorne gave me my gift, a brown leather purse. She was pleased with the scarf I had chosen for her and kept it over her shoulders at dinner. Mrs. Woeste had baked an enormous turkey which rested on a great platter at one end of the long table, but it seemed almost wasteful for just the two of us.

I missed Adrianne all day long. I had made Christmas a gay time for her, wrapping up small gifts she delighted to open, and reading to her the Christmas story from the Bible, and telling her the story of Tiny Tim. On her table there would be a little live tree I had cut in the woods, which we had decorated with paper chains and popcorn and a silver star on top.

After dinner Miss Hawthorne went to her rooms. I sat in the library and read. It began to snow late in the afternoon. I poked up the fire to make the room more cheerful. Finally, tired of reading and bored with my own company on a day that should have been joyful, I bundled up in my old plaid coat, wrapped a wool scarf over my head, put on my boots, and went for a walk. The great, old trees along the road were fast becoming lined with snow. A few solitary winter birds hopped in and out of the stripped hedges. It was a windless day, and the soft snow stuck everywhere it fell. It was almost bus time when I reached the gate. I decided to wait and watch it pass, just to know some other people were alive. In a few moments it came looming down the highway, its headlights already on. In their long beams the snowflakes glittered and spun. As it passed, going more slowly than usual, the windows were steamed, and I could not see inside. Beyond the gate it stopped. The door opened and a man got off. He carried a suitcase; his coat collar was turned up, the brim of his felt hat pulled down over his eyes. There was something familiar about his height, his walk—

"Mr. Clay!" I cried.

He was equally astonished at sight of me. "Keturah, what are you doing here?"

"I was taking a walk. I'm so glad you came," I burst out. "Now it does seem like Christmas, with someone here."

He smiled in spite of himself. It still did not come easily to him. "I got into New York yesterday," he explained. "It seemed the loneliest place in the world on Christmas Eve. I decided to come out here."

"It's been lonely here too," I said.

As we went up the road through the thickly falling snow, he had little to say but the silence was not awkward. I was glad I had been down at the gate so he did not have to walk the long road alone. As we rounded the bend the white house rose against the darkening sky. The lights were on downstairs. Mr. Clay put down his suitcase and rested a moment. The house looked warm and secure in the steadily falling snow. It looked more welcoming than it ever had before. Mr. Clay quoted some lines of poetry about a house waiting on a cold night for a weary traveler. Then he picked up his suitcase again and we went on.

Miss Hawthorne had seen us coming. She opened the door as we came up the steps. A glow of pleasure lit her face. "Clay! What a surprise." Mr. Clay kissed her lightly on the cheek. It was the first show of affection I had seen him give her.

"I thought you sent Keturah down to the gate to meet me," he said jokingly, and I hastened to explain to Miss Hawthorne how I had happened to be there.

Mrs. Woeste had left after dinner but there was plenty of food in the kitchen. Miss Hawthorne asked me to go out and warm it up for supper. She urged Mr. Clay to stay up at the house for the night as the cottage would be cold. While he unpacked, I heated up the leftovers. There was a good deal more than leftovers. The turkey had scarcely been carved, the vegetable bowls were full, the surface of the cranberries almost as smooth as at noon. There was an untouched pumpkin pie and a mince pie.

In the flurry of setting the table and getting the food on, I forgot half the necessaries. I was constantly up to fetch and pass. But Mr. Clay and Miss Hawthorne were busy chatting and did not seem to notice. Mr. Clay *had* changed. He not only looked better, he had put on weight. He talked as if he hadn't had anyone to talk to for a long time; in fact, he was alive again.

Afterwards they went to the library, while I cleared up and washed the dishes. When I went in to say good night, they were listening to music coming over a radio that Miss Hawthorne had brought from her room. I stood a moment in the doorway, not wanting to disturb them. Miss Hawthorne looked up. "Come in and listen, Keturah," she invited. "It's Handel's *Messiah*."

I sat on a chair near the fire and became lost in the music. The sweet, strong scent of the untrimmed pine tree rose in the room and mingled with the music. When the music finished I was so far away I was on the edge of sleep. Miss Hawthorne's voice roused me.

"It's been a good Christmas after all." She was standing up, stretching her arms. "Almost like old times." She turned the radio off. "It's way past our bedtime, Keturah."

I stood up slowly, still entranced with the beauty of *The Messiah*. "It was so lovely," I said. "It seemed to come right down from heaven. I wonder if Adrianne heard it."

It was the wrong thing to say. Miss Hawthorne's eyebrows lifted, Mr. Clay stared sharply at the fire. But there was no taking it back. I said good night and went upstairs, leaving behind me an open door I should have left closed. The silence trailed me all the way up the stairs.

◅§ 22 §▻

The snow stopped by morning. It lay thick and soft on the fences, the hedges, the trees. The whole countryside sparkled as the sun rose. Mrs. Woeste came back and Mr. Clay went down to the cottage to stay. The first few days he came up to dinner in the evenings, but after a long-distance call he became completely involved in his work again, and since Mrs. Woeste was afraid of slipping on the snow on the uneven path, I carried dinner down to him.

The first evening I had to tell him twice his meal was ready before he stopped writing. The next night he was out in the yard, wearing a heavy, plaid wool jacket and smoking a pipe. "Dinnertime already?" he greeted me. "I just came out for a breath of fresh air."

I stopped beside him. "Don't you ever get any rest, Mr. Clay?"

He looked up at the sky that was as clear and pale as it had been in the early morning. "Not when I have something to do."

"I should think your head would hum with nothing but reading and writing all day long."

"It does sometimes," he admitted. He followed me into the house. "If you think I need to relax perhaps I should play some records. Music always soothes me."

While I set the table he chose a stack of records and put one on. Slowly, as if coming in on tiptoe, the music began to flow through the room, first the violins, soft as scurrying mice, then the deeper notes of the horns, the cellos, and finally the rumble of the drums, all weaving together in pure, clear sound. I stood listening.

"Why don't you stay and hear it all?" Mr. Clay said, noticing my rapt attention.

I glanced up at him. "May I?"

"You can sit here by the fire. I'll eat my dinner if you don't mind."

I took his big chair beside the fire and watched the logs burn as I listened to the music. When the record was finished I did not move at once.

"Do you want to hear the other side?" Mr. Clay asked.

I did. But I realized suddenly that Miss Hawthorne would be waiting dinner for me. I told him so, slipping back into my coat that I had taken off beside the warm fire.

"You can hear the other side tomorrow night," he offered. "You like music, don't you?"

"Yes. But I've never heard much but hymn singing."

He raised an eyebrow. "Do you mean Aunt Alice has neglected your musical education?"

So she must have discussed my lessons with him. I laughed.

"She doesn't often care for it herself," he went on. "She considers it too sentimental. And Aunt Alice, as you must know by now, is not sentimental."

Since he had finished eating, I put the dishes back in the basket. "I hope you won't let her disturb the essential qualities in you," he said, watching me.

I looked at him quickly, not sure what he meant. But he was not going to explain. He picked his pipe up from the desk and began to light it.

As I hurried up to the house I thought of what he had said. "The essential qualities . . ." Did he mean that I had something I should hold on to against Miss Hawthorne? Did he mean I shouldn't become like her, that if I liked music I should not let her sway my opinion of it? Was he warning me against something? I could not decide.

When I came with his dinner the next evening, he was nowhere about. I was keenly disappointed as I had looked forward to hearing the other side of the record. The door was locked. He must have gone for a walk or a ride and forgotten the time. I carried the food back up to the house. Mrs. Woeste tossed it off lightly when I told her.

"He'll just have to do without, then," she said in a hurry. She was getting ready to catch the bus, for she had New

Year's Day off. "Unless he has sense enough to come and get himself something later on. When his brain's working hard, food don't mean a thing." She shook her head on which floated her big, untrimmed, black felt hat, the brim riding over the knot on the back of her head. "Now if you'll give me a hand, we'll get dinner on the table. Then I'll be off for my bus. The party will be on at my sister's by the time I get there as it is."

Parties and Mrs. Woeste seemed unmixable, yet every holiday she attended one at her sister's house. And a gay time they must have had from the tales she told when she got back. They were a subject of conversation for weeks to come. They were the only times in the whole year Mrs. Woeste got out of her kitchen, but however much she enjoyed them, she was always glad to get back.

"I'm getting on," she would sigh the day after. "One knows he's getting old when he's all done up after a party, sober as I was all through it."

Miss Hawthorne had a cold and ate very little at dinner. She was sorry that Mr. Clay had missed his, but she did not concern herself about it.

"He's been getting along without anyone to look after him for a long time," she said, shrugging her shoulders around which hung the blue scarf I had given her for Christmas. She took only a spoonful of pudding and pushed it aside. She thought it better not to eat when she had a cold. She sipped her tea and rose from the table. "I think I'm going to bed." She dabbed at her nose that was red at the tip. "I want to start the New Year feeling well. I have to drive Clay to the city tomorrow to catch his train."

The long, lonely evening stretched ahead of me. I wandered through the empty rooms, touched the piano keys in the living room just to make a sound. The piano was all out of tune. No one ever played it. I lightly struck each key all the way up and down the piano. Their notes fell like broken glass into the quiet. In the library the fireplace was gray with ashes. I wished for a fire but it seemed foolish to build one at that time of the night. I turned out the lights and went upstairs. The moonlight fell through the windows. From the upstairs hall I saw it shining on the snow, masking the world in silver; the snow-clad trees along the drive might have been faintly sketched with a black pencil. As far as I could see, nothing stirred. I was suddenly overwhelmed with loneliness. I thought of Mrs. Woeste at her party, the laughter, the dancing, the good things to eat.

At the Dennys', New Year's Eve was the one time we sat up after midnight. Just before twelve o'clock Mr. Denny would take out his silver watch, see that it tallied with the clock on the mantel, and we would solemnly wait for the old year to die. All evening Mr. Denny reviewed the past year, taking from his pocket a little black notebook in which he kept a record of the weather year after year and jotted down important events. He would leaf through it, recalling on what day such and such a thing had happened, which had been the coldest day in the year, the hottest day. He would recall all the sad and happy events of the dying year, counting up the people who had married, the new babies born, the ones who had died. Mr. Denny gathered the whole year up in a basket of remembering and sorted out the blessings. And each year, he decided, had been a good year, in fact the best year, and he was reverently grateful and thankful for it. At the stroke of twelve he opened the door and shouted a Happy New Year out to the frosty night that was only a quiet countryside, with no one to hear but the animals down at the barn, the squirrels curled up in the hollows of the trees, and the mice snug in their holes waiting for a scrap of cheese from the lunch that always followed. There was always a piece of herring for luck and a glass of gingerale for each of us, which was a real treat in the middle of winter.

How long ago it seemed. The stars began to wink until I had to blink to see them clearly. I went to my room and picked up Mr. Denny's silver watch from my dresser, rubbing my fingers over its smooth back to get some of the feel of Mr. Denny. Each time he had taken it out of his pocket he had rubbed his fingers over its smooth, silver back. "Happy New Year, Mr. Denny," I whispered. "Happy New Year, Mrs. Denny." Holding the watch, I skimmed over the past year, and all that had happened. The winter when Adrianne had been so ill, the nights I had crept about in the cold making a croup tent, bending over her bed until her breathing became regular again. The night we took her to the hospital, the day she was buried, Miss Hawthorne coming back from the South of France and making me her companion. Derrick and Wendy's visit, Mr. Judson's arrival, Christmas evening when Mr. Clay came. I thought of him alone in his cottage without any supper. "He's been getting along without anyone to look after him for a long time," Miss Hawthorne had said. But was it the way he liked to get along? There was such a loneliness about him. Perhaps right now he was hungry. . . . I longed to go and take Mr. Clay something to eat.

It was a wild idea, something I would ordinarily not have dared to do, but the idea began to possess me. It was the one night in the year people did something out of the ordinary. Miss Hawthorne was asleep. Mrs. Woeste was gone. Surely there would be no harm in my going.

I crept down to the kitchen, careful not to make a sound on the stairs, fearful of waking Miss Hawthorne. But there was no light under her door. I found the cold turkey and made sandwiches, filled a jar with cold cranberries, wrapped pickles in wax paper. There were two puddings left over. I put them both in the basket. From the fruit bowl on the sideboard I took apples and nuts. Then I ran down to the cellar and got a jug of cider since there was no gingerale. I left only the small night-light burning in the kitchen. If Miss Hawthorne should stir out of her rooms, she would think nothing amiss.

I stepped out into the cold, silver night. The stars fairly danced up in the cold sky, the moon laid a tracery of tree shadows on the glistening snow. The sharp air rushed into my lungs, and it was suddenly wonderful to be alive on the last night of the year. The year was dying but I was not. Life flowed warmly through me, spreading a warm, comforting circle about me as I carried my basket down the path. Lights shone from the windows of the cottage. As I came up the porch steps I saw Mr. Clay sitting at his desk. I had slipped Mr. Denny's watch in my pocket, and I reached in and touched the watch again, hoping Mr. Clay wouldn't be angry at my coming at that late hour. I knocked on the door.

He looked up, startled. Then spying me through the glass, he hurried over and opened the door. "Is something wrong?" he asked at once. "Aunt Alice?"

"She went to bed with a cold." I clutched the watch. "I thought you might be hungry since you missed your dinner." I held out the basket. "I've brought you something to eat."

A curious expression crossed his face. Whether he was touched or angry at my intrusion, I could not tell.

"It's New Year's Eve," I reminded him. "There's a piece of herring for good luck."

He did not move from the doorway. His hair was mussed, his coat wrinkled. He looked infinitely tired. At last he stepped aside. "Come in," he said, as if he were still not quite sure whether he should invite me or not. "I'd forgotten about food, I guess."

Books were scattered on the floor beside the desk, papers strewn about the overflowing wastebasket. Mr. Clay ran his hand over his rumpled hair. "Come to think of it, I am hungry."

I began unpacking the basket on the coffee table in front of the fire. "It looks as if you've brought enough for two or three people," he mused, watching me. Then he added, as if the thought had just struck him, "Perhaps you'd better stay and help me eat it."

Why not? I thought recklessly. "Will you play the other side of the record if I do?" I asked.

"If you like." He put it on while I drew his chair close to the table and pulled up a footstool for myself.

The bright fire, the food, the soft music, began to relax Mr. Clay. I could almost see him unwind, the tiredness move out of his face. He began to talk as if it were perfectly natural for me to be sitting there with him at that hour of the night. Way back in my mind I had a dim vision of what Miss Hawthorne might think if she knew, but I did not let it trouble me.

"It was Mrs. Woeste's party and remembering Mr. Denny on New Year's Eve," I confessed, "that gave me the idea." I reached in my pocket and took out the silver watch. "This was his. I treasure it more than anything I have."

"What did Mr. Denny do on New Year's Eve?"

As I told him he sat with his chin in his hand, his elbow resting on the chair arm, completely thoughtful.

"It's quite remarkable," he said, when I finished.

I looked up, puzzled.

"To find someone as completely natural as you are."

I thought it over a moment. "Is it a good thing to be?"

He nodded. "It's being what you are. Without sham or pretense."

"Is that what you meant about Miss Hawthorne not disturbing the . . . the essentials?"

"Yes. 'To your own self be true.' "

I felt a sudden, warm confusion at Mr. Clay looking into me the way he was. To cover it, I dove down into the basket and brought out the bottle of cider. "I brought some cider. We had gingerale at the Dennys'. Since there wasn't any I thought cider would do as well. Would you like some?"

He smiled slowly. "A good glass of cider will be just the thing."

I went to the kitchen and brought back two glasses, filled them with the cloudy, amber cider. I handed him one. He held it out to the fire.

"To the coming New Year," he said.

I held mine out likewise. "May it be a good one."

The cider was prickly. "I think it's beginning to turn," Mr. Clay noted.

"It's almost as bubbly as gingerale," I said happily.

He turned his glass around in his hand, peering through it. "What was the nicest thing that happened to you during the year?" he asked.

I flew back in my mind. I remembered, with a stab, Adrianne, the bad things always flying into your mind first. I glanced quickly at Mr. Clay, hoping he didn't see it there, but I could see it had popped up in his mind too. I closed my eyes. When I opened them Mr. Clay was still waiting for me. "Getting to stay on here," I told him.

It was evidently different from what he had expected. "But isn't this a solitary life for you?" he protested.

I shrugged. "Tonight it was. But not often. I'm busy with my studies. Miss Hawthorne is going to make a lady out of me."

He threw back his head and laughed. For a moment I was offended. But it was the first time I had heard him laugh. It so completely transformed him I could not remain miffed. I became amused along with him. "Is it so impossible?" I asked.

He sobered quickly. "Forgive me for laughing. It's just that you say such unexpected things. I've never heard a girl say that was her ambition, at least seriously."

"But I am serious."

"Why?"

I couldn't tell him about the picture in the magazine. I couldn't tell him that because I was nobody I wanted to be somebody. I looked into the fire. "You can just want to be something without really knowing why, can't you?"

"Yes. I always wanted to write," he said. "It was something that was born in me."

I felt I understood, then, why he worked so hard. Because it was like a passion in him. A log that had been burning brightly fell apart, and the red embers flew up the chimney. "I wonder what time it is," I said, suddenly aware that a great deal of it had passed.

He looked at his watch. "Five minutes to twelve."

I jumped to my feet and began putting the things back in the basket. "I've stayed much too long." I got into my coat, hung the basket on my arm. I turned and faced him. "I didn't intend to stay so long."

He said nothing, smiling a bit, so that I knew he didn't

hold it against me. He followed me out to the porch. It was light as day outside. In the distance rose the clump of dark woods. In the clear night the hills stood etched against the sky. Way off somewhere a church bell began to chime. It was so beautiful we stood and listened until the last chime died away.

"A herald of the New Year," Mr. Clay said.

I started slowly down the steps. Mr. Clay had been standing behind me as the bell pealed. He had been standing behind me as he had that night at the hospital when his hands were on my shoulders to steady me. A warm feeling rushed over me as we stood there on the porch listening to the faraway bell. I waited for it to go away but it did not leave. As I reached the foot of the steps Mr. Clay called down: "Thank you, Keturah." I looked up at the tall, lean figure above me, clearly outlined in the bright night. I was caught for a moment by the dark eyes gazing down at me. Then I turned and fled up to the house. At the kitchen door I caught the cold, white knob in my hand. I looked up at the sky. The stars fairly crackled across the heavens. It was like the night I had come to the Dennys', the first time something wonderful had happened to me. The stars witnessed again. "I must be in love with Mr. Clay," I told the stars in astonishment, and quickly opening the door, escaped inside.

Daylight came and I was still far from sleep. My bed was cast like an island in some far-removed place, and nothing could invade the warmth that wrapped me. But with the cold, gray light of dawn I found myself back in my room at Hawthorne. The impossibility of my situation spread over me like a cold gray mist. There were two worlds: Mr. Clay's and mine. Briefly I had stepped into his, and out of it again.

I had read too many novels, I told myself severely. I had only imagined myself in love with him. Nothing could ever come of it even if it were true. My mind tossed restlessly back and forth. Of one thing I was certain: Mr. Clay would never know.

I did not go down to breakfast. I was too worn out from not sleeping. I was suddenly so tired I could not get out of bed. I must have fallen asleep. I awoke to a knock on my door. Miss Hawthorne was calling my name. I ran over and opened the door without putting on my robe. Miss Hawthorne was standing in the hall huddled into her bathrobe. I wondered if she had found out about my visit of the night before. Had she come to reprimand me?

"You weren't down to breakfast," she said, her voice smothered in her cold. "Are you ill?"

"I must have overslept," I said cautiously.

"My cold is worse instead of better." She was not scolding me. So she hadn't found out, she hadn't heard me come in. "I can't drive Clay to town. *You'll* have to go with him and bring the car back. He wants to leave by ten so you'll have to hurry."

Drive Mr. Clay to town . . . I almost shouted that I couldn't. Not this morning . . . not now . . . If only I had said I was ill. I was caught, and there was nothing to do about it. I dressed quickly, putting on my new, brown wool dress. Suddenly all that mattered was that I was going to be with him again. All the sane arguments of the dawn left me. I was going to be with him again.

As I went into Miss Hawthorne's study, she called to me from her bedroom. I went in hesitantly. It was the first time I had been inside it. It was all silver and white like herself. There were no frills, everything was plain and severe, but there was a brightness about it, the room had a cheerful air.

Miss Hawthorne gave me a few brief instructions from her bed about driving carefully. She did not even remark on the fact that I wore my best wool dress. She did look ill against the white pillow.

I stopped for a glimpse of myself in the long, hall mirror. My face fairly glowed under the yellow hat. No one would guess I had had a sleepless night.

Mr. Clay was waiting in the car. At sight of him I became calm again, feeling safe and secure in his presence. I slid into the seat beside him with no more than a brief "Good morning." He made no reference to the night before, in fact he talked very little, evidently having something on his mind. He asked if I minded driving back alone.

I didn't, although I had never been alone in the car. I told him I wasn't sure of my way out of the city.

"Just go back the way we go in," he said. "I'm sure you can manage."

I wondered that he had such confidence in me. I watched carefully as we entered the city, making mental notes of streets and buildings where we made a turn. As we waited for a traffic signal Mr. Clay glanced at his watch.

"I had planned to take Aunt Alice to lunch before my train left," he said. "Would you like to come along instead?"

"Me?" One surprise was following another so that I could not keep up with them.

"Why not?"

What would be nicer than having lunch with him? I threw all caution to the winds, immediately agreeing to go.

We went to the same hotel where I had once eaten lunch with Miss Hawthorne on a shopping trip. The hotel was transformed for the holidays. An enormous tree was still standing in the lobby, covered with lights from top to bottom. I had never seen such a large tree except in the woods. I stood entranced before it. On the very top was a shining silver star, as bright as the ones I had gazed up at the night before at the kitchen door.

"I'd like to let you stand and admire it," Mr. Clay said, "but if I'm to catch my train we'd better have lunch."

In the dining room the walls were hung with great green holly wreaths tied with red satin bows. On each table was a decoration of silver ornaments and a red, lighted candle. As I slipped out of my coat and the waiter tucked it over the back of the chair, I was glad I had worn my brown wool dress. The menu in my hands, I couldn't make up my mind what to order. Seeing I was having difficulty, Mr. Clay ordered for me: a soup, a fruit salad, and French pastry. He ordered the same for himself. He handed the menu back to the waiter and looked across the table at me. The Mr. Clay of the night before returned. "I must say that yellow hat becomes you."

Yet we had little to say at lunch. I was content just being there, sitting across from him, hearing the soft tinkle of china and glass, the music drifting softly through the room, the well-dressed people at the other tables. As we were finishing our dessert, he said without looking up, "I'm sorry Aunt Alice has a cold but I can't say I'm unhappy that it had to be now."

"If it weren't for the cold I wouldn't be here," I said.

He raised his eyes. "That was what I was trying to tell you."

I laughed. I felt suddenly free again. I dared to say: "You're not so unhappy anymore, are you?"

He was thoughtful for a moment. "No," he admitted slowly.

"The shadows aren't as thick around Hawthorne anymore, either," I said.

"Could a place remain dark and gloomy with you in it?"

To cover my confusion at his words, I found myself telling him about Mr. Judson's visit. "I thought maybe they would marry," I told him.

"Aunt Alice!" He laughed. "Never."

"But Mr. Judson once asked her to marry him a dozen times."

"And I'm sure she told him no a dozen times." He leaned toward me across the table, his eye shining with amusement. "Aunt Alice doesn't like music, men, or prying. If she knew you knew that, she might send you packing."

"Oh no!" I exclaimed. "I want to stay at Hawthorne forever."

The amusement changed to seriousness. For one long moment he held my gaze. Then he glanced quickly at his watch. "I'm sorry, but it's time to go." He pushed back his chair, stood up, and came around to help me with my coat. The moment was gone.

As we left the hotel and started back to the car, the knowledge that we would be apart in a few moments rushed over me. "Couldn't I go down to the train with you?" I asked rashly. "I love to see the trains."

"Then come along," he agreed. "If you'll remember where the car is parked."

At the station he put a hand under my arm to steer me through the thick crowd of holiday travelers. Everyone seemed to be taking off for somewhere, people were bidding each other good-bye, students returning to school, families that had been to visit, leaving. It was all gay and exciting with the big engines hissing and steaming in the frosty air, waiting to carry people away.

"Aren't you glad I came along," I shouted to Mr. Clay above the noise at the gate, "so you'll have someone to say good-bye to?"

There was scarcely room for him to set his suitcase down while he fished in his pocket for his tickets. The crowd surged about us, pushing us into a tiny space that contained only the two of us. Holding the tickets in his hand, he gave me a quick glance and as quickly looked away. Then his dark eyes were back, studying my face. His arms came suddenly reaching out, catching me against him. In his tight clasp I felt swept into some safe harbor I never wanted to move from. "All aboard!" the conductor called from far away. "All aboard!" Mr. Clay as suddenly let go of me, reached down and picked up his suitcase. "I'm sorry," he murmured. "That shouldn't have happened."

He looked so forlorn, so regretful, I reached out and put my hand on his arm. "Don't be," I said. He covered my hand with his. But the crowd was already pushing him away from me, through the opened gate. I watched him walking down the platform beside the hissing train, swinging along with the crowd. He never looked back.

Miss Hawthorne had told me to be careful driving home. I don't believe I saw the road at all. I don't remember passing another car. All I saw was Mr. Clay's face, his dark eyes sad again as he murmured "I'm sorry." Was he really? For himself or for me? For both of us? I thought of that longago time with Floyd. How different this was. The quiet standing in his arms for just that moment. The peace. And yet I was on fire from the contact with him.

23

There was absolutely no mail from Mr. Clay the rest of the
winter and the following spring. Miss Hawthorne remarked
that he had not even acknowledged the holidays he'd spent
at Hawthorne. "He needn't be that busy," she said, speaking more sharply of him than was her wont. I did not reply.
I knew now that he had spoken the truth when he said he
was sorry, that he realized the great gulf between us, and
his way of letting me know was to cut all ties with Hawthorne. I doubted if he would ever come back again.

Spring found us often in the fir-walled garden after I'd
finished my lessons in the afternoons, the long, dreary
months since New Year's fading into the past. We sat and
watched the flowers grow, and if I was quieter and less apt
to respond than before, Miss Hawthorne made no comment.
Only one thing of interest happened.

On a trip to town to buy the special flower seeds Miss
Hawthorne always bought each spring, we stopped in the
ten-cent store for a few knickknacks she needed. While
Miss Hawthorne looked for them, I wandered over to the
jewelry counter, drawn by the glitter of beads, rings and
earrings. A ring with a large, blue glass stone caught my
fancy. I slipped it on my finger. It was too tight and I had
trouble getting it off again.

"May I help you?" a voice behind the counter asked.

There was something about the voice that made me look
up quickly. I gazed into the bright blue eyes of Georgia

Lee. We recognized each other in the same moment. "Georgia Lee!" "Keturah!" she cried.

And then we stood there, unable to find the first thing to say to each other. She had changed; her hair was bleached, her long lashes painted black, and her skin, that had been soft as a baby's, was dry under the heavy powder. Her rayon slip shone under the flimsy white blouse. But her eyes held the same wide innocence, they were still the same impossible blue. She smiled, and I noticed her teeth were going bad. "Honest-to-God," she said at last. "I never hoped to see you again."

It all came rushing back, the night in the barn, the morning Floyd's parents had come accusing me, the news that she and Floyd were married. For just a moment the old wound was opened, then it closed again. Georgia Lee might be a stranger who had never touched my life.

"Well," she said brightly. "I guess a lot has happened to me since I saw you last." She leaned her elbows on the counter. "I'm not married to Floyd anymore. We got a divorce. We never did get along." She paused, picking up a string of bright beads and letting them slide up her arm. "I got married again. He left about six months ago."

"Your baby?" I asked for something to say. I remembered she had been named K after me but I had no desire to call her that.

Georgia Lee smiled briefly. The baby at least still meant something to her. When she smiled she was still pretty underneath the change. "She's going to school next fall. She'll be six. Think of it." I did. Six years had carried us in such opposite directions, spread us so far apart. "Thank God she's the only one I had," Georgia Lee went on. "I had a couple of misses but they only kept me off work a few days."

I could see her taking in my yellow hat with the pheasant feather on the crown, my brown coat. "You're looking mighty prosperous yourself," she summed up. "Are you married?"

I shook my head. "No. I'm a companion to a lady." I suppose there was a note of pride in my voice. I wanted to let her know I had come up in the world even if I didn't have a husband.

"You talk different," she said. "Like you was educated."

I laughed. And suddenly I was immensely sorry for her, realizing what she had done to herself, what life had done to her. Georgia Lee whom I once had wanted to be like more than anything else. She had never been able to help herself really, with all the odds against her. She had been too pretty too soon. There had been no one to show her a better way. I said, grasping for a straw, "Did Mr. Atwood ever find you?"

"No," she said firmly, the old spirit rising in her. "But if he were to walk in here now I'd spit in his face." All the hardness that was in her bloomed for a moment in her eyes, then slowly wilted away. I could see that she was tired, not just tired from standing behind the counter on her feet all day, or tired of being polite to customers, or tired because she'd not slept well the night before. But tired of life itself. She wasn't much past twenty yet, and I think she was tired enough to die. I wanted to help her, to do something to ease the tiredness a bit. I could see her going home some night and turning on the gas, or jumping into the river, or simply lying down and not opening her eyes again. I opened my purse. I had a five-dollar bill in it. I took the bill out and held it out to her. "Buy something for your little girl," I said. I hoped she recognized the fact that I wanted to do something to ease things a bit, that I wasn't trying to let her know I was better off than she was.

She eyed the five-dollar bill hungrily, pressing her red nails on the edge of the counter. Slowly she reached out and took it. "Thanks, Keturah," she murmured, her voice softer. "You always were good to me."

Miss Hawthorne came down the aisle looking for me. "I've got to go now," I said quickly. "Good-bye, Georgia Lee."

Her eyes clung to me. "If you come to town again look me up, will you? I'll be right here."

I promised her I would.

The next time we were in the city I made an excuse to go to the ten-cent store. I went straight to the jewelry counter but Georgia Lee was not there. I asked another clerk about her. She was a larger Georgia Lee, too blond, too much makeup, but her eyes lacked the luminous quality of Georgia Lee's. She shrugged. "She left about a month ago. She got married or something."

Or something. . . . Nothing Georgia Lee had ever touched went right. She had never had a real break in her whole life. She seemed to have been born unlucky. She may have brought some of it on herself, but what could a girl like Georgia Lee do with no one ever on her side? I was the only one who had ever befriended her, I suppose. Floyd had probably tried but he had been too weak himself. I would always be glad I had given her that five dollars the last time I saw her. It may have brightened an evening, or a single moment. At least she had still regarded me as her friend.

24

"You've calmed down, Keturah," Miss Hawthorne said one evening as we sat on the terrace. It was the first really warm evening of summer.

I smiled, saying nothing.

"I wonder, aren't you contented here anymore?"

I looked up at the dusky sky, the first brushstrokes of night drawn across it. "There isn't any other place I'd care to go." I evaded a direct answer.

"Perhaps," Miss Hawthorne went on, "you ought to meet some young men and look ahead to getting married." She might have dropped a glass that splintered on the flagstones, for all she startled me. "Have you ever considered the idea?"

I shook my head, blushing with confusion. "Once long ago," I recollected. "But the boy married someone else." I pressed my hands together in my lap. Was she baiting me? Did she have some idea . . . ? Did she suspect . . . ?

"For your own good, I wonder if you shouldn't go to the city and find work."

Or was she trying to get rid of me?

"I don't want you to stay here if there is something better for you."

"But I love Hawthorne," I protested. "I wouldn't feel at home anywhere else. I belong here."

A faint smile trailed the corners of her lips. She sat silent for a time. "Tomorrow," she broke the silence, her voice brisk again as if she had the situation in hand, "I want you to come to my study right after breakfast. I think it's time you learned more about Hawthorne. No one has ever kept the books but myself since my father died. If I should be ill or go away for a time, perhaps it would be a good thing for you to know how."

So I learned about the inner workings of Hawthorne, how much it cost to run the house and keep up the grounds, how much the help was paid, the amount of taxes, the cost of repairs. Miss Hawthorne taught me how to write a check, and sometimes I wrote them for her at the first of the month, leaving the space blank for her signature. She went over each one carefully before she signed it with her fine pointed pen. I was proud that she never had to give one back with a mistake on it. There was never any fuss about money. She merely checked to see that it had not been foolishly spent, but she had no complaint with either Mrs. Woeste or Mr. Hodges. And no further mention was made of my meeting young men.

Derrick and Wendy came the day after school was out and stayed until the first of September. Miss Eloise's new husband didn't like the country so they did not come. The months flew by with the children there. They were old enough now to take daylong hikes through the fields and woods. Sometimes I took them off in the car to the village where we bought ice cream cones or bags of candy, and on Saturday nights we drove in to the weekly movie. My unhappiness lifted and I was almost content again.

At last Miss Hawthorne had a brief note from Mr. Clay. He was still in New York.

"I suppose he'll be marrying again now that he's free," she remarked offhandedly, folding the note back into its creases.

The idea came as a shock to me. When I raised my eyes I saw that Miss Hawthorne was watching me. I forced myself to smile. "It would seem strange," I managed to say, "Mr. Clay having a wife."

"I just hope it will be someone who will understand him," she said, as if it were all settled that he would marry, and I wondered if he had hinted at it in his note. "Also, someone who would be at home here. Hawthorne is in the very marrow of his bones. He wrote so tellingly about it. Some day, I'm sure, he'll realize again how much it means to him."

I didn't reply. The awkward moment had passed. But that night and the nights that followed, I ended my prayers with the plea that Mr. Clay wouldn't get married until he came back to Hawthorne one more time. I didn't want him to be married the next time I saw him.

The last day of summer the answer came. The September morning was golden and still. The sky hung overhead like a deep blue canopy, the air was light and cool. It was good just to be out under the sun. I went down past the barn, down the path Adrianne and I had taken so many times. Thick clumps of goldenrod bloomed along the way, purple ironweed, yellow jewel weed; golden glow lifted brown-eyed daisy faces. The old pear trees sagged with their russet burden, apples hung rosy in the unkempt orchard, beneath the oak trees the acorns scrunched dryly under my feet. It was the ripe time of the year, the harvest full, waiting to be plucked. I thought back to the spring when the first green was beginning to show, the blossoming trees like brides, seeds blowing in the wind. Here was the culmination of it all. Spring had stepped softly into summer; summer strode through its lush green course arriving at the threshhold of autumn in a last burst of russet, purple and gold. I reached the spot where I could see the white house on the hill. It stood empty, the desolate pond cluttered with lily pads, the old rowboat still caught on the bank. The place looked unkempt and unused, overgrown with weeds, but in my mind's eye I could see the dark-haired girl with the doll in her arms coming down the hill. I saw again the white skirt sticking up out of the lily pads, like a duck upended in the water.

Miss Hawthorne had mentioned once that she thought Mr. Clay ought to sell the place but he didn't have the heart to do it. Or else it was just too much bother for him to take the time. I felt the latter was more likely, since she spoke of his marrying again. He had probably forgotten all about it.

I closed my eyes and thought how it used to be with Adrianne standing there beside me, her little hand in mine, her legs tired so that I would have to pick her up and carry her back up the path. When I opened them I saw that the door of the house was standing open. At almost the same moment a man walked out onto the front porch. He came down off the porch and stood looking down at the strangled pond. My heart slipped into my throat. It was Mr. Clay.

He could not help seeing me. Whatever would he think of my being there gaping at the empty house? I stood rooted to the spot, unable to move away as he came on down the hill. He was past the pond, nearing the fence before he spoke. "Keturah! What in the world are you doing here?"

His voice was so sharp I was sure he was angry. I remembered those last moments at the station, how he had taken me in his arms. I could find nothing of that person in him now.

"I was taking a walk," I said, with an attempt at a coolness I didn't feel.

"You seem to be always taking a walk," he said, and I recalled that snowy evening the past Christmas when I had walked down to the highway to see the bus and he had been on it.

"Yes," I said.

His eyes burned into me. When he spoke his voice was as I remembered it. "I came down to sell the place. I have a buyer. They want it right away."

With his explanation everything fell into place. "I didn't know you were coming."

"No one did. I came here first."

How glad I was that he hadn't written or called or given any notice. I wouldn't have been in that particular spot at that precise moment if he had. We might have met under more difficult circumstances, under Miss Hawthorne's watchful eye, or my bringing his dinner down as a servant.

"Would you like to see the house?" he asked suddenly.

"I can't get over the fence."

"There's a stile down the way." He started toward it, and I followed on my side of the fence. The old, wooden stile was hidden in a clump of weeds. The boards were weathered but firm enough. I went up one side and down the other, and we went up the hill together, past the pond which neither of us mentioned, up onto the porch and through the open door into the house.

"The furniture didn't belong to me," Mr. Clay said at my surprise at finding the house bare. "It went to Laura's relatives." It was the first time he had mentioned her name. It somehow made it easier to talk to him, it established something I could not name, as if he had taken me into his confidence.

He raised the blinds in the living room and let the sunshine in. It was a beautiful room with shining floors and white walls and woodwork, smaller than the living room at Hawthorne but prettier, with its tucked-away windows and wide window seats. Mr. Clay stood gazing into the white marble fireplace. "I remember the first time I came here," he said quietly. "Laura was standing there by the mantel, not as tall as the shelf. She looked as if she had stepped out of some romantic novel. I was hooked then and there."

I saw his face in the gilt-framed mirror above the mantel. There was a faint blue shadow along his jaws, his eyes were dark, brooding. I stood almost even with him in the mirror, and Laura had come only to the shelf. He raised his eyes and we met in the mirror. I blushed to think of what he read there, catching me all unawares. He turned and led me through the next room and on through the house. In the dining room a summer scene was painted on the wall, a river flowing through a meadow, and great weeping trees against the sky. In a small back room there was a smaller fireplace with hand-painted tiles. We came back through the hall, past a white staircase that twisted up to the second floor, but Mr. Clay did not go upstairs. He went on to the porch. As I came out behind him I asked: "Shall I close the door?"

He had said only two or three words since we left the living room. I had admired the rest of the house in silence, feeling he did not want me to talk, that he was walking through a memory in which I did not belong. But once outside, the memory was behind us in the house, and I could recall him to the present.

"Yes," he flung over his shoulder. "I'm not going back in again."

He was saying good-bye to the place forever, the good

and bad times, all of it. He rested against one of the tall, white pillars of the porch, his shoulders sagging a little. Beyond us the dark oaks spread a thick shade. A dry leaf fluttered down, an acorn fell. I don't know how long we stood there. I noticed the sun high above the house. It was time for me to be getting back for lunch.

"I must be getting back," I said, my words falling hollowly into the stillness. I don't think Mr. Clay even heard me. I wondered how he was getting back, if he intended to go to Hawthorne. He had probably rented a car and parked it down on the road. Since he seemed to have forgotten me, I left, going down past the pond again and over the stile. As I walked along the fence I looked up toward the house again. Mr. Clay was coming down the hill. He was coming very fast. At the pond he fairly broke into a run. He climbed over the stile and breathlessly caught up with me. Catching hold of my wrists as if he had hurdled the last of the memories that plagued him, he searched my face. Then he took me in his arms as he had at the station. For a long moment he held me. Gently, at first, he began to kiss me. All of ripe September was in that kiss he pressed upon my lips.

"I love you, Mr. Clay." The long held words escaped as he released me. "I've loved you ever since . . ." But there was no time to go back to. I couldn't remember not loving him.

He looked at me for one long, intense moment. He bent his head and tugged at his black tie. "Stop calling me Mr. Clay," he said roughly. When he looked up his eyes had changed so I couldn't believe it was the same man who had kissed me. "Don't say you love me," he said between his teeth. "Everything I love is taken from me. . . ." He turned half away from me. "Keturah, this can't be."

"Why?" I heard myself shouting at him.

"Because you're you and I'm me," he shouted back full of anger.

In one ridiculous moment I lost everything I had ever gained, everything Mr. Denny or Miss Hawthorne had taught me. All of it slipped from me, stripping me bare. I was a poor orphan girl with no background, without a penny in my pocket, in long, black stockings, in a dark cotton dress with damp spots spreading under the arms, my unruly hair caught in a bone barrette that had come in a missionary box. I was standing on a platform being auctioned off; I was standing in front of Mr. Clay (and I could not in all this world think of him then as simply Clay), the brother of Miss Hawthorne, the father of the child I had loved and cared for. I was standing before a man who wrote books, who had traveled everywhere, who was at home in Paris or London or New York, who was famous for all I knew. He had said, "Because you're you and I'm me." I could not remember anything else he had said. Those words were dinning in my ears. For one wild, panicky second I sought his face for some sign of rescue. Finding none, I turned and fled up the path, the weeds tearing at my stockings, past the barn, around to a back door, and up the backstairs to my room. I stayed there pretending to be ill, until I thought Mr. Clay had had time to sell the house and leave.

25

When at last I came down to breakfast, chastened and un-
loved, Mrs. Woeste greeted me soberly in the kitchen. She
had brought food to my room but I had had little appetite
to touch it. She had carried the trays back down unhappily.
"Well now, you do look peaked," she noted, as I sat down
at the table. "I hope you have more of a mind for food this
morning."

"I think I can start eating again," I told her. Over my
cereal I asked casually: "Has Mr. Clay gone?"

"Mr. Clay? Why, I haven't seen him since last winter."

"You mean . . ." I forgot myself. "You mean he wasn't
here?"

She looked at me closely from a pair of black, beady eyes.
"What makes you think he was?"

I had to think quickly. So he had never come to the
house. So he had run away too. "I thought I saw him out
riding."

For just one moment longer Mrs. Woeste remained sniffing something going on behind her back. Then she relaxed.
"That must have been the Vet come over to see what was
the matter with the horse. Mr. Hodges said the horse had a
limp and he was calling the Vet. I didn't know he'd come."

The days in my room had seen me at the bottom, and
now my spirits began to rise again. I had been hiding all
that time for nothing. Mr. Clay was gone and would probably never be back. He was most likely off finding himself

a wife, someone suited to him. The very idea made my blood rise. I would show him, I decided bitterly. I would show him. I would get to be a lady in spite of him.

Miss Hawthorne was pleased to see me at lunch.

"You're such a healthy person," she said. "It was so unlike you to be sick."

"Probably too much fresh fruit," I said, not wanting to discuss my illness.

After lunch I sat in the library and read. Fall had put summer to flight while I was up in my room. The blue sky was gone. A light rain fell. The air was chilly. It was cool enough for a fire but there was no wood in the basket, and I didn't feel inclined to go down to the barn for it. When Miss Hawthorne rose from her nap, she called me, and together we worked on the bookkeeping. At five o'clock she glanced out the window. "It's stopped raining. It looks as if the sun were going to shine before it sets. Would you mind taking Mr. Clay's dinner down, Keturah? Mrs. Woeste was complaining of her rheumatism and I don't like for her to go out in the damp."

"Mr. Clay!" The moment I spoke his name I realized I had been too surprised. Miss Hawthorne glanced at me quickly.

"He's here. Didn't you know?"

"But he . . ."

"He's been staying in town." She ignored me. "I didn't know until he rang up shortly after lunch. He came right out."

How was I going to tell her that I couldn't take dinner down to him? That it was impossible. That I wasn't his servant. Could I suddenly become ill again? Miss Hawthorne put the big, black bookkeeping books back into the safe behind a picture on the wall. She turned the lock. She wiped her hands against each other as if they had gathered dust from the books. "In fact, Clay requested that you bring his dinner down," she said, and sat down at her desk and began to write.

He requested it! I would not go. I would not wait on him. Did he want a chance to insult me further? Did he want to let me see more plainly how unsuited to each other we were? But beneath my anger I knew I could not disobey Miss Hawthorne. I could not refuse without her finding out everything, and then I would have to leave. I preferred staying at Hawthorne to anything Mr. Clay could do to me.

Stopping in the hall to put on my coat, I went out to the kitchen to pick up the basket of food. Mrs. Woeste had it ready. "Why that man can't eat with other people, I don't know," she fretted. "His wife's gone, his child's gone, his house is sold. He's nothing more to lose."

Why did what she say bring tears to my eyes? They blurred my vision as I went down the wet path to the cottage. Why must I always go back to feeling sorry for this man, even after I'd spent the last few days hating him? Around the front of the cottage I stopped to look at the view, gaining courage to go inside. The sky had turned a brilliant yellow, the whole valley beyond was bathed in a curious light. The stream was yellow, the grass and trees faintly tinted with an edge of gold, even the far hills rose goldenly against the thick cloud banks. The bad weather was breaking. I took a deep breath and went up the steps.

I knocked on the door. No one answered. I tried the knob. The door was unlocked and I went in. Mr. Clay was lying on the couch asleep, an arm crooked under his head, his hair rumpled. He looked tired even in his sleep. I could put the food on the table and not wake him, I thought quickly. But as I crossed the floor a board creaked. The sound woke him. He opened his eyes and lay staring at me.

"I brought your dinner," I announced, and began setting out the food. I hurried out to the kitchen for a glass of water. When I came back, Mr. Clay was sitting up. He had smoothed his hair a bit but it was still untidy. He looked oddly young sitting there with his chin cupped in his hands. I picked up my basket and started to leave.

"Keturah!" The sound was as sharp as a twig snapping.

I stopped but did not turn around. Standing there with the basket hanging on my arm, I was sure I looked every inch what I was, his servant. But I no longer cared.

"What are you thinking?" His voice demanded.

I lifted my shoulders. "What is there for me to think?"

"Did you think I ran away?"

"Yes."

"Turn around and look at me," he ordered.

I was torn between marching out of the door and facing him again. Slowly I turned around. His eyes burned like live coals in his face.

"You're the finest person I know," he said, his voice even. "You have everything in you that I wish was in me. You're like a light shining back here when I'm away."

"Then why . . . Why did you say I shouldn't love you?"

"Because it isn't fair."

"Fair?" Anger flared up in me again. "You don't have to keep reminding me," I flung out. "You don't have to keep telling me I'm not good enough for you." I flew out the door and around the house. The world was all lemon-yellow and unreal. Great, dark clouds loomed in the west, and between them the sun hung like a red ball of fire. It looked like the end of the world. I ran up the path to meet it, hoping it was.

Under the oak tree Clay caught up to me.

He blocked my path, breathing hard from running. "You little fool," he cried. "Do you think your past makes any difference to me?" With strong arms he pushed me back against the trunk of the tree, pinning me there. "It was you I didn't think it was fair to. I don't have anything left to give you."

His dark face was squarely in front of mine. I could feel his breathing, the strength going from him as he released me and put his hands gently on my shoulders. "Oh, but my dear Keturah. Help me to find happiness again."

In the yellow light each small line was visible in his face. Everything that sorrow had etched was there. It was for me to wipe away. The tears ran down my cheeks as I took him in my arms. We held each other under the oak tree while the yellow light faded. Over Clay's shoulder I saw the first star. I made a long, long wish on it. And I knew that through the years it would come true, not once, but many, many times. We would be happy together. I would give back to Clay more than he had lost.

As we moved from under the tree Clay said: "Shall we go up and tell Aunt Alice?"

I laughed softly. "She'll be my Aunt Alice too, won't she?"

"Will you like that?"

I considered it as soberly as I could. "I'm so used to Miss Hawthorne. It will be hard to think of her as Aunt Alice."

He clasped my hand tightly. "It will be as easy as not thinking of me as Mr. Clay."

Laughing, we walked up the wet path together. A bright

red leaf burned on the maple tree. The season had turned. The last, faint sounds of summer stirred in the insect voices that rose upon the evening.

"Miss Hawthorne will be surprised," I said.

But would she? And it all came to me then that maybe this had been a part of her plan, that this was what she had been preparing me for. This was what she had hoped would happen. In her strange, cold way she did have a romantic streak in her. Because it had not risen to fulfillment in herself, perhaps she longed to see it come to bloom under her roof.

Just before I had left her study that afternoon, she had done a most momentous thing. She had looked up from her desk as I was about to turn on my heel and leave.

"I want to talk to you a moment, Keturah," she had said.

I wondered if she were going to try to uncover my secret. Her face revealed nothing. Her eyes were as coolly gray as ever. The coils of gray hair were wound tightly over her ears, not a hair was out of place. Her forehead was faintly lined. She looked suddenly old again. And tired. I became panic-stricken with the thought that maybe she was thinking she might die.

"I'm going away this winter," she said. "I'm getting on and I don't like the winters here anymore. They're too long and too cold. I'm going back to the South of France."

I breathed a sigh of relief. She was not going to die. It was on the tip of my tongue to ask if Mr. Judson was still there. But I refrained.

"Now that you know the workings of Hawthorne I think you can take over. I have great confidence in you. And you've had sufficient schooling for the present. You can go on learning from your reading." She looked directly at me; behind her cool eyes was a flicker of warmth. "I want you to have Hawthorne. You have a feeling for the place. I've left it to you in my will. Some day it will be yours."

Tears sprang to my eyes. I was deeply touched. But in the next instance I remembered I did not have a right to what she was offering.

"But your niece . . . Mr. Clay . . ."

"Eloise would only sell the place. Clay . . . I've thought about him, but he's too footloose. He'd let it go to seed while he was away. Besides, both of them have enough money of their own." She smiled slowly, almost sadly, as if the idea of Hawthorne belonging to someone else was not easy to think about. "I know you'll treat it well, Keturah."

I closed my eyes and felt the tears pressing against them. I was to have Hawthorne. It was to be mine. And into the dazzling picture a cloud sailed. If Mr. Clay knew, would he feel differently about me? Never, I decided quickly, never would I have him if he turned back to me because of it. I opened my eyes. "Does Mr. Clay know?"

She shook her head. "No one knows. No one else is going to know until I'm dead and my will is read. It's none of their business." And with that she caught herself back into the familiar pattern. The moment of softness was gone. The coolness spread about her, enveloping her.

"I don't know how to thank you, Miss Hawthorne."

"By taking care of Hawthorne." She looked away, above me, at the wall, at a picture hanging there, or perhaps merely at nothing, but away so that I knew I was dismissed.

At the door I looked back. Miss Hawthorne had not moved.

"I'll have to be a lady," I said, "if I'm to run this place as well as you do."

As we approached the house I wished I could tell Clay before we went in to see Miss Hawthorne. It would not matter between us now. The light was burning in the library. Miss Hawthorne was probably there waiting for us. But I had to keep the secret. It was not mine to tell. There had always been secrets at Hawthorne; it had been a house of secrets, of shadows, of hidden things, of unasked questions. I hoped this would be the last secret. I looked up at the Evening Star. It had led us up the path. It would stay over us while we were in the house, while we slept. I thought of Mr. Denny. "Mr. Denny," I said silently, "the cream is up."